Praise for *Our Little Histories*

Our Little Histories is historical fiction at its finest and most original. Like the very best and most engaging books, this one is always on the move, full of surprising and stunning twists in tone and storytelling, each chapter revealing new remarkable characters and profound thoughts, ones that will reshape and enrich your understanding of Jewish history. Through intimate, innovative, and absorbing prose, Weizman steadily and brilliantly guides the reader backward through modern Jewish history, prompting the reader to consider how the family stories most hidden from us are ultimately the ones that prove most impactful in shaping our own little histories.

— Avner Landes, author of *Meiselman: The Lean Years*

Our Little Histories will leave you breathless. Intriguing, moving, formally inventive, and gorgeously written, this sweeping novel, which traces a fractured branch of a Jewish family, comes together like a jigsaw puzzle, one riveting piece following another. When the last piece snaps into place, the reader is left with a heartbreaking picture of what it means to be human — that is, to play a small, often unknown, role in a tremendous story.

— Jessamyn Hope, author of *Safekeeping*

In *Our Little Histories*, Janice Weizman ingeniously spans 165 years in the life of a single extended family through individual stories that are funny and sad, moving, and eloquent, all brilliantly told. From Chicago to Tel Aviv, Vilna to Belarus, *Our Little Histories* is a masterful sweep through Jewish time that entertains and enlightens without ever losing sight of its heart. A wonderful novel of love and loss and the enduring ties that bind.

— Joan Leegant, author of *An Hour in Paradise* and *Wherever You Go*

Our Little Histories

Toby

Janice Weizman

Our Little Histories

The Toby Press

Our Little Histories

First Edition, 2023

POB 8531, New Milford, CT 06776-8531, USA &
POB 4044, Jerusalem 9104001, Israel

www.tobypress.com

ISBN 978-1-59264-599-2, *paperback*

Printed and bound in the United States

For my parents, who gave me my past,
for my children – the future,
and for the murdered millions
and their lost histories and futures

There is no history of mankind, there is only an indefinite number of histories...

– Karl Popper

Table of Contents

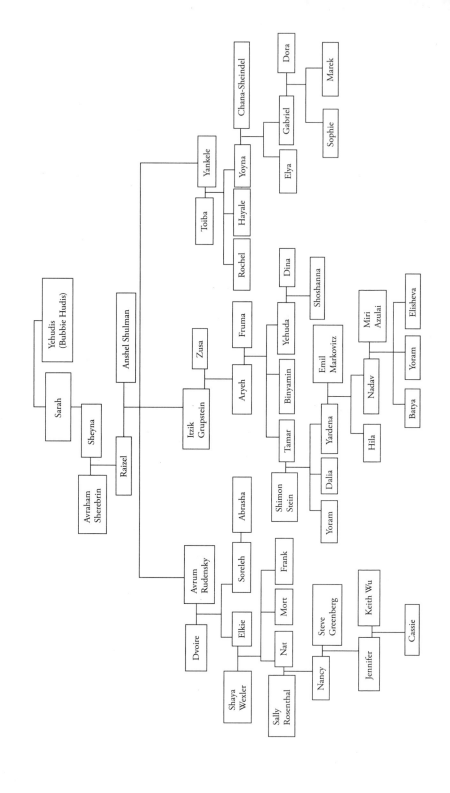

Reality

(Jennifer – Chicago, 2015)

"You're wearing *that*? On the plane?" My mother stands in the doorway of my bedroom staring aghast at Cassie, my daughter, her granddaughter. We're packing for our midnight flight to Minsk and Cassie is decked out in her Goth Girl attire: plaid miniskirt, Alien Sex Fiend T-shirt over a white blouse, and on her feet, her cherished combat boots. A heavy streak of dark eyeliner and a tiny metallic ball over her right eyebrow complete the look, but that's old news. I know that if anything has given my mother pause, it's the oversized wooden crucifix around Cassie's neck.

"It means nothing," I say, looking up from the pile of socks I'm counting on the bed. "It's just a fashion accessory."

"Well, you certainly look dressed to kill," Mom remarks jauntily, and stares into Cassie's face. "I see you have a new eyebrow thingy."

"My friend Marcy took me to this studio – it's all totally hygienic. Do you like it, Grandma?"

I have to smile at the poetic justice – Nancy Wexler forced to reimagine teenage rebellion in the form of her fifteen-year-old granddaughter's jewelry. *The* Nancy Wexler – renowned feminist, puppeteer, art teacher, protest journalist, and activist. Though twice married, she'll always be Ms. Nancy Wexler, revered among academic and grassroots feminists alike for her polemical writing on the Pill and female empowerment.

She's come over at this late hour to say goodbye, wish me luck with the project, and to show me "a surprise." I watch as she opens the used Walmart bag she's brought and gingerly draws out a faded blue booklet. Its cover sports a crudely drawn picture of a sun rising over a horizon, set under a bold-font title in Hebrew letters. The only intelligible thing is the year, 1914, which appears to be the date of its publication. As I stare at its stiff dusty cover, I get this weird feeling that I've seen it before. In fact, I'm positive; the art-deco logo of a sun rising over the hills is not something I would easily forget. "Where have I seen this?" I ask aloud.

"You haven't. It's been sitting in my basement with Grandpa's old LIFE magazines for half a century. After Grandma Sally died, I couldn't bring myself to throw them away, so I rescued the whole pile from the trash heap." She gazes wistfully at the journal. "I actually remember my dad showing this to me when I was kid, a few years after the war. He told me it was from the old country, and that there's a poem in here that was written by a relative of his mother. It's in Yiddish, you know. The letters are Hebrew, but it's Yiddish. Since you're going to the place it came from, I thought it would be neat to show it to you."

But I barely hear what she's saying because I'm under a spell of déjà vu. Those letters. That funky picture of the sun. Something about those frail, hundred-year-old pages intrigues me. I ask my mother if she'll let me take it to Slawharad, and when she agrees I pack it carefully with my files.

Later that night at the airport Keith hugs us in turn, me affectionately, Cassie anxiously. This is her first trip abroad, and neither of us is at all sure that it's going to be a success. Her original summer plans, the ones avidly arranged months earlier, involved a stint as a counselor-in-training at a small arts camp in Upstate New York, but last week crisis struck; the director was charged with molesting young boys, the camp was shut down, and Cassie was left in the lurch with not a plan B in sight.

Cassie Greenberg-Wu. Gorgeous sui generis, fortune-kissed daughter of not one but two weighty civilizations. Jewish Mom. A dad born in Hong Kong. Survivors of the fates. Like her grandma Rose Wu, she knows how to smooth-talk destiny. Like her grandma Nancy Wexler, her instincts are her spirit guides. But most of all she's a searcher. She wouldn't put it that way, but Keith and I know how much she yearns to belong to something. Keith, being an anthropology professor and having some authority on the matter, claims that the issue is only natural for a mixed-racer: too much history, too many roots, as he puts it. It's a conundrum that lurks under the surface of everything she does; Asian plus Jewish equals...what? No matter how much we insist that the only thing she needs to be is her own charming self, the equation is always waiting for an answer.

She's a great kid, always has been. The only thing that gives us cause for concern is that her Halloween-style clothing has come with a new group of friends. As far as we can tell from the little that Cassie has let on, the "Goth Girls" are into soft drugs, suicide-themed music, and casual nihilism. Ever since Cassie admitted that one of the posse was caught self-harming in the school bathroom, we've taken to casually monitoring her every move.

For the first few days after getting the bad news about the camp, she moped around the house in a depressive funk. "Why does stuff like this always happen?" she despaired to her friends on the phone. "I'll probably kill myself out of boredom!" Keith and I surmised that in the absence of concrete plans, Cassie would be spending her summer moping and doping with the Goth Girls. There were basically two choices: she could either stay at home with Keith and look for a job – an unlikely proposition at this late stage – leaving her to spend long days in the company of her loser friends, or she could come with me on my gig to Belarus. I was actually relieved when Cassie unhappily opted for the trip. The insanity of taking a spoiled fifteen-year-old to the wilds of Eastern Europe doesn't escape me, but this whole Slawharad project is so insane anyway that I'm hoping, somewhat optimistically, that the two insanities will cancel each other out and this trip will do all of us some good.

Once we're settled in our seats Cassie inflates her neck pillow and falls asleep immediately. But I put on the headphones, find the classical music channel, set the seat back, and replay, like a surrealist film, the curious accretion of events set in motion last winter that have brought me to this moment.

They began, as most things do these days, with an email.

Dear Mrs. Jennifer Greenberg-Wu,

Hello from Minsk. My name is Maxim Pranovitch, owner and CEO of Belarus Mineral, from the country of Belarus. I have written this email with the help of my lawyer, Mr. Pavel Drozd, because his English is very good.

Some days ago, I was visiting Chicago and my guide took me to your "Daily Life of the Ancient Egyptians" show at the Museum of Ethnology. He explained that you call this show a Living Installation. I liked it very much. I stayed for a very long time to watch the woman in the white tunic playing the harp like in the ancient drawings, and also the priest making a sacrifice to the gods, and also the two little boys writing on papyrus. For me it was like a play in the theater. Ever since I was a young child and my mother read to me the Bible stories about the pyramids and the temples, I have wanted to see the things that the people do in that show.

I want to tell you that this show has put an idea in my head, and I want to make to you a very special proposal. I have made a research about your professional reputation. I see that you have worked as a museum curator in many places and that you are now a freelancing woman, and that you possess a solid name in the field of Living Installations. This is all excellent. And now I will tell you my idea. It is my dream that you will put on a Living Installation in the town where I was born. It is a very small place, very very humble, called Slawharad. But this show will not be about Belarusian people. It will be about Jewish people.

The reason I want to do this is an amazing story. You see, Mrs. Jennifer, a few years ago my grandmother shared with me a secret that one of her own grandfathers was Jewish! You would not believe my surprise when I heard this thing. He died when my grandmother was a child, and we know very little about him. However, because of his Jewish blood that is in me, I feel that I am also in a small way part of the

4

Jews. It is a very strong thing that I feel about everything that has a connection to Jewish people.

Do you know the television show, Big Brother*? I'm sure that you do. It is where a group of strangers all move into a house to live together with no leaving allowed. Here in Belarus everyone loves the show. My idea is that I want to build one of your Living Installations, but where Jewish people will be the stars. It will be just like the people in* Big Brother*. We will find a Jewish family, real Jews, not actors, and they will be living like my ancestors in a traditional Russian cabin, which we call an* izba*, but this* izba *will have a glass wall so that everyone will be able to see what is happening inside. They do not have to do anything special. They will be in their Jewish lives, and visitors will come to observe how they make their life with all of their special behaviors and habits.*

Though I myself am living in Minsk, I want to make this izba *installation in Slawharad, the home of my grandmother's family, in honor of my Jewish great-great-grandfather. I would like for Belarus people to be able to watch the family and see how Jewish people make their religion, and so they will know about the Jews who used to live right here, in the town and all over the country of Belarus.*

Mrs. Jennifer, I want to invite you to come to Slawharad and curate this living Jewish installation. I am a very busy man but if you can give to this project a mere two weeks in the coming July, I will make myself available. As for financing and your own fee, I will say that I am a man who has worked hard all his life, and I know to pay very nicely for the things I want, and also to show my gratitude to people who help me to achieve my goals.

If this project interests you, please answer to Pavel, his address you will find in the cc.

With very much respect,
Maxim Pranovitch

The first thing I did was google Maxim Pranovitch. A slew of links came up, most from the financial pages of international newspapers. The headline, "Belarusian Mineral – Maxim Pranovitch's Golden Ticket" was the first, followed by several more about the sale of a percentage of Belarus Mineral to an "unnamed Russian investment group." There was also a video tour of Maxim Pranovitch's luxury yacht, and a lively excerpt from what appeared to be an appearance on a talk show.

A Jewish reality installation! What a joke. But still! It was preposterous, yes, but it also, I had to admit, worked perfectly with the concept behind "Living Installations," the format I had been staging in museums for the past five years. The concept is simple: rather than tell, show; offer people the chance to witness cultural customs and practices, enacted before them in real time. Before the Ancient Egyptians show that had so inspired Pranovitch, I had curated and staged the goings-on at a Greek temple, a Roman senate, an Inca court, and even, my most successful show, a Native American prayer ceremony, co-curated with representatives of Illinois tribes.

Given that Living Installation formats involve real people performing authentic acts of cultural affiliation and tradition, wasn't a *real* family of religious Jews living out their day-to-day life a logical next move? Portrayed in the right way, it could be bold, challenging, powerful – an amalgamation of both performance and ownership, the most real that reality could be. I could feel the nebulous core of it starting to take shape. To invite people into a space where the distinction between illusion and reality is blurred, enacting the indisputable fact that what is unfolding before them is, in the simplest sense of the word, true. Done right, it could be nothing less than thrilling.

But when I told Keith about it, he failed to share my enthusiasm. "Living their Jewish lives?" he said, making a face. "That's pretty patronizing. The whole idea sounds ridiculous."

"I know," I agreed, "but in a good way. Imagine it – like a reality show, but with actual religious content. It's not reality, its hyperreality! It's…it's a simulacrum! It's the imitation that becomes an actualization. It's edgier than edgy. It's state-of-the-art fabrication of the real."

"You do see the irony," he said dryly.

"What irony?"

"Well, you're not exactly a model Jewess."

"Don't you Jewess me, you banana."

"You're not even a model Jew."

"He doesn't only want me for my ethnicity."

"How do you know? He's probably under the illusion that you actually know something about the subject."

"I know enough."

"You may have a handle on the basics, but hard-core Orthodox Judaism? Admit it, Jen, you'll have to do as much research for this as you did for the Egyptian show."

Deep down, I had to admit that he had a point. My mom's family was never into religion, and my stepdad isn't even Jewish. Religion was just never a thing for us.

"OK, I'm an atheist," I conceded, "but a Jewish atheist."

"Are you going to tell that to your Belarusian tycoon who thinks you're the real deal?"

"Not a problem," I had replied breezily. "I can educate myself if need be."

Or that's what I thought then. But now, when Pranovitch's dream is about to unfold in real time, a small voice in my head is whispering, like a brutally honest friend, *"What if Keith was right?"* His skepticism which, truth be told, was not misplaced, is now pitted against the months of research I've put into creating this show. What if I've somehow forgotten some essential detail, or made some inexcusable mistake? What if something in this outrageous show is going to screw up badly? What if I've gotten myself, and the teenager sleeping beside me, into something I may live to regret?

——— . ———

It's already afternoon when, one connecting flight later, we touch down in Minsk. Cassie and I stumble inelegantly into the arrival lounge where a driver is holding a sign with large black letters that says *Mrs. Greenberg-Wu.* "Hi," I greet him with an outstretched hand. "I'm Jennifer Greenberg. You're taking us to Slawharad, right?"

"No English," the driver replies as he grimly shakes my hand and takes our suitcases. Hoping for the best, we follow him out to his black BMW. The highway landscape is dull and unremarkable with its endless stretches of fields and forest. I'm keenly aware that this place, Belarus, is the land my great-grandparents left for America over one hundred years ago, yet the drama of encountering it now doesn't excite me. I feel little connection to these forests, these endless miles of fields. Though I've slept for most of the flight, I soon doze off, waking only when the driver taps me on the shoulder and wakes me with the words, "Madam, Slawharad."

I blink open my eyes. A security guard is waving us into the parking lot of the warehouse which houses the set, a place I'm very familiar with, having seen it hundreds of times on Skype. Pranovitch in person is somehow better looking than he appeared on my computer screen: part oligarch part indie-film director, in an expensive leather coat and black jeans, with wavy longish hair and a sharp little goatee. "Mrs. Jennifer!" he exclaims. "You are here! Welcome. Welcome to Belarus. Welcome to our Slawharad."

He embraces me, and over his shoulder I see two familiar figures approaching – Vlad, the burly, cheerful construction engineer hired to build the set, and Polina, Pranovitch's sweet, quick-witted niece, just out of design college, who has been acting as my assistant. We greet each other warmly, as if we're old friends, which we sort of are. Over the past several months we've become an intercontinental creative team, using Skype, Dropbox, and Instagram as our mediums of choice. Vlad and I have spent many an evening (for him, many a morning) hammering out the final sketches for the *izba*, while Polina has been invaluable in furnishing it as authentically as possible. With the help of her cell phone screen, we've scrounged together through local flea markets, secondhand furniture shops, and even homes of recently deceased old-timers, where I've watched her bargain with bereft relatives over the perfect wooden bench, an embroidered tablecloth, a handmade bookshelf.

"And this must be your daughter," Pranovitch says as Cassie slides, a little dazed, out of the car. He extends his hand and she shakes it limply. He points to a large Winnebago camper van standing at the far end of the parking lot. "This is where you and your daughter will stay. I have acquired for you a beautiful trailer. Brand new. I apologize that it is not a hotel. A hotel would be better, but there are no hotels in Slawharad. I hope you will be very comfortable. If you need something, you will tell Polina and she will bring it for you."

"No hotels?" Cassie says, incredulous.

"Come," Pranovitch says, gallantly ignoring my daughter and leading the way into the warehouse through a sliding metal door with Russian writing on it. "It says, *Stay Out. Private Property*," Polina translates.

I couldn't have thought of an edgier effect if I tried. "Fantastic!" I exclaim, invigorated by all the excitement.

We step into a black entry hall lit with small bright spotlights. A ticket counter with an electric marquee runs a banner in Belarusian. "This will show the prices," Pranovitch says. "Not very expensive, but we are not going to offer the entertainment for free." A flat screen hangs on the wall behind the counter, displaying what appears to be the interior of the cabin.

"This will show what is happening in the *izba*," Polina explains, "but it will just be a taste. To see it properly the people will have to buy a ticket. Now come. You must be very much wanting to see how your plans came out." They lead me down a corridor, also black and brightly lit, to a second door which opens onto something that resembles a makeshift theater. On our left, men are assembling aluminum bleachers that face a giant glass wall, behind which is an authentically furnished nineteenth-century one-room peasant home. "There is place for 150 people, fifteen in each row," Vlad reiterates the details. I follow them around the back of the stage to a small entryway, then up a narrow staircase and through a sliding glass door.

— • —

Everything is in the details. Get them right and the spectators will find themselves transported into a foreign environment as surely as Martians stepping off a spacecraft. To create the set for the show I examined hundreds of documents and photographs from what is known as The Pale of Settlement, a region of unstable borders in which, from 1791 until 1917, all Jewish inhabitants of the Russian empire were forced to live. Most of the rural population lived in one-room cabins made of wooden planks with thatched straw roofs and small windows. The winters were long and brutal, and heat was a constant challenge. The central feature of a home, if the family was lucky, was a huge wood-burning oven called a *pechka*.

As I pored over the material, the phrase *nasty, brutish, and short* often came to mind. The miserable towns, with their ramshackle wooden buildings and muddy market squares, were bleak and depressing. Hardship was etched into the faces of the people and obvious in their scruffy and ill-fitting clothing. The men, with their thick beards and shabby caps, appeared weary. The women wore long dresses, heavy shawls, and kerchiefs on their heads. The children were scrawny with big eyes and patched coats. Nobody looked particularly cheerful.

I drafted plans for a one-room *izba* cabin with a large *pechka* set in the middle, a roughly hewn wooden table with two long benches, and some beds pushed together on one side. Due to the absence of plumbing there would normally have been an outhouse in the yard, but in a concession to modern comforts I added a bathroom behind the stove before sending the final version off to Vlad.

⌒ • ⌒

I've viewed this space from every possible angle on my computer screen, but now, stepping into the actual creation, I'm delighted with how authentic it all feels. Here is the main room, with its worn wooden floors and small windows hung with lace curtains. Here is the giant brick *pechka* oven with the flat top and open fireplace, built specially for the set by a master stove builder whose family has been in the business for generations. Here is the kitchen table, complete with water stains and scratches, which Polina's sharp eyes picked out in the home of her sister-in-law's great-grandmother who had passed away two months earlier. Here are the wooden benches, bought from a secondhand furniture dealer in Mogilev. With satisfaction I survey the roughly cut shelves, the iron pots and pans, the chipped dishes, the crudely-made ceramic cups. On the opposite side of the cabin four beds, three singles and one double, are made up with thick woolen blankets. Between them, parallel to the wall, a large antique clothes cupboard borrowed from

Polina's uncle provides a small space, blocked from the spectators' view, where the family can change clothes.

"I think it came out very nice," Vlad says proudly. "Just like in the pictures you sent, yes? I bring my grandfather here, and he can't believe it. He says to me, 'Vlad, this is just like my grandfather's cabin that I used to visit when I was a boy before the war. Exactly the same!' Do you see this stove? My grandfather loved this stove. It almost made him cry. I think that all of the people will cry when they see this house. It is a house from our past."

"And now," Pranovitch says, "you must see the secret places. They are very special." Polina leads us behind the stove where a crawl space has been made comfortable with purple carpeting and colorful stuffed pillows. On the wall hangs a 34-inch screen which is hooked up to a computer. A brand-new keyboard sits on a low table. This space was a last-minute addition, built after it dawned on me that we could not put three kids in a fake cabin without some sort of access to screen time. Cassie plops down on a pillow. "This is so, so awesome. Mom, can I live here too?" I shake my head sharply, hoping no one else has heard her.

"And look," Polina says, opening a small fridge in the corner. It's been stocked with a carton of milk, a pack of processed yellow cheese with Hebrew writing on the label, and other kosher foods for clandestine snacking. "Yum. Is that hummus?" Cassie asks.

Polina smiles with satisfaction. "I ordered this food from a special supermarket in Minsk."

"And that's the bathroom, right?" I say, peeking through a narrow door in the wall. I poke open the door and see a prefab toilet, sink, and shower.

"In there," Vlad chuckles, "it is the twenty-first century."

Pranovitch shows me down the hallway outside the set to a series of small offices — one for me, one for himself, and one for Polina and Vlad. Mine is fitted with a desk, two chairs, a lamp, a stand with an electric kettle, coffee, tea and sugar, and a small fridge. I take a look out the window, which offers an uninspiring but clear view of the neighborhood. Polina murmurs something to Pranovitch, and then suggests that we head out to the parking lot to check out our Winnebago.

It's in pristine condition, right out of the factory. Cassie gets over her initial disappointment and actually seems satisfied. She tries out the adaptor I bought for our phone charger and tries to get Wi-Fi. I take a quick shower and then head back to the warehouse where I set up my computer, plug in my cell, and boil the kettle for a quick cup of the Taster's Choice coffee I take wherever I go. As I sift through some last-minute notes I made on the plane, I come across the old Yiddish journal that Mom gave me the night we left. I show it to Polina and she suggests that we place it on the shelf beside the holy books. I stay to help her and Vlad, who are trying to light a fire in the *pechka*. Just when we manage to get a flame going, a workman appears and announces something in Russian. Polina clasps my hands excitedly. "They are here!"

—— · ——

Finding candidates to participate in Living Installations is actually harder than it sounds. The whole concept dictates that they can't be actors. They have to be "normal" – agreeable, easy to get along with, willing to follow instructions, and uninhibited about appearing in public as a version of themselves. It's rare to find candidates who fit this bill, and I've learned that it's best, whenever possible, to work with people whom I know personally. But this project presented a special challenge. I needed an actual family, all of whose members would be OK with being under the scrutiny of spectators. Though Pranovitch was willing to compensate generously, I had to find the *right* people.

It isn't like I don't know any Jews; I know plenty, except they aren't the types whom anyone would actually pay to see on display. Could I actually call up, say, Alexa Lifshitz, a badass girl when we were in college but now a corporate lawyer, married with two preschoolers, and ask her if she'd like to dress up in long skirts and pretend that she believes in God? Or send off an email to Carrie Feldman, my Pilates instructor, to feel out if she and her family might want to fly to Belarus to take part in a fun reality experiment involving traditional religious Jewish practice? Even Keith's tennis partner, Jay

Litwin, a sensitive soul who flirted with Jewish observance in grad school, was not going to be right for this. I drew up a mental list of every Jewish person I knew and rejected all of them. But then, just when I was thinking that I might have to give up the whole project, I remembered my Israeli "cousins," Nadav and his younger sister Hila, relatives so distant that I wasn't sure exactly how we were related.

I first met Nadav Markovitz twenty years ago when I made a detour south from my summer trip to Europe, and at my mother's urging visited his mom, Yardena, in Tel Aviv and his grandmother, Tamar, on her kibbutz. Hila had been travelling at the time, so I literally knew her in name only, but over the years Nadav and I had kept loosely in touch. For a while we wrote occasional letters, but our correspondence never made the switch to email, and all I knew of him now was what my mother passed on, isolated tidbits of information that I only barely registered. He had married his girlfriend, Miri. Together they had become religiously observant. They had three kids. He had been teaching physics and computer science for years at a local college.

It was as though the forces of the universe had somehow aligned. I wrote to Nadav, and in spite of our having lost touch he was happy to hear from me. Over a series of Skype conversations in which we caught up and held photos of our respective families to the camera, he warmed to the idea, admitting that the innovative and experimental nature of the project appealed to him. Serendipitously, and more to the point, he had long dreamed of leaving his job to open a startup, and the money Pranovitch was offering could finally make that happen. Miri was initially skeptical, but after Nadav agreed to the idea of a family trip to Scandinavia following the show, she changed her tune. The younger kids, ten-year-old Batya and twelve-year-old Yoram (named, Nadav explained, for an uncle who was killed in the Yom Kippur War), were on board from the start, jubilant about the idea of starring in a reality show. Only his older daughter Elisheva dissented, calling the idea "totally idiotic," but after a few family discussions in which she found herself outnumbered, she grudgingly agreed to go along with it.

Pranovitch was elated. We drafted a contract, fine-tuning the terms. Only kosher food would be provided. Miri asked for a small yoga studio on the premises. Yoram and Batya requested that the site include an outdoor basketball court. Nadav mentioned that Yoram's bar mitzva was coming up in the fall, and they'd like to use the time on the set to practice his Torah reading. When I explained this to Pranovitch he gave me a big smile and a thumbs-up. During a three-way Skype conversation, Miri asked about sightseeing in the area. "Ah yes," Pranovitch said, frowning. "Well, it is a very small place, a quiet place. There are a few monuments for the soldiers who fell in the Patriotic War, yes. But it is a place mostly for simple, serious people. It is not Paris. It is not New York."

─── • ───

We head down to the parking lot where the Markovitz family is emerging from a large black van. Pranovitch is welcoming them as the driver hoists out their luggage. "Jennifer!" Nadav exclaims, setting down the knapsack he's carrying and opening his arms for a hug. After months of talking over Skype, it's strange to see him now in person; the skinny guy with a head of curly rust-colored hair whom I met twenty years ago is now balding and middle aged. Only his eyes haven't changed. They're bright, alert, taking everything in. "I've always hoped we'd have a chance to meet up again," he tells me, "although I didn't think it would happen exactly like this."

"I know. It's…a little bizarre. Thanks so much for doing this."

He grins and shrugs. "I'm looking forward to it."

I turn to Miri, short and plumpy, already looking the part in a long polyester skirt, her hair covered, *Fiddler on the Roof* style, in a kerchief. We hug and she reintroduces me to Batya, also in a polyester skirt, Yoram, a fidgety, wide-eyed preteen, and Elisheva, a pretty but sullen-looking teenager whom I notice is wearing fashionable, faded jeans.

"It's so great that you're finally here," I tell them. "Everything is all set up and ready for you. The cabin is like a real peasant house. You're going to love it."

"We are very happy to be here," Miri says. "And we are also very excited about our trip to Scandinavia."

Elisheva murmurs something in Hebrew in a grumpy tone that reminds me of Cassie on a bad day. "Is everything OK?" I ask. "She's going through a stage. She doesn't want to be religious anymore," Nadav explains apologetically. "She refuses to wear skirts."

Pranovitch seems, or at least behaves, as though he is unaware that anyone is anything less than thrilled to be here. He picks up two of the knapsacks and leads the entire party inside. We all pause in front of the bleachers and I watch their mixed expressions as they stare through the glass wall at the set. "It's one-way glass," I explain. "The spectators will be able to see you but you won't be able to see them." Yoram says something that sounds like he thinks it's cool. Elisheva gives him a swat.

Single file, we climb the stairs behind the stage and enter the cabin through the sliding door. At first they just gaze around the set, taking in the giant *pechka*, the wooden table and benches, the beds, and the dark wall of one-way glass. They've all seen this on Skype so it's not exactly a shock. "Incredible," Nadav says. "It's right out of the *shtetl*. We might even forget who we really are! We're going to need psychological treatment afterward."

"Psychiatric," Miri corrects him.

"So, you are the person who got my parents to come to this crazy place." I turn around and see Elisheva. I'm surprised by her fluency in English, and make a note to ask Nadav about it later.

"Yup. I'm to blame," I reply, trying to sound jocular. "I think your dad really likes the idea."

"My dad likes anything that is weird."

"He mentioned that you've been having doubts about being religious," I say, trying to feel out whether this could affect the show.

"Isn't it obvious?" She glances defiantly at her jeans.

"So you'll just be acting when the show opens."

"Show!" she snorts. "I can't believe anyone would pay just to watch us."

"Why not? People are really interested in learning about the lives of others."

"Well, I told my father that I will pretend for this crazy thing, but after that I'm leaving."

"You're leaving...home?"

"I'm leaving religion. I am going to be a *ĥiloni*."

"What's that?"

"Not religious. A free life."

It's a sentiment I can get behind, and I give her a thumbs-up. We show them the yoga studio at the end of the hallway of offices, and as we gaze out the studio's large window that overlooks the parking lot, Pranovitch points out the regulation basketball court he's put in on the side of the building, complete with new nets and white lines on the pavement. Yoram complains that he's hungry, and I tell them that we've arranged for some kosher meals to be brought in from Chabad in Minsk, and that we'll all meet up again in the bleachers after they have a chance to eat and freshen up.

I'm back in my office when Polina comes in with a pile of printed booklets sporting a big Star of David on the cover. "This is the Russian translation of your guidebook," she says and opens one to show me. I glance at the cryptic Cyrillic script and nod approvingly, trying to conceal the fresh wave of anxiety they've brought on. Researching the project, I've become aware that not only has Judaism accumulated centuries of rituals and traditions, but there is often dissent about how to perform them. I decided early on to follow what mainstream Orthodox Judaism dictates, but even that, I've seen, is open to debate.

——— . ———

"I'm putting together a guidebook to explain to the spectators what they're seeing on the set," I told Nadav during one of our Skype conversations. "Would you mind taking a look at it when it's done, just to make sure that we're all on the same page?"

I can still see Nadav's expression, frankly amused, as though he has come upon a dirty little secret. "You don't actually know very much about Judaism, do you?"

"Well, I'm not a practicing Jew, but I've been doing a lot of research. That's always a big part of any project." I didn't share my feeling that my lack of first-hand experience was actually turning out to be helpful, enabling me to write the guide from the viewpoint of a novice.

"I get that," he replied, "but are you only learning this stuff now?" It felt like a trick question, as though he was suggesting that I was some sort of imposter.

"I didn't exactly grow up with it, if that's what you mean," I replied, a little defensively, "but whatever I did or didn't grow up with is irrelevant. Anthropological research is part of my job. All that matters is that I learn it and present it in an artistic context."

"True," he conceded. "It can be learned. Look at me. I spent my childhood in a socialist commune. I also didn't grow up with it."

—— . ——

An hour later, Pranovitch and I hold an orientation in the bleachers with Polina, Vlad, and the Markovitz family, the adults seating themselves on the lowest row and the kids climbing higher up until Pranovitch invites them to come down for a talk. After the preliminary welcomes and a little speech about how glad he is that the project is finally opening, he asks them, "Do you know why I have dreamed of this show? It is because I found out that I am a little bit Jewish."

Nadav and Miri exchange a glance, which Pranovitch catches. "It is true," he insists. "One-sixteenth percent Jewish, from my great-great-grandfather. This is a big reason why I am making this whole show. The older people remember a time when there were many Jews here. Today we miss the Jewish people. We think about the times that they lived here and we are sad."

"Except for the anti-Semites," Elisheva mutters, but loud enough for everyone to hear.

"What kind of people will be coming to the show?" Miri asks warily.

"Well, I suppose it will mainly be made up of the local population," I say, not sure how to describe the sullen-faced Slawharad Belarusians I observed from my office window, returning from the small supermarket down the street, or smoking in the clean but uninspiring yards that surround the Soviet-style apartment blocks. "People who know nothing about Judaism and are perhaps coming with some preconceived ideas."

"They are not anti-Semitic. Not at all," Pranovitch says, a touch insulted. "OK, maybe a few of the old-timers, or some crazy people and idiots, but most do not hate anyone except for the fascists who murdered so many of our people. But this show is not about sad things in the past. It is about remembering the good things that we have forgotten. People know that Jews used to live here, and they are very curious. They want to know all about the Jewish religion." He glances at me and I can see that the subject has made him uneasy. "OK. Right now we must talk about the show. Please, Mrs. Jennifer, explain how it will be." I take a deep breath and open my tablet to where I've made a list of the daily events to be enacted on the set.

—— • ——

"So, let's run through the schedule together. Basically, the first spectator period will be from 8:00 a.m. to 2:00 in the afternoon. After that you'll have a break until 4:00 and then the second period will run from 4:00 till 8:30 p.m., except on Friday and Saturday nights, when the day will run longer so that the spectators will be able to watch the Shabbat and *Havdala* ceremonies.

So, each morning after you get up, wash, dress, etc. Nadav will put on *tefillin* and recite the morning prayers with Yoram. Miri and the girls will say private prayers. The more observant viewers may notice what they're doing, and in any case there's a note explaining about women's prayer in the guidebook. There's also a blessing to be said before eating breakfast, right?"

They stare at me, perhaps a little overwhelmed, but Nadav gives me an encouraging nod and I continue. "Now after breakfast, since we're trying to show a very traditional sort of Judaism, Nadav and Yoram will open the holy books and do their studying or preparation for Yoram's bar mitzva – it's up to you. And Miri and the girls will start to prepare the midday meal – there's a recipe section in the guidebook that will help the viewers to follow along. If there is extra time, it can be spent doing typical traditional activities: knitting, sewing, cleaning, whatever. Then at 12:30 you do lunch – with blessings before and after, and then you," I say, pointing to Nadav, "do your midday prayers. At two in the afternoon everyone leaves and you get some free time. You can hang out on the set, use the computer space, watch some TV, go outside for some basketball, do yoga, aerobics, whatever. Then at 4:00 you all come back in. More studying for Yoram and Nadav while you guys," I turn to Miri, "are in the kitchen cooking the evening meal. After that there will be dinner with all the accompanying blessings etc., then evening prayers, and at 8:30 the spectators leave and that's it until tomorrow. Now, Friday nights, that is, Shabbat evenings, are going to be the real highlight, and we'll allow spectators for an extra hour at night – till 9:30. People are going to want to see all the prayers, rituals, singing, the blessings after the meal; whatever you do, it's all good. And…" I glance over my notes, "I think that's about it." I face them all brightly. "Any questions?"

"Beautiful!" Pranovitch exclaims. "You have done a wonderful work! Hasn't she? But you must tell her if she has left something out."

A tense, perplexed silence hangs in the air. "It is very strange to hear it in this way," Miri says finally, "but everything you have said sounds OK."

"Great!" I say, and even though all of this has been discussed and confirmed weeks ago, I feel a surge of relief. "Now, if you need to tell us something while you're on the set, all you need to do is go into the bathroom and text me or Polina. Our phones will be on 24/7 so whenever you have to get in touch, send us a message."

"Sveta, my PR lady, has publicized the show everywhere, internet, newspapers, radio too," Pranovitch tells them. "Many people will come, but we will only allow 150 people at a time, and only for a period of thirty minutes. After that they will have to leave and a new group of 150 people will come in. I believe that there will be some people who come not only once, but many times."

— • —

The next day, Pranovitch and I, as well as Cassie, who has ambled in, watch from the bleachers as Polina outfits the Markovitz family. Batya emerges from behind the cupboard dressed in brown boots that lace up, thick wool stockings, and a smock dress. Yoram has traded his sandals and shorts for pants that end just past his knees and a boy's tunic shirt, belted at the waist. Miri steps out, grinning playfully in a floor-length grey skirt and a peasant blouse, but the best is Nadav, dressed in a long-sleeved undershirt topped by a vest and baggy work trousers. The four knotted fringes of his traditional *tzitzis* undergarment, which he normally tucks into his pants, now descend visibly from his shirt. Both he and Yoram have exchanged their crocheted skullcaps for small black caps. Elisheva appears last, sour-faced, yet nonetheless fetching in a long skirt and fitted blouse with small buttons down the back.

Cassie stares admiringly at the set. "Elisheva looks amazing."

"You should tell her. She's not too happy about doing this."

"Why? It's like she gets to act out this whole other character – like in a movie."

"Tell her that too. We tried, but it sounds much better coming from you."

Final preparations. A mezuza nailed to the doorway. Silver candlesticks, a cup for the *Kiddush*, a *Havdala* candle, and a very old set of holy books, all on loan from the Markovitzes, are set out on the shelves. Polina shows Miri how to boil water. Vlad helps the kids navigate the Belarusian internet. That night the Markovitz family sleeps on the set.

We open at 6:00 p.m. on a Thursday evening. There's been a lot of local curiosity about the installation, and all the tickets for the first few days have been sold online but nonetheless, by midday a queue of hopefuls has formed outside the warehouse, policed by hefty bouncers hired by Pranovitch, who apparently knows his people. He's also hired a few locals to man the ticket booth, show people to their seats, and hand out the guidebooks. Cassie and I are up in the bleachers, watching people's reactions as they file in.

It's been decided that when the spectators first enter, the lights on the set will be dimmed, so that nothing can be seen through the glass wall. Pranovitch addresses the inaugural audience with a speech. Though I don't understand a word, it's an emotional moment for all. I can feel the anticipation radiating from the spectators, who applaud as Pranovitch steps down. And then the lights come on over the cabin and there are the Markovitzes, sitting down to their evening meal of boiled potatoes with herring and black bread. When they're done eating they chant the prayer after meals, and I see the audience consult their guidebooks. Miri clears the dishes and washes them in a wooden basin with water provided earlier by Polina. Nadav and Yoram take up their prayer books and recite the evening prayers.

When the half-hour time slot is up, the staff gently urges the audience onto their feet and shepherds them out so that the next group can take their place. The bleachers remain filled until closing time, with group after group filing through as the Markovitzes, oblivious to the fascination their activities elicit, go about their business. I run back and forth between the ticket booth, Pranovitch, and Polina who is kept busy attending to last-minute logistics, but through it all I notice that Cassie remains in her seat, following the action and reading the guidebook.

After the last spectator is gone, I go up to the *izba* to check in. The kids have settled down to watch a movie in the computer room. "You guys were fantastic," I tell Nadav. "You looked so realistic!"

Nadav rolls his eyes and unbuttons his vest which, I see now, is a bit too tight for him. "I'm not even sure what that means anymore."

Miri comes out from behind the clothes cupboard wearing bright pink lycra pants and a matching top. It takes me a few seconds to realize who she is. "It was a little strange, but also sort of fun, like performing your own life in a play," she muses, and then asks if I want to join her for some yoga. I want to say yes, but Polina has asked to go over some last-minute logistical issues, and I decline.

Sveta posts a schedule of the day's "events" on our Facebook page, and when the ticket booth reopens at 7:00 the next morning, early risers are lined up to watch Nadav don his *tefillin* and perform the morning prayers with Yoram. Eager to begin the day, I'm up before the audience enters. I dress quickly and drink a fast coffee, trying not to make noise, but just as I open the door of the Winnebago, I hear

Cassie murmur, "Wait, Mom. Are you going to watch the Markovitzes? I'm coming with you." She throws on a pair of jeans and an old Phish T-shirt and we head out together.

In light of the burgeoning interest in the show, Pranovitch has told Vlad to add an extra row of seats. The crowd, still bleary eyed, files in quietly. For the first time, I observe them carefully, not just as spectators at the show, but out of curiosity about who these people are. They have a look about them, a homogeneity that one can't miss. Tall bulky builds. Wide round faces. Smallish eyes. The same palette of hair shades. Cassie and I, not to mention the Markovitzes, deviate strongly from the prototype.

Nadav is already up and dressed. The spectators watch as he taps Yoram lightly, rousing him awake. He slips behind the cupboard to change from the nightdress that Polina found in a vintage store in Minsk into his *tzitzis,* peasant shirt, and knee pants and then tiptoes to the kitchen table. The audience watches, mesmerized, as Nadav takes the little black boxes with the leather straps from their pouch. A few soft gasps are heard as he rolls up the sleeve of his shirt and begins winding them around his bare arm, and then fixes the second box on his forehead. The audience is confused, captivated, fascinated. "Look, Mom," Cassie whispers, pointing to Miri, who has in the meantime risen from her bed, dressed in a floor length skirt and blouse and, prayer book in hand, is swaying in a corner of the kitchen. "Why doesn't she put on the…" Cassie consults her guidebook, "*tefillin*?"

"Religion's a man's game, honey," I tell her. "Male-only rituals are integral to the patriarchy."

Prayers out of the way, Miri lights a fire in the stove and hoists a pot filled with water, set out last night after closing time by Polina, on a hook over the flames. After the Markovitzes eat their breakfast of cooked oats, the spectators, who are awaiting the blessing after meals, seem disappointed to find that rather than chanting it aloud, each family member mumbles a few quick, unintelligible words. *All blessings should be recited aloud clearly*, I type into my tablet, along with all the other things I need to remind them.

Nadav and Yoram sit down at the kitchen table with a large leather-bound volume. Nadav reads out a line and says something to Yoram, who responds in Hebrew, clearly in disagreement. In the meantime, Miri and the girls begin preparing the Shabbat evening meal. I watch along with the crowd as Miri pours copious amounts of salt over a raw chicken. Polina has arranged to have chicken brought in from a kosher butcher in Kiev, but we've agreed that Miri will go through the motions in order to show what a *shtetl* housewife would have had to do. The rest of the menu we've planned – gefilte fish, roast potatoes, apple compote, and of course homemade challah – is of great interest, not only as characteristic of Jewish culinary tradition, but also as an authentic demonstration of pre-industrial cooking.

During their afternoon break, the Markovitz kids organize a basketball game, the three of them against Cassie, Polina, and Vlad. I stop to watch them for a moment, pleased that my daughter has disengaged from her smartphone. Later in the day a reporter from *Zviazda* comes to write up the show and a camera crew from *BelT* asks to film a few minutes from the bleachers. "It is wonderful," Pranovitch enthuses. "People all over Belorussia are talking about this. They're coming from Mogilev, Vitebsk, Minsk. There is even a bus coming in from Kiev!"

But not all of the attention is positive. Later in the day Polina informs me that two groups of protestors have gathered outside the lot. One of them, a group of right-wing neo-Nazis, are protesting against "Jews taking over our history," and the second, a small but vocal crowd of left-wing activists, are urging people to boycott "Zionist colonialist cultural appropriation." "But don't worry," she reassures me. "My uncle has made a phone call to the Regional Chief of Police. They'll take care of everything." I'm not sure which of these reports is more disturbing, but I suppress my concerns and resolve to ignore them both.

Nonetheless, the coverage of the show is overwhelmingly favorable. The Shabbat dinner is touted the next day in the local press as "a cultural experience of the highest degree," a description that's sure to bring in good crowds for the Saturday night *Havdala* ceremony. According to the Jewish lunar calendar *Havdala* must take place after sunset, which, given the fact that its summer and that we're in the northern latitudes of Belarus, will be around 11:00 p.m. The late hour only adds to the exotic aura of the rituals, and I can sense the excitement of the crowd even before the ceremony begins. Cassie and I observe, as engrossed as the spectators, while Nadav chants the blessings over the braided candle, the exotic-looking spice box, the hallowed cup of wine. "It's so cool, Mom," Cassie whispers. "They want to make a clear separation between Shabbat time and regular time. Sacred and profane."

"*Kodesh ve'hol,*" I murmur the Hebrew words I've learned from writing the guidebook.

"It's like there's this whole other world."

The next few days pass like a fevered dream. I'm needed anywhere and everywhere. Polina consults me about discreetly slipping a Hebrew cookbook onto the set with recipes for borscht, kasha, and *tzimmes* so that Miri can expand her repertoire. Vlad wants to upgrade the lighting. Pranovitch suspects an error in the guidebook. Miri burns a *kugel* in the *pechka*. Batya can't get her favorite series online. Elisheva has promised to teach Batya to knit a scarf and is asking for some wool. Miri has spilled some oil on one of her dresses, which is now draped over the chair in my office. And Nadav despairs about forgetting to bring a particular medieval text that he wants to consult with Yoram. When, one morning, Batya practices a religious hymn to be sung at Yoram's bar mitzva, I get word from Polina that the audience wants to see a translation. Nadav slips into my office and takes up the task. *I will compose songs and weave poems, for it is you that my soul desires,* the first line reads. It sounds good, and so I trust that the rest is OK as well, and hurriedly give it to Polina to render into Belarusian.

Through it all I keep an eye on Cassie, who spends most of her time in the bleachers, following the Markovitz family with the enthusiasm of a devoted soap opera fan. Pranovitch reports that scalpers are selling tickets at double the price. I suggest telling the police, but Pranovitch just smiles and pats me paternally on the shoulder. Once a day, Polina and I meet with Nadav or Miri in my office for a quick rundown of problems on the set. "The toilet is clogging up," they complain. "The kids are asking for more hummus." "We need to do laundry."

One evening into the second week of the show, Nadav knocks on my door, the Yiddish journal in hand. "Where did you get this?" he asks, incredulous, and I too do a double take, as I've completely forgotten about it.

I explain how my mother showed it to me before I left, saying that it was her father's. And then something strange happens. I take it in hand and stare again at the sun logo, and all at once I remember where I've seen it before. It was twenty years ago, when I was in Israel, staying with Nadav's grandmother Tamar, on her kibbutz.

Everything comes back to me: her small house, the darkness outside, the dim glow of the lamp that cast a warm light over her simple room. I had asked her a question – something about the family she had left behind in Europe, and instead of replying she brought out the journal from a file in her bookshelf. I remember her saying that a cousin in Lithuania had sent it to her before the war, but that he and his family were all murdered in the Holocaust, shot in the forest outside the city where they lived – Vilna, I think she said. That would be the Yiddish word for Vilnius, which I know is just over the border from here.

"This is incredible," Nadav is saying. "It's exactly the same journal that my grandmother showed us when you visited her. Do you remember?"

I shake myself out of the trance that has come over me. "I didn't at first," I murmur, "but I remember now. This must be another copy. When my mom showed it to me I thought it would fit in on the set, and it felt sort of appropriate. Like closing a circle."

Nadav still looks puzzled. "But how did your grandfather get it?"

"That's what's so amazing. According to my mom, this copy was also sent by a cousin in Lithuania. It must have been the same person. She had no idea who he was, but obviously my grandfather had been in touch with him too. Where is your grandmother's copy now?" I ask.

"Who knows. I don't think I ever saw it after that. It's possible that my mother has it. Or my aunt Dalia."

I wait for him to continue, but he doesn't. "So this is maybe the last copy in existence."

"I guess."

"It's sad to think about it that way."

He shrugs. "Not really. Nothing lasts forever."

It's not the kind of platitude that you can really argue with, yet something about his attitude upsets me. Maybe it has to do with the doomed, forgotten Lithuanian relative of ours and his family, shot dead in the forest somewhere that's probably not too far from here. I'm about to say something to that effect when my phone rings. It's Polina, letting me know, ironically enough, that there's a delegation from Vilnius that wants to meet me. Nadav leaves the journal on my desk and heads back to the set.

The next morning Miri texts me saying that she's found a recipe online for potato knishes and she's going to try it out. As I sit in the bleachers watching her knead dough with the girls, something seems very different about Elisheva. I observe her closely, and soon perceive that the girl dressed in Elisheva's long skirt and blouse, with hair done up in two long braids, is not Elisheva. She fumbles with the dough, as though she's a little scared of it. I try to get a look at her face but she's looking down, giving the task her full concentration. When she finally looks up a soft yelp escapes me. It's Cassie. But how is that possible? Is my Goth Girl actually dressing up as a religious nineteenth-century Jew?

I manage a calm front as I rush through the narrow door and up the stairs. At the rear of the set I motion to Yoram, who has just emerged from the bathroom. "Can you tell your dad to come out a sec?" I whisper, and half a minute later Nadav strolls out from behind the curtain. "Cassie's in there making knishes," I tell him, trying to keep my voice down. "We've got to get her out of there."

His grin infuriates me. "No, we don't. She's doing fine."

"She has no idea what – " I hiss loudly, and then catch myself. "She has no idea about being a religious Jew. She'll make a mistake."

"Relax. They're just baking."

"She isn't supposed to be there. It says 'a family of five' in the program. Everyone will know that something's wrong."

"Who's everyone? The locals who stopped by on their way home from the pub?"

26

"Cassie doesn't fit in there! She doesn't know anything about being religious. She's not even fully Jewish."

At this point Pranovitch appears looking perturbed. "Mrs. Jennifer. Have you seen what your daughter is doing? Enough with the games. I ask you, please remove her from the cabin."

"I was just telling Nadav that he needs to – "

"Wait," Nadav cuts me off. "Why does she have to be removed?"

"Have you seen her eyes, Mr. Nadav? They are very special, but they are not Jewish eyes." He has spoken, of course, of what everyone can plainly see. Cassie's very identity plays out in her eyes – the same hazel shade as mine but with a subtle slant, like her father's. "Everyone will know that she is not a real Jew," Pranovitch is saying. "They will think we have brought in an actress. And the whole point of this show is that – "

"Cassie is a Jew because her mother is a Jew. That's all there is to it," Nadav interrupts again, flashing me an indignant glance. "Jennifer, you of all people should know that."

"Well Jew or not, she could seriously mess things up."

"No, she won't. We'll help her. She'll be fine," he insists, and then turns his attention to Pranovitch. "Mr. Pranovitch, Judaism recognizes any person who has a Jewish mother to be a Jew. Today, there are many who accept even those who only have a Jewish father. There are blond Jews because we accept the children of Jewish women who were raped by peasants and Cossacks; there are black Jews because there are blacks who took on the Jewish faith. And there are Asian Jews," he winks at me, "whose mothers fell in love with Asian men. It's that simple. By having Cassie on the set with us, you are affirming the principles of Judaism, not negating them. And isn't this exhibit about teaching people what Judaism is, and not just acting out stereotypes?"

Pranovitch appears to be considering this point, but I hardly notice. For Nadav's words, spoken almost offhandedly, have moved me. It dawns on me that this whole time I have harbored the suspicion that he and Miri do not accept my child as a member of their tribe. Of my tribe. But here he has clearly declared that they do. She is as much a part of these customs and these blessings and this history as they are. As I am. "OK," I agree. "But make sure she doesn't make any mistakes."

Nadav nods and his reassuring gaze tells me that he has read my thoughts. "Of course," he says. I look to Pranovitch. He seems confounded, as if the debate has gone far beyond his scope. "You say that her daughter is a Jew?" he asks, and then without waiting for an answer, shrugs in resignation. "I don't understand about such things," he says. "Do what you think is best."

From then on, Cassie makes appearances on the set and I'm impressed and puzzled by how seamlessly she blends into the Markovitzes' daily activities. Keith and I have always tried to make our home unreservedly atheist, free of the prejudices and dead weight of religious narratives. Is this thirst for rules and stricture what constitutes teenage rebellion in the face of absolute freedom? I want to talk with her about what this all means, but that conversation will have to wait.

The truth is that I am tired. I try to deny this as I run around the warehouse all day. But each night, when I finally crawl into my bed in the trailer, sleep evades me. Even when I close my eyes I see the set: Nadav listening to Yoram chant his bar mitzva portion, the girls knitting by the *pechka*, Miri stirring a pot over the fire. I see the lines of spectators that file through every half hour, eager to experience the foreignness and mystery of stepping briefly into the lives of others. More and more, I question what they're seeing.

Whatever it is, I'm haunted by a growing suspicion that it bears little resemblance to the lives of the people who stare out of the old photos on my laptop. I couldn't see this before but I see it now, because I can feel their presence in these restless silent hours. I see, in stark vividness, the pale faces with their somber gazes. And I can only wonder: what was it that compelled them to uphold their ancient customs and cling to their faith as they lived out their days in these dreary villages, among people who hated them, ultimately enough to murder them?

As I gaze out the trailer window into the dark sky, I see in my mind's eye a row of frail houses, endless snow-covered fields, muddy roads in spring. I see thick-bearded men as they emerge from the synagogue, women in long skirts, sleeves rolled up, hanging laundry in the shade of leafy trees. Children posing gravely for the camera, as if they've seen an intimation of the future and it does not bode well. A sliver of moon comes into view, casting a thin light across the wall, and I'm overcome with a sadness so searing that I want to cry. What I have created here is not a work of entertainment or edification. It's a study in tragedy. Why did I not see that? Why, as I researched and studied and constructed this world, did I not notice how sad it is?

Perhaps it is that sadness that makes me think again of the Yiddish journal which lay in my grandfather's basement for seventy years, sent to him by a relative from the city of Vilna. That relative would have been around my grandparent's age. His children would be just a little older than my mother. Instead, they were all shot in a forest outside the city. Murdered. In a place scarcely four hundred kilometers away. I slide out of bed, grab a sweater, pull it over my pajamas, and step out into the chilly night air.

I wave to the security guard in the booth as I slip into the warehouse. Passing the bleachers I glance at the darkened glass wall and then tiptoe up the stairs to my office, close the door, and switch on the light. I pick up the faded blue journal and sit down to examine its dry pages, searching for the poem written who knows when, who knows why, by my unknown, forgotten ancestor. But the pages, with their typed Yiddish script, all look the same. The impenetrable words stare back at me, mute, and I cannot read a single one. Why is that so? How did it happen that this language, which once gave form to the world for so many, can now only be deciphered by so few? How did it happen that it became a language for museums?

A light rap on the door startles me. It opens and I see Nadav, looking all too authentic in his nineteenth-century peasant nightshirt, a ghost of distant times coming back to speak from the grave. "Why can't we understand this?" I ask him, as though we are in the midst of an ongoing conversation. "They all spoke Yiddish, didn't they? It wasn't that long ago, just our parents' parents' parents."

He shrugs. "It pretty much died along with most of the people who spoke it. The Nazis killed it. Stalin killed it. And the people who remained, our own grandparents, they killed it too."

"What do you mean?"

"The majority of Jews didn't want to speak it any more. My grandparents, all the old-timers on the kibbutz, they just refused. And in America, the Jews wanted to speak English."

"That's true," I muse. "My grandfather understood Yiddish, but he never spoke it. Unless it was to tell a joke."

"They wanted to forget it. Just like they wanted to forget their lives here."

"And now it's dead."

"Not entirely. Some ultra-orthodox Jews still speak it."

"I rest my case."

"Yes. Jews like you speak English. Jews like me speak Hebrew." He gives me a little smile. "I think it's been a good trade-off for everyone, wouldn't you say?"

"For everyone except the people who actually spoke it, like for example, the folks you're pretending to be on the set."

Nadav looks at me quizzically. "Are you OK?"

"Show me the poem," I tell him. "I know I won't understand it but…could you just show me which one it is?"

He opens the journal, turns through the frail pages, and deciphers the titles until he stops at one and hands it to me. "It's this."

I stare at the unfathomable letters and fold down the top corner of the page, to mark it. "What's it called?" He studies it and shakes his head. "I don't know. I mean, I can read it, but I don't know what it means."

"And what about this?" I point to the letters over the rising sun logo.

"What?"

"The name of the journal. What do the words mean?"

He glances at the Hebrew letters and grins. "My grandmother once told me, and I still remember because it's kind of…ironic. It's called *New Yiddish Horizons*."

$$\sim \cdot \sim$$

The project's two-week run has passed in a blur. On the last day preparations are underway for Sabbath eve, which will be a sort of grand finale. I hold a staff meeting, delegating tasks to make sure all the logistics are taken care of. Pranovitch proudly tells us that the spectators this week have been not only Belarusians, but also Russians, Poles, Lithuanians, and even Germans. A TV station from Berlin has asked for permission to film a five-minute segment and interview me, as well as Nadav and Miri.

The installation has been written up in the Belarusian press as an important historical statement, proof that the country has undergone a "deep change" in its attitude toward "those who once lived among us." Pranovitch is being hailed as a man of vision and a cultural innovator. The Markovitzes are preparing for their trip to Scandinavia. Early Sunday morning Pranovitch's driver will take them to Minsk, where they'll fly to Copenhagen. Polina has received two job offers. Vlad is a local hero.

Normally all of this would give me a tremendous buzz, but what I'm really feeling, at the bottom of my heart, is a sense of melancholy. I pick up *New Yiddish Horizons* and open it to the page I folded down. As I stare at its archaic words, typeset in a world that no longer exists, the poem seems to give off something that I've been blind to, something I couldn't see – not twenty years ago when Nadav's grandmother pulled it from her bookshelf to show us, not a few weeks ago when my mother gave me this copy, forgotten in her father's basement, and not even yesterday, when Nadav and I pondered its journey to us.

The thing that I see now, on this grey afternoon here in Slawharad, is that all that the Markovitzes have been doing, all that I planned for them to do, is a lie. And the only thing that's true are the words set down on the pages of this journal, this remnant of the world as it appeared to those who lived in it.

And I know this: a daughter of this bleak place, my ancestor, recorded in the only language she knew some lines that gave her thoughts shape and form. But I, encountering those very lines, will never fathom them, not even if I could translate every word.

A peculiar sorrow, sobering and dark, descends upon me. I miss Keith. I miss home. I miss my life. I miss reality.

Someone is knocking on the door. It opens a little and I hear Nadav say, "Can I come in?" I stare at him quizzically. "Everyone's looking for you. Cassie said you weren't in the bleachers and Pranovitch wants you to meet his brother-in-law. And there's a reporter from Moscow who wants to interview you."

I put my head in my hands and groan. "I don't know what's with me today. It's sort of like I'm done."

"What do you mean *done?*" He gives me an amused, sardonic grin. "You're a star."

He's laughing at me, my charming, straight-shooting Israeli tenth cousin, or whatever he is. "Shut up," I say. "It's been an insane few weeks."

"Too much fun and games?"

"You know what's really weird? It's like, if you really think about it, this project, it's not a success. It's a failure. I mean, what can we ever really know about the lives of the Jews who lived here? This show is nothing but a failure of my puny imagination."

Nadav is staring at me with a sympathy reserved for those who have lost it. I'm not sure if he even understands what I'm saying. "No," he says kindly, "the show is many things, but it isn't a failure." He holds out his hand. "Hey. Come with me."

"Come where?"

"For months now you've been telling me what to do. Now do what I tell you. Let's go. Get up." Like a child I give him my hand and he leads me out to the corridor and onto the threshold of the set. "No. No way," I pull back. "I'm not going in there. Forget it."

"Come on. It's the last night."

"I can't. I'll ruin everything. I'm not dressed properly."

He glances around and picks up the dress with the oil stain, still draped over the chair, and hands it to me. "So put this on. Just come."

They're sitting around the table, laid with a white tablecloth and adorned with the objects of ceremony and ritual. The warm light of the candles gives the scene a sort of enchantment, and I feel a strange pull of something calling me to join them, to take up my place at this table, which is both a simulacrum of countless other

Sabbath tables and, I see this now, an actual Sabbath table. "But I have no idea what to do," I whisper to Nadav.

He squeezes my hand. "That's exactly what will make it a little bit real." I follow him into the cabin. Elisheva and Yoram make room for me between them on the bench. Across the table, Cassie is gazing at me.

There is nothing accidental in this scene, for I have planned its every detail: the tablecloth, the chipped crockery, the orange flames in the silver candlesticks, the wine cup, the challah loaves baked by Miri and wrapped in an embroidered cloth. A family, gathered together on wooden benches around a table. The scene is so familiar, yet I've never truly known it.

Everyone rises and even Cassie, who seems to have learned the Hebrew words, begins to sing the song that welcomes in the Sabbath. I close my eyes and listen to the melody, to the rise and fall of the enduring lyrics. The spectators behind the glass wall, the town of Slawharad, the country of Belarus, the continent of Europe, the entire world, have all disappeared and all that's left is this. Nadav raises the wine cup and chants the ancient words that bless the wine. I gaze around the table and for a moment, I am comforted.

Encounter

(Yardena – Tel Aviv, 1968)

It's a balmy morning in April, and a munificent sunlight warms the streets, the bright storefronts, the sidewalk cafes. Yardena, twenty-five years old and happily pregnant, is sitting at an outdoor table at Café Kassit. She's five months along, the bump under her pale green dress is pleasantly visible, and when she takes off her sweater, letting the light breeze run over her bare arms, she feels as lovely and fortunate as a goddess. Certainly that's the feeling that Emil gives her, sitting on her right at the small Formica table, his knee brushing against her thigh, his hand clasping hers under the table. On her left sits Nancy Wexler, her cousin from Chicago. Not really a cousin, she explained to Emil, but a distant relative, her mother's second cousin's daughter. Something like that.

Nancy's clothes are like a blaring radio broadcast. She wears a bright orange T-shirt with a blue peace sign, a pair of tie-dyed jeans, and a braided leather headband that reins in her light, wavy hair. She's attractive in a sort of an exotic way, not exactly pretty, but exciting, different, original. Emil, for whom English is practically a mother tongue, loves to pick out the slang words she uses. Every time she says "groovy" or "far out" or "that's boss," he grins to himself. "Those words – it's like she's speaking a dialect," he said after he first met her, driving back to Tel Aviv after a visit to her parents at the kibbutz, where Yardena's mother, Tamar, has set up a stint for Nancy as a volunteer.

Yet there's something that Emil and Nancy have in common; they're both foreign, with the slightly off-center perspective of outsiders. Nancy because she's so obviously American, and Emil because he is like a fractured mirror – one part still the child he was in Poland, another an orphaned teenager in wartime Manchester, and still another an immigrant who finds himself in Tel Aviv, a translator and freelance journalist, yet always at heart a little bewildered. She sees this union of theirs, this pregnancy, as a new beginning for him, a chance to finally belong somewhere.

Nancy reaches into her Native American style purse with long leather fringes, digs out a pack of American cigarettes, and offers them around. Emil takes one eagerly, but Yardena refuses. The lab at the hospital research institute where she works is studying cellular behaviors related to cancer, and she takes the reports on the link between smoking and lung cancer seriously, far more seriously, it seems, than everyone else in the café.

Emil lights Nancy's cigarette like a gentleman. Her foreignness is different from Emil's; it's proud of itself, defiant, but at the same time weirdly naïve. Her whole anti-war attitude, for example. "Man, I just don't get the way everybody is cool with the draft here," she told Yardena one Friday night as they walked from the kibbutz dining hall back to her parents' house. "War is a patriarchal, capitalist, racist game. It's The Man's way of getting rich and powerful on our backs, not to mention the stupid waste of life. Our generation has a moral duty to stand up to that. We have to start fresh, to build a society based on brotherhood and sisterhood. Love and peace aren't just slogans, they're our birthright."

It was hard to hear her speak this way. She's like a child who doesn't yet understand the world. When the Six-Day War broke out last June Emil was called up, and even though he was almost forty, he put on his uniform and went down to the Sinai like everyone else. The whole country had heard Nasser declare on the radio that he was waiting for General Rabin, that the Arab armies would drive the Jews into the sea. It took Emil, and many people like him, right back to childhood, like the second act of a tragedy. People believed Nasser. They believed Assad and King Hussein and the masses of ecstatic mobs that cheered them on. And it's easy to laugh now, the enemies vanquished, Jerusalem liberated, the country tripled in size. But then, in the weeks before it happened, all anyone could think about was leaving, or if they had nowhere to go, preparing the bomb shelters. She would have liked to have heard Nancy's ideas about "dodging the draft," as she calls it, if she had been in the country then.

There's a radio playing inside the café, and when the news comes on, they raise the volume and people's ears prick up. When it's over everyone settles back into their conversations around the tables. Nancy orders a beer, Emil a Turkish coffee, and Yardena a glass of cold tea. Nancy is a bit of a flirt with men, with Emil too. She flips her hair and gives him a teasing smile. Yardena is used to this sort of thing. Her husband, with his charismatic but soft-spoken manner, his pensive eyes, and his full head of dark hair, is appealing to women. "At first I thought he seemed a little old," Nancy confided last night. They were at the beach walking along the shoreline, and Emil had gotten ahead of them. "But actually, he's a pretty cool cat. He has this hip vibe that's kind of intellectual and sexy. It's far out that you're going to be the mother of his child!"

Emil takes a long drag and Yardena sees his restless eyes scan the scene. The café is a favorite spot of theater people, writers, journalists, and the like, and the talk is loud, animated, passionate. Well-known figures come here to hold court and discuss the events of the day. The women are self-assured and expressive, the men opinionated and witty. They crowd around the small tables, messy with coffee glasses, beer bottles, ashtrays, little plates of pretzels and olives. Beyond, people are strolling down the wide sidewalks, entering and leaving the shops in a blur of motion, while the cars and buses make their way down Dizengoff amongst the wily pedestrians. A line from the old Tchernichovsky poem comes to mind, *"Everything is submerged in a sea of light and above it all, the blue,"* and really the sky is so blue today, and the light falling on the streets a little bit golden, and the clink of glasses mixed with talk and laughter washes around them like an ebullient sea.

An expression comes over Emil's face, a look that doesn't match the mood. "What is it?" Yardena asks him in Hebrew.

"Nothing," he murmurs, shaking his head, and then adds, "this whole scene – it just reminds me…the smart people smoking around the tables, the discussions, the arguments, the jokes. The poses. It's the Café Ziemianska in Warsaw, come back to life."

She loves when he does this – when he calls up images and impressions from his childhood before the war. She loves when he talks about his parents, his older sisters, the family textile store in Warsaw. The childhood games in the courtyard of their apartment building, the building itself – a self-enclosed community inhabited almost exclusively by Jewish families, wary, on edge, yet incapable of imagining what was to come. She loves to hear about the Polish school he attended, the teachers who openly hated Jews, and the few liberal ones who defied the spirit of the times. And the decision, taken at the last minute, that he would travel to England in a *Kindertransport*, "just until it was safe to come home again."

Yardena's mother was also born and raised in an Eastern European city, but she refuses to speak of anything having to do with the life she had there. Not just memories of the place, but also her parents, brothers, friends. "Everyone has their own way of mourning what was lost," her father had once said to her. This was a few years ago, when the whole country was following the Eichmann trial on the radio, hearing the dreadful testimonies, and all that was never mentioned, never clearly put into words, was suddenly filling the front pages of the newspapers. Her father didn't miss a single broadcast. Her mother refused to listen to even one. "For me, it's the talking that helps, bringing up the old memories, remembering the people," he told her, "but for her it's focusing on the work at hand – building the kibbutz, her work on the committees, and you. And Dalia and Yoram. The three of you. The future."

"She has so many questions, that Nancy," her mother remarked last Saturday afternoon after Nancy had gone off with one of her new friends, another volunteer. "She's nosy. And rude. Americans are like that. They just say or ask the first thing that pops into their minds. Like children. No sense of propriety or convention."

"That's what some people say about Israelis," Yoram, who had come by after dinner, had remarked.

"I'm talking about something else. I'm talking about having a sense of what's appropriate and what isn't." Yardena couldn't agree more. Nancy has a way of speaking and behaving that often leaves them all a little bowled over. It's not just her cavorting with the other volunteers – an international assortment of young people who supposedly are interested in the kibbutz as a socialist experiment, but are in fact mainly there to "let it all hang out" as she's heard them put it.

"Hey Yardena, I need to ask you something," Nancy said to her in conspiratorial tones about a week after arriving. They were sitting on her bed in the volunteers' dormitory, Yardena watching with interest as Nancy unpacked the contents of her duffle bag – the patterned miniskirts in gaudy colors, the torn denim shorts, the big belts, a coffee-stained copy of *The Second Sex*. "Where is it possible to get some Mary Jane around here?"

At first Yardena had no idea what she was talking about. Her English is that of a high school student who's good with languages, but her textbooks and the scientific articles she had to read in university didn't cover the latest slang. When Nancy explained it to her, she was surprised and disappointed. She had heard about Americans and Europeans who extolled the benefits of what they called "getting high" and what the older kibbutzniks sternly referred to as "destroying your mind." "We don't do that here," she told her severely. "We prefer to live our lives, not escape from them."

Also unnerving were Nancy's long diatribes on what she called "feminism." Yardena tried to explain that kibbutz ideology upheld complete equality between men and women, and that kibbutzim were in fact models for the best and most enlightened way to live. Men did kitchen duty. Women drove tractors. Equality was a value. "So you dig it," Nancy said impressed. "You know where it's at. That's boss. But back home us sisters have a lot of work to do."

It seemed that Nancy's default stance to anything was rebellion, a desire to turn everything normal on its head. Yardena couldn't understand it. Wasn't it obvious that the life experiences of older people were worth more than the whims of kids who knew nothing? When she put the question to her, Nancy showed her the lyrics to a song by Bob Dylan that talked about how the times were changing, and how those who failed to change with them would be left behind. "My parents don't need any more change," Yardena tried to explain. "They left everything they knew in order to come here, to build a new life, to create a Jewish country. The job of our generation is to continue what they started."

One day Nancy got hold of a Beatles record, and as it spun on the record player in the *mo'adon*, she talked about the time she saw them play in Comiskey Park. She described the screaming, the fainting, the crazy electricity in the air. When Yardena told her that the government had refused to allow the Beatles to perform in Israel, Nancy was nothing short of amazed. "That's unbelievable! How did people take it? If anyone would have tried to pull that crap in Chicago there would have been rioting in the streets!"

Yardena shrugged. "The authorities thought they would be a bad influence on the youth." She doesn't tell her that what scared them was the idea that Israeli teenagers would start to behave like Nancy did.

"Yeah, well you're missing out on some fab music. Not just the Beatles. Have you heard of the Stones? Jefferson Airplane? The Who?"

"The Who?"

"That's their name. The Who." She started jumping around the room like one of those crazed rock and roll musicians she's seen in newsreels, as though playing a guitar, and singing. Yardena had smiled, trying to look like she wasn't laughing at her. But then a volunteer, recognizing the song, came rushing into the room and joined her, as though he too was wildly playing a guitar. Clearly she, and most of the people she knows, are missing out on something, but she can't see the appeal of it. She likes quiet, sober songs, especially when they're based on poems. Last month Emil brought home a wonderful record of songs by Jacques Brel. Though she doesn't understand the French, the passion in his voice is stirring and profound. Reflective. Romantic.

These are qualities that first attracted her to Emil Markovitz and she wasn't wrong about him. They met in Jerusalem at a talk he was giving at the university on modern Polish poetry. Yardena, a biology major, would not have normally been interested, but her roommate asked her to come after her boyfriend couldn't make it. Emil spoke about the challenge of writing poetry in the wake of the war, and the issue of freedom of expression under Communist regimes, and he read from the work of several modern Polish poets. Poetry didn't often move Yardena, but there was one, a brief philosophical poem by Milosz called "Encounter," that caught her attention. The poem recalls a moment on a winter morning, a memory from childhood. The moment is lost, but its visceral elements are recalled "not out of sorrow, but in wonder."

After the reading she approached Emil and asked about the poet, and where she could read more of his work. He showed her a volume entitled *Modern Poetry in Translation,* which had come out in England, and suggested that they continue the conversation at a café. Speaking with Emil was like visiting a lost land where something of what had once comprised her parents' world and her mother's unspoken family history still existed. Like a subterranean force, it exerted a mysterious pull. He asked if he could see her again, and she eagerly agreed. They would meet in cafés or parks around the city, delighted and surprised by what felt like an innate chemistry. For the first time in her life she had met someone who made the world seem wider, fuller, more beautiful.

Their attraction seemed to work on contrasts – his age and her youth, his love of literature and her preference for science, his world-liness and her communal kibbutz upbringing. The fact that he had had love affairs, long and short, with many women fascinated and excited her. After their third date she hinted, as subtly as she could, that she wanted to go to bed with him. She was curious about what it would be like, how it would differ from her less than satisfactory experiences, two in number, with boyfriends her own age. He told her they should wait, so as not to ruin everything through hastiness. His abstemious attitude came as a pleasant shock and seemed to her so courtly, so quaintly romantic, that she felt herself falling in love.

Nancy behaves quite differently with men, and seems to have no use at all for romance. She's on "the Pill," and she doesn't buy into "all the BS about saving yourself for marriage." "This place is like the United Nations," she observed with a lascivious wink soon after she arrived, "and I want to visit all the countries." Again, Yardena was dismayed. What kind of girl spoke this way? She doesn't believe that Nancy has actually slept with that many people, but she's slept with enough. There are no secrets on kibbutz. Gossip is rampant. There are ugly names for this sort of carrying on. But what does Nancy care? She's clearly oblivious to shame.

Everyone notices her. As she walks through the kibbutz, people call her over and try to practice their broken English. Girls make chain necklaces like hers and tie dye their clothes in their dormitory sinks. Boys vie for the chance to sit beside her at meals. They sidle up to her as she peruses the volunteer bulletin board outside the dining hall, eager to impress her. When Yardena visits her parents, old schoolmates, people with whom she has barely exchanged a word in years, come over to say hello. One day Matty Bluestein, the neighbor's son, still in high school, begs for an introduction. "Your cousin is a very interesting woman," he says. "Do you think she'd like me?"

It's sometimes hard to believe that they're related at all. But when Yardena comes for lunch on Saturday afternoons and they all sit on the front porch and drink tea and crack sunflower seeds, Nancy has a way of bringing up the subjects that remind everyone of their family connection. And, oddly enough, those subjects are the ones that Yardena most yearns to hear about. "So, you grew up in Minsk, right? That's what my dad told me," Nancy says to Tamar one Saturday when Emil has stayed behind in Tel Aviv.

Yardena watches her mother's face and sees her flinch. Unfortunately, Nancy doesn't know who she's dealing with. She expects that her mother will offer a platitude or two and then change the subject without Nancy even noticing. "Your father is a charming man," Tamar replies, her little-used English sounding surprisingly fluent. "I hope I will meet him again one day."

"Yeah, my dad's a pretty good guy. He knows what's what. And he was actually really jealous that I was coming. I think he'll try to make it over here after he retires from the newspaper. I know he'd love to see you again too. But the thing I really wanted to ask is about you.

Your life. Like, growing up in Minsk. What was that like? I mean, it might as well be on the moon, for all the chance we have of seeing it. And your family – I'd just love to hear more about them."

"Maybe later, dear. Would anyone like some more tea?"

"Before I left, my father told me that right before the war you were in touch through letters," Nancy perseveres, a guileless bull in a china shop. "He said you were trying to help a cousin get out of Europe."

"What cousin?" Yardena asks.

"You don't know about it? My dad and your mom were trying to help a cousin of theirs in…I think it was Lithuania? They wanted to help him and his family to leave the country, to escape the war."

Yardena glances, a little timidly, at her mother. "Who was he?"

"Yeah, my dad only told me a little about it," Nancy says. "What was the story?" Yardena tries to appear casual, like she isn't that interested, but her breath has gone thin, as if there is less air available. There's no way her mother is going to answer. Her expectation is that of waiting for a volcano to erupt, or the onset of an earthquake. But something in her mother's mind must have switched tracks. Her expression is calm, almost openhearted, as pleasant as a stranger's. It's like she doesn't see Yardena, and it's just her and Nancy in the room. And then, as though this is a normal conversation, she begins to speak. Yardena decides to just act natural and let whatever happens next take its course.

"Well, your father and I had a cousin, really he was a second cousin, Gabriel Shulman, and he had a wife called Dora, and there were two children, Sophie and Marek. His father, Yoyna, was my father's cousin. They all lived in Vilna – today it is in Lithuania, but in those days, it was part of Poland. In the years before the war I thought about Gabriel often, and I would write him letters telling him to leave Vilna and to come here, to the kibbutz. But he didn't believe…well, none of them could have imagined what was going to happen. Just like my parents and my brothers – we all thought they were safe in Russia, with Stalin in charge. But with Gabriel I felt that I had to convince him to leave. To come join us here. To go anywhere that would take him. I was very worried about him and his family.

That was why I wrote to your father, to see if he could help get visas for America. And I know he tried too. We all did what we could."

"That's so sad," Nancy says, visibly moved. "It's hard to believe the terrible things your generation lived through!"

Yardena can hardly speak. How is it that with Nancy, a person they barely know, her mother speaks so freely, revealing things she refuses to tell her own children? "Do you still have any of his letters?" Nancy asks.

"No. I should have kept them, but I didn't." Again, her mother asks if anyone wants more tea. Nancy says that she'd love something cold, and her mother says she has a bottle of soda water in the fridge. Yardena wants to tell Nancy to keep asking questions, offer more openings, but she can't do this without her mother hearing or noticing. When she comes back with a tray of glasses and the soda water, her mother says, "But I have something else he sent me – a Yiddish magazine with poems and stories. There is a poem inside it written by my great-grandmother."

"No way!" Nancy cries out. "I know it. My father has the same one – he showed it to me. It's a literary journal, light blue, right? And it has this funny drawing, like a sun rising, and the date – 1914 – on the cover, right? He told me about that poem. He said it was written by an ancestor of ours, and it must be her. Your great-grandmother? She must be my dad's as well! He marked the page. We couldn't understand a word of it, but I know we have it in our basement in Chicago!" She glances excitedly at Yardena, and then says to Tamar. "Where is your copy? Do you have it? You must know Yiddish, right? Maybe you could translate the poem for us!"

Yardena feels dizzy, but she tries not to show it. "I'm sorry, but I don't have it," her mother is saying. "I gave it to a special library for Yiddish books in Tel Aviv, and that was many years ago."

"You gave it away?" Nancy says, disappointed, and perplexed. "Why? Didn't you want to keep it as a memento?"

Yardena understands perfectly why her mother would not want to keep it. In fact, the Yiddish library sounds like exactly the right place for it. "What for?" Tamar shrugs. "At least in the library, people who are interested in that sort of thing can read it."

"But…it's like part of your family."

Her mother frowns. "It is not my family. It's an old magazine for people who wrote little poems and stories in Yiddish. That's all." Nancy opens her mouth to speak, but appears to be at a loss for words. If her mother were not present, Yardena would explain that both of her parents, like the entire kibbutz and everyone else they know, make a point of speaking nothing but Hebrew. All foreign languages are discouraged, but Yiddish in particular is considered outdated and a little distasteful. Yardena has never given this any thought, probably because it has always made perfect sense to her. But looking at Nancy's puzzled expression she muses, for the first time, that perhaps it is a little odd – such a total negation of one's mother tongue and the time when one spoke it.

"Well I, for one, find this whole thing really far out," Nancy says after a few seconds of rumination. She looks at Tamar with new resolve. "But you do speak Yiddish, right? Say we were to go to this library and find the magazine and take it out, if they let us. Or copy it down. You could translate it, couldn't you?"

Yardena is expecting a firm no. The whole scheme is ridiculous – a Yiddish library, a journal from 1914. Sitting on the shelf for how long? Probably since the end of the war, or even before that, and it's doubtful that it's still there. But again, her mother is accommodating, agreeable. Her Yiddish is rusty, out of practice, but she is willing to give it a try.

A plan is put in motion. Yardena will tell the head of the lab that she has a doctor's appointment that day. Nancy will ask for a day off work and take a bus to Tel Aviv. She'll stay over at Yardena and Emil's apartment, and the next morning the two of them will go and look for the library.

— . —

They don't have a spare bedroom so Nancy sleeps on the sofa. After the long weeks on the kibbutz she's excited to be in the city and asks for them to take her out on the town. Yardena wants to see *The Graduate*, playing at the Mugrabi, but Emil, who knows a thing or two about nightlife, suggests a bar on Ibn Gavirol. There's live entertainment too, a guitar player, and Nancy earnestly sings along with his renditions of "Michelle" and "Yesterday." Afterward, dance music comes on and though it all sounds like noise to Yardena, Nancy recognizes the song. She sways instinctively to the beat and then gets up to join the dancers near the bar. Yardena has seen this sort of dancing in movies and on TV – dancing where it looks like the dancer is in the midst of a controlled fit, with arms swinging and odd gyrations, yet somehow Nancy seems to know how to make it look graceful and harmonious. It really is a mystery; how can this woman, who dresses like a little girl and likes to behave like a silly teenager, be so interested in a Yiddish poem?

Over coffee in their small kitchen the next morning Yardena opens a map of the city. Though she's been living in Tel Aviv for two years, she doesn't like to linger among the pushy crowds and commotion of the bus station, and she's unfamiliar with the small streets that surround it. She locates the address her mother has written out for her. As they board a bus that will take them to the south side of the city, Yardena wonders if the library is even still there. Nothing about the world is the same as it was twenty years ago. The war in Europe had just ended. Refugees had emerged from the camps to find themselves widowed, orphaned, destitute, and homeless. And the country, barely just created, was fighting for its life.

It isn't difficult to find the street, but not all of the buildings have numbers. Luckily Tamar mentioned that the best way to recognize it is by the fig tree growing in the yard, and sure enough they find such a tree by the entrance to a three-story building. It looks like a regular apartment building and a woman with two small children passes them as she comes down the narrow walkway that leads to the entrance. Yardena checks the mailboxes in the entry hall and sure enough, there is one labeled *Di Yiddishe Biblyotek*.

They head up the three flights of stairs, and on the top floor there is a small Yiddish sign on the wall by the door on the left. Yardena enters tentatively, with Nancy following behind. The air in the room is warm and musty and smells of old books. A man of about her father's age, in suit pants, a vest, a white buttoned shirt, and a black tie held with a gold clip, sits behind a small wooden desk, a pencil tucked above his small, almost delicate ear. He looks up from the book he is reading. "Can I help you?" He asks politely.

The room is lined with metal shelves containing what must be thousands of volumes, many of their titles faded into their dark, worn covers. Several more rows extend across the room, so that the librarian at his small desk appears a castaway, stranded on an island, surrounded by a grave and silent sea of books. "We're looking for an old Yiddish journal," Yardena tells him. She reaches into her purse and finds the paper with the name that her mother wrote out. "My mother thinks it might be here."

"*Der Nayer Yiddisher Horizont,*" he reads out. "*Friling 1914.*" He sighs, as if this has saddened him, and asks, "Do you know what *friling* means?"

Yardena shakes her head.

"Spring," he replies. "What an innocent place the world was then. Well, let's have a look." He rises from his seat, turns to the lettered drawers of the wooden card catalogue directly behind him, opens one, and leafs slowly through the index cards. Nancy stands by his side watching, but Yardena soon grows restless.

The place has the creepy stillness of an old museum that no one ever visits. Or worse, a morgue. She wanders into one of the rows and pulls a random book from the shelf. *Di Dray Musketirn.* When she opens the cover a light cloud of dust erupts. The words, *Far Leyeleh,* are inscribed in finely shaped Hebrew letters. She replaces it and pulls out another volume, *Der Printz.* It has no inscription, but its pages are marked with neat rows of handwritten notes. A third volume is called *Mayses,* by Chekhov, and on the title page someone has scribbled a fine, virtuoso doodle of two cats. She opens a few more: *Death in Venice, Madame Bovary, Don Quixote* – all in Yiddish translation.

"Miss?" The librarian calls. "I think I've found it." They follow after him down the length of the shelves, narrow as tunnels, to the back corner of the room. He points to a row of binders lining the bottom shelf, and drawing the pencil from behind his ear, taps on one of them. "According to the catalogue," he says, "it should be somewhere in here."

It doesn't take long to find *Der Nayer Yiddisher Horizont.* There actually is such a thing. Or at least there once was. *"Friling 1914,"* Yardena reads out the Hebrew letters in the bottom corner. "Yes! That's the one my father showed me," Nancy says. "The exact one, with this same exact drawing on the cover. Can you believe it? Try to find the poem."

But there is a problem; her mother didn't remember the name of the woman who wrote the poem, and Nancy isn't sure of it either. Yardena scans the table of contents and finds a poem by an R. Shulman. Like Gabriel Shulman. The poem is brief, three short verses, still easily legible. "I think this is it," Yardena tells her, staring blankly at the Hebrew script.

"Can you read it?" Yardena can, but when she speaks the words they sound like gibberish. She asks to check it out. The librarian is reluctant to allow the frail, aging journal to leave the premises. *As if anyone else will ever want to see it,* Yardena thinks, but when she tells him, "Please. It's for my mother, on kibbutz. Her whole family died in the war, but she's related to one of the writers in here," he relents.

When they step out of the building into the open air it's like waking from a strange, disturbing dream. The air is fresh and fragrant, birds are chirping in the fig tree, and the sounds of the city are familiar and comforting. Nancy wants to get some lunch and Yardena takes her to a small place on the other side of the station in Neve Sha'anan, where they order a plate of hummus and a bottle of nonalcoholic malt beer. "Man, did you feel the vibe in that place?" Nancy says as they take a seat at a small table at the back.

"What do you mean - vibe?"

"The whole atmosphere – it was heavy. Really heavy."

"Serious, you mean?"

"Exactly. All those old books. Who do you think even reads them?"

"Old people, I guess."

"Right. I mean, people our age, would they even go in there?"

Yardena laughs. "No. No one like you or me. Only old people. Or maybe people who came from Europe, after the war."

Nancy considers this. "Makes sense. Tell me something. Most Israelis, are they like your mom? Like, they refuse to speak Yiddish like that?"

"Yes. When people came to this country, the first Zionists, their plan was to be new Jews – completely different from the Jews they left behind in Europe. And part of it was that speaking Yiddish wasn't allowed, so that everyone would go back to speaking Hebrew, like we did in the times of the Bible. It was like a national project."

"A national project? That sounds a little scary."

Yardena shrugs. She's getting tired of Nancy's weird expressions and distrust of any kind of authority, and her general cluelessness.

"Telling millions of people that they have to forget their mother tongue and speak something else – isn't that a bit…fascist?"

"Fascist??"

"OK, fine. I didn't mean that."

"We're trying to build a new country. A Jewish country, where people speak the original Jewish language, not something that's just a mixture of other languages. Yiddish is a language for people who don't belong anywhere."

"That's a little harsh."

"Then why don't you speak it?"

"OK, yeah, I don't speak it. But at least I can respect it. Just like I can respect my family's history. Which is more than I can apparently say for your mother."

Yardena is speechless. Nancy's chutzpah knows no bounds. "Don't you dare judge her," she says, trying not to lose her temper. "You don't know anything about her, about what she lived through."

Nancy turns up her palms, gesturing as though backing off. "OK. Sorry. You're right. Sometimes I just say what's on my mind without thinking."

"Yes."

"But I can tell you this: when we were in that library, and I saw all those old Yiddish books, do you know what I was thinking? I was thinking that my grandparents – my dad's mom and dad who came from Russia, they must have had read some of those books when they were growing up. I had this weird feeling that I had a connection to those books – that they're part of my family history. Just like your mother must have read them, and so they're part of your history. And I was thinking that all the places where those books were once read are gone now. Once the people who know how to read them die out, no one will ever read them again."

"Listen, Nancy," Yardena says, "this conversation is depressing me. Enough." Nancy stares at her, surprised and hurt. Perhaps she has spoken too forcefully. "All my mother wanted was a normal life, in a normal country with a normal language. But this country isn't really normal. Not yet. Everyone who is here left a place where they weren't wanted. Can we ever be normal? I don't know. Maybe not."

"That's a pretty rough thing to say, considering that you're going to be bringing up a child here."

"Yes. But at least he will be in his own homeland. That is what is most important."

"Or she."

"Yes. Of course. He or she. You know what I mean."

Nancy finishes the last of the beer and says she has to be getting back to the kibbutz. Yardena walks her back to the bus station. Nancy apologizes for the hurtful things she said. Yardena forgives her easily and wishes her well. They hug, and promise to spend more time together. There at the ticket counter in the station it's easy to promise this, but in fact, not only will they not spend any more time together, they will never see each other again.

That night when Emil comes home, he asks about the trip to the library. Yardena doesn't want to think about it anymore, so she tells him yes, they found the journal, and yes, it contains the poem. She shows it to Emil, and he translates the short verses. The poem sounds to her like something a child would write, simple and naïve.

"Maybe I should go in there to take a look around," he says pensively. "I'd probably find a lot of the books that I read as a boy in Warsaw."

"I wouldn't recommend it. It's a gloomy place. And we were the only ones there. They'll probably close it down one of these days."

Yardena is looking forward to a quiet evening, perhaps continuing the game of chess they started several days ago, when the doorbell rings. It's a couple from downstairs, Rina and Hezi. She had almost forgotten that Rina mentioned yesterday that they would drop by. Emil puts on the Jacques Brel record. Yardena makes coffee and puts out some dates and cookies. Rina is also pregnant, with a due date two months ahead of her, and Yardena is very interested to hear about how her final trimester is going. Emil talks about a new book he is translating from Polish. Hezi tells about an article he is writing on the Apollo space missions. He believes that they are very close to being able to put a man on the moon. "It could happen soon, even in the next year or two," he tells them.

Evening settles over the city. The days are getting longer and the air outside is cool and smells of trees in full flower. When Rina and Hezi leave, Yardena is unusually tired. She gets into bed and settles onto her side, her burgeoning belly rubbing up against her bent knees, and falls into a deep sleep. She doesn't notice when Emil gets into bed later on, but when she wakes, in the quiet hours of the night, he is sleeping by her side. She has been dreaming, she realizes, of the library. The long shelves loomed large, with their rows of books holding funny little inscriptions inside their dark covers. In the dream she felt like a small child, with the books watching over her like kindly aunts and uncles. *Di Dray Musketirn. Der Printz. Mayses.* They stared down at her, recognizing her as one of their own.

She rises from her bed, goes to the kitchen, and pours herself a glass of water. Nancy was right. Her mother must have had books like those in her home as a child. She must have read them. She has heard her mother discuss such books in detail, yet they were nowhere to be found on her shelves, or in the kibbutz library. Ghosts.

Emil appears in the doorway of the small kitchen. She apologizes for waking him, but he claims he couldn't sleep anyway. "Most of the people who once read those Yiddish books are dead," she tells him. "Those books are what's left." He nods thoughtfully. Somehow he knows exactly what she's talking about. "They wanted to be the kind of people who read important books and knew what was written in them."

"Yes," Emil agrees. "That's exactly what they wanted."

"And that's why my mother won't speak Yiddish. That's why she won't set foot in that library. It's not that she didn't love those books. It's that she loved them too much."

The next day, when she passes the Café Kassit on her way to work, she pauses to look at the people sitting around the little tables, smoking, drinking coffee, debating the events of the day. It's then that she feels, for the first time, a strange flutter like a little fish, moving inside her stomach. When she goes to the kibbutz on Saturday, she will tell her mother. Hearing about it will be a solace to her, a small consolation.

Comrades

(Tamar – Kibbutz Givat Hadar, Oct. 1946)

I t's the strangest thing. When I lie in my bed at night, Shimon snoring lightly beside me and the kibbutz still and quiet after tireless days of labor and debate about our future, my mother's image comes to me. She's in the kitchen of our apartment in Minsk, embroidering a handkerchief for me with small blue flowers. It is only now, when I'll never see her again, that I know I should have been a better daughter. I wish I had told her, when it was still possible, that if not for her love I would never have had the strength to venture away from her, to forge this life of endeavor and struggle.

Lying there in the darkness, I see also my father, my brothers, my quiet, gentle sister-in-law Dina, my little niece Shoshanna. They are waving to me from the platform as I board the train in Minsk. Their images accompany me as I fall asleep, but when morning comes and I open my eyes, their faces, so clear in the dead of night, have evaporated away like steam.

We rise at 5:00, pull on our work shorts and shirts, boil water for a quick glass of tea. It's harvest time in the fields and Shimon's tractor awaits him, just as the baskets of dirty clothes await me and the girls in the laundry, and piles of work shorts and shirts await mending in the warehouse. Work is the cure for all that ails the soul, but today will be a day of reckoning, a Yom Kippur that forces one to face what one has done, to beg forgiveness in one's heart, knowing that there can be no absolution, only the weight of carrying what can never be revealed.

Yesterday evening, after I returned from tucking in the children, and Shimon had left for the Defense Committee meeting, I retrieved Lotte's letter, stuffed between Alterman and Koestler on the bookshelf, and reread it.

Dear Frau Stein, it begins, and continues in a Yiddish spiked with German. *We have never met, but we know, or have known, someone in common. I am speaking of my nephew, Otto Fischer.*

Last week I found the letter lying in wait for me in our mailbox by the entrance to the dining hall. It had no return address and at first I opened it carelessly, but when I caught sight of the signature I panicked and I stuffed the letter into the pocket of my shorts, reading it only after I had locked myself in a toilet stall in the new bathrooms.

He spent the first years of the war in Palestine and was later sent back to Germany to do espionage work for the British.

My heart stopped, then found itself and beat wildly. A vision of Avner, sharp as a photograph, rose in my mind: thin, so that he appears taller than he is, awkward in khaki pants that are a little too big for him. His hair, the color of rust, parted to one side. The smile – sad, ironic, weary.

Otto managed to perform valuable work for a full eighteen months before his identity was discovered and he was betrayed. As you may have been informed, he died in Dachau, probably sometime in the autumn of 1944.

Well, I had not been informed, and reading about it there in the bathroom stall, a cry rose in my throat and I had to strangle a stifled wail.

"Are you OK in there?" someone had said – I guessed it was Miriam, one of the Palmachniks stationed with us, and I remembered myself. But reading those lines again now, there is still a stab of horror. A horror that has become all too familiar, yet every time I encounter it anew, I feel sick. *Him too?* I wanted to scream. I had so hoped that he had somehow escaped. Imagining it was a consolation, like a fairytale with a happy ending.

Some months ago I came to a decision: I cannot think about what happened. There is no other way to carry on. I must lock away all thoughts of my father, my mother, my jokey brothers, the courtyard of our apartment near the market in Minsk that always smelled of cabbage and onions, the view from our window, the bustling street below. Also, all recollections of my school teachers, my comrades in our Zionist youth group, Lena and Sonia, my best friends. And Kiva Zilber, the handsome, serious boy who once declared his love for me as we walked in Governor's Garden on a warm spring day.

I am all that remains. The single seedling that survived the fire. The fragment of shooting star that still burns. The ant that escaped the annihilation of the anthill. But survival comes with a duty and a calling: we must be brave, steadfast, courageous. Deterred by nothing.

I am writing to tell you that I will be coming to Tel Aviv next month for a brief visit. The purpose of this visit is to meet you, so as to discuss a matter regarding Otto which has recently come to my attention. I will be staying at the Hotel Gat Rimon, where I hope to meet with you on Thurs. October 3rd at 1:00 p.m. in the hotel lobby. Such a trip may be difficult for you, but I very much hope that you will take the trouble to see me. I am coming at great personal expense and I do not expect to travel to Palestine again. Please, if only as a last respect for Otto's memory, come to the hotel to meet me so that I can set this matter to rest.

Sincerely,

Lotte B. Haussler

Every few minutes I glance at the small clock on the sewing table. When it shows 10:30 I put down the shorts with the hole in the crotch, which will have to wait till tomorrow. "I'm off," I say breezily as I fold the shorts and put the needle and thread in the sewing basket.

"Give them to me," Hayale says, holding out her hand. "I'll do them after I finish this button. You're taking the 11:00? What time is your meeting?" A meeting. That's what I told the girls in the warehouse. That's what I told Shimon. A meeting with an old friend from

Minsk. She's here with her husband and they're only in the country for three days. This afternoon is the only time she's free. "It's at one," I blurt out, and regret saying even this.

"Where?" Hayale asks.

I glance again at the clock. "I have to go. I'll tell you about it later. Promise," I call as I dash out and head down the path behind the dining room to the newly built housing units across from the cowshed.

I draw the curtains shut, slip out of my shorts and work shirt, and pull the dress I've chosen from the warehouse's ample supply over my head. It's light blue, with tailored short sleeves and a smart little belt around the waist. It came into kibbutz possession from Rosa Mandel, a refugee from Bucharest who arrived six months ago, and as I smooth down the neckline I wonder where Rosa, who spent the war years hiding in the forests of Transylvania, got it.

I splash water on my hair to calm its frizziness so that I can pin it up, and dig out a tube of lipstick, bought for special occasions with three months' savings, from a tin at the back of the cupboard. The black leather handbag I retrieve from under the bed. The change purse too. What else? My handkerchief – the one embroidered with blue flowers. And the photograph, of course. Isn't that the reason for this meeting?

How do I appear now, all dressed up like a European lady? Am I a vision of what I once was? What I might have been? I wish I could see myself in full but the only mirror we have is the size of a postcard, hanging over the bathroom sink. Enough for Shimon to shave with. Enough for me to comb my hair.

If the children were to see me like this they would surely be startled. When I pass the preschoolers' dormitory on my way to the bus stop, I spy Yardena with the little Herzfeld girl, the two of them immersed in their play as they dig their shovels in the vegetable garden. I resist the urge to call out to her. It makes me unspeakably happy to think of the children and what they're doing right now. Yoram, raising his hand to solve a mathematical equation, Dalia copying out Hebrew letters into her penmanship notebook.

After I read Lotte's letter in the bathroom stall I held it over the toilet, about to tear it to pieces, but then stuffed it back into my pocket. For the next few days I carried it around with me, taking it out and rereading it whenever I had a chance. What did this woman want? What would happen if I simply didn't show up? But she had asked me to come as a gesture of respect for his memory, and how could I refuse that? He's dead. They're all dead and I'm alive. To meet with the woman would be unpleasant, but not to go would be worse.

Two days ago I went to Zorik and told him that I would be going to Tel Aviv. It was short notice but Zorik is not one to miss an opportunity. "Tel Aviv? On Thursday?" He nodded in his curt manner. "Very good. Same as usual. I'll make the necessary notifications."

— • —

I've never understood the appeal of hotels. Such a bourgeois notion, paying an exorbitant sum for a night's sleep! I put on an agreeable face as I enter the cool lobby with its fancy marble tiling, and stare straight ahead – the best way to mask my discomfort. I stride past the bar where a group of British soldiers are gathered, glasses of beer in hand, and head into the hotel restaurant, where I identify Lotte immediately, sitting at a table by the window. Everything about her is foreign: the cut of her dress, her styled hair, the very way she sits, straight-backed and self-possessed, yet full of feminine charm. She sees me and gives a little wave. She's older than I expected, perhaps fifty years of age or more. "Frau Stein?" She calls tentatively, and I respond with a nod.

She extends her hand politely and I shake it, saying, "It's Sela now," without explaining that Shimon and I decided to Hebraicize our family name after the war, when he returned from Africa. "But you can call me Tamar."

"And you can call me Lotte," she replies in a Yiddish that to my ear sounds stiff and oddly ceremonial. She gestures to the chair across from her. "Please have a seat. I've ordered a cup of tea. May I order one for you as well?"

As I sit down, smoothing my dress under me, I glance around the room, taking in the starched linen tablecloths, each adorned with proper table settings and a small vase holding a sprig of pink bougainvillea. Two men in suits are at a table in the opposite corner, their heads bowed in conversation. A couple, clearly foreigners, are both writing in their notebooks, journalists perhaps. Waiters glide by carrying pots of tea and plates of sandwiches on bronze trays.

"Thank you for coming today, Frau Sela. I appreciate it very much. You must forgive my Yiddish. I have not spoken it for many years, since my grandmother passed away."

I don't expect that she's aware that the only language that we speak on the kibbutz is Hebrew, or that I too have not conversed in Yiddish for many years. Likewise, I don't let on that I speak a serviceable German.

"I may as well say right out that I know all about you and Otto," she says.

Of course she does. Why else would she have sailed the seven seas to come here. "How?"

"After the war his diary came into my possession. He recorded many details about his time in Palestine, and it's clear that even after he left the country, he continued to receive news about you," she pauses and smiles sweetly, "and your family. You see, he had no other remaining relatives. And except for two second cousins now living in Brazil, neither do I. Your connection to him, and what has come of it, is the reason I've made this trip." The soldiers and the bartender burst out in loud laughter and clink their glasses, and Lotte glances at them, mildly annoyed. "I realize that neither he nor you wanted anyone to know about your liaison," she says, pronouncing liaison with an awkward French accent. "And you can rest assured that I intend to honor his memory by keeping all that I know to myself."

Hearing her speak the words so plainly is unnerving. "Please come to the point," I tell her.

"Yes. In good time. But first I'd like to tell you a little more about myself. I spent the war years living under a false identity, working as a maid for the Haussler family. My first husband was Mr. Haussler's lawyer, you see. They lived in a small town outside Düsseldorf."

"And they hid your family?"

"Only me. My husband killed himself several days after the Kristallnacht events. My two sons died in Dachau." She opens her handbag and dabs her eyes. "My sister and her family…no one is left."

We hear these stories often from the refugees the Jewish Agency sends us, sole survivors of their families and villages, with nothing to their name and nowhere to go. I'm about to offer some words of sympathy, but a waiter appears with a pot of tea and two china cups, and we refrain from speaking until he moves on. "I don't have to tell you, Frau Sela," Lotte begins again, "that war changes everything between people. Frau Haussler died toward the end of the war. Today, I am the second Frau Haussler."

"I see," I reply, suppressing the urge to excuse myself and leave. There is no one in this country who has not suffered the losses that she has, and I have no interest in the sordid details that have spared her life.

"I'm not a young woman," Lotte continues, "and if there is anything I've learned it's that one mustn't judge others. The only reason I've made this trip is because I need to know. That is the only thing that I want from you. You must understand me, Frau Sela. I am too old to start again elsewhere, but my life in Germany is far from easy. Not because of what people say to me, but because of what they don't say. Do you understand me? The knowledge that there is a child, a remnant of what was once our family, would be a great comfort to me." She pauses and then adds, "Even if she doesn't carry our name. I swear that I will tell no one what you tell me. I swear on the memory of my sons. But I must know."

I must know. What I say to myself, each morning when I rise for work in the warehouse and each evening when I tuck Yoram, Dalia, and little Yardena into their beds in the children's dorm, is that *I must not know.* Better to remember them as they were the last time I saw them, at the train station in Minsk in the fall of 1927. My mother, trying to put on a brave face but repeatedly breaking into tears. My father embracing me in his strong, sturdy arms. Yehuda, his wife Dina, little Shoshanna, a yellow bow in her curly black hair. And Binyamin, who had confided to me the night before that he was going to ask Regina Applebaum to marry him.

It was a sorrowful scene, but inside I was joyful. I had spent six months at an agricultural training farm in Germany that spring and when I returned home all I could think of was how I would soon meet my friends and comrades from the movement in the Land of Israel. Many of them had already made the journey, and I longed to join them. *To build and to be rebuilt,* as the famous song says. To exchange the grey streets of Minsk for the blue skies of *Palestina.* The worn hominess of Yiddish for the lovely, clear tones of Hebrew. The stench of the market for the scent of the orchards. And instead of the rot of a bourgeois way of life, a community of equals. What fate could be better?

"I still can't believe that you're actually doing this," Yehuda had grinned. "The rest of us are all talk – you put us to shame! Promise you'll write the second your boat sails into Jaffa."

Binyamin took my hands in his and said with mock seriousness, "I hereby appoint you the official representative of the Grupstein dynasty in Palestine," and we had all burst out laughing.

Even my father declared, "I'm not sad that you're going. I'm happy. This is the happiest day of my life."

Only Mama had wept. "I should have danced at your wedding and here I am sending you off to a desert," she sniffed as she handed me the handkerchief I had watched her embroider the night before at the kitchen table. Even now I can recall her fingers stitching the small blue flowers, the sounds of the street below, the sweet smell of the onions she had just fried, wafting in the air.

"Don't forget us, my darling brave girl," she had whispered. "God willing we will see each other again."

"Do you even know what you meant to him?" Lotte is saying. I'm shaken out of the place where my family is still alive, and stare, incredulous. As if this woman really expects me to give her an accounting. Again, I feel an urge to get up and leave.

"No," Lotte answers her own question. "Perhaps you don't. Otto was a very private person. And perhaps you, too, are a very private woman. But Otto is dead. As are his parents and his younger brother. The secrets he kept are gone with him. And all of his reasons, his plans, his hopes, they are gone too. All that is left is one little child."

I cannot get up. I can barely even move.

"Frau Sela," she continues, "I am neither young nor naïve. I understand that it is perhaps best for you and for your daughter that Otto's life, and your part in it, be stricken from the record. I do not object to this. In fact, I applaud it. In your situation, I am quite certain that I would do the same. And so I've come here, to this country which is not really a country, to ask a kindness from you. Perhaps you would prefer to simply walk away from me, but I am asking you to stay and to tell me, once and only once, and then I swear that you and your family will never hear from me again. You must have cared for him," she says, and I no longer know whether this is an accusation or a reprieve. "And now that he is gone you have barely mourned him. I see that now. So let this be your tribute to him. A gift to a man who deserved far better than fate accorded him. An act of witness, if you will."

My eyes squeeze shut. It has come to this. Like a child I have tried to hide, vainly hoping to avoid this moment when I find myself standing before a judge who is not this woman but me, myself. Or to recall Alterman, I am the sin and I am the judge. And this bourgeois hotel restaurant is to be my court.

Through the arched oriental window behind Lotte, I see, in the distance, the shimmering blue of the sea.

— • —

When I was a girl, a distant relative of my father's whom we called Aunt Rivke was a frequent visitor to our home. Her hair was the color of straw in the sunlight, and when seen from behind, you might imagine that she was an attractive woman. But when she turned around you would balk in horror; instead of a nose, she had an odd-shaped lump of flesh, and a long, deep scar ran down the side of her face. I was told only that as a child Rivke had survived a pogrom in her village, lucky to escape with her life. Later, when I was older, I learned that drunken peasants had cut off a piece of her nose. Whenever I think about what has brought me here, to this life,

I believe that above all, it was Rivke. Even now, her face is the most convincing argument I have ever known.

I've thought of Rivke often in these past years, her image a reminder, rising in my mind whenever our situation seemed dire. I recalled it, for example, in the summer of '40, when a general meeting was held in the dining hall to discuss the voluntary enlistment of kibbutz members in the British army. The Allies were losing the war in Africa and we had no illusions about what could happen to us. Italian planes had just dropped bombs over Haifa. The Nazis had practically walked into Paris, and now all French territory, including Syria and Lebanon, were theirs. The French Foreign Legion had declared loyalty to the Vichy government in Syria and the British were reinforcing defense lines in the Galilee.

When the vote was called on the issue of sending volunteers to the British army, every last hand was raised in the dining hall. The mood in the room was grim but resolute. Shimon took the floor that night and put forth a motion that it should be the older members, the fathers and husbands who had deep roots in Givat Hadar, who should be sent to enlist, because it was they who would best withstand a long separation from the kibbutz community. When he sat down everyone turned to me, as though asking for my approval. As though my agreement would be my contribution.

The evening before, Shimon and I had gone walking in the fields and something had led him to speak of things he had never shared: the Polish boys who would wait for him and his friends as they walked home from school, mocking them, pelting them with sticks, stones, rotten vegetables. He told me of being accosted, pushed to the ground and beaten, barely eight years old. A gang of boys had buried him in the snow, and he fell ill with pneumonia, which he survived only thanks to medicines bought with his parents' meager savings. The air was sweet with the smell of ripening fruit, and the first stars flickered in the darkening sky. We had come to the edge of the field, by the road which in the daytime was busy with passing cars and trucks but was now silent and still, and we turned to look back at the kibbutz houses, their lights shining in the distance.

"I support the motion that the kibbutz allow members with the most seniority to volunteer," I declared that night at the general meeting. Two weeks later Shimon was in the group of fifteen "old-timers" who left for a British army training camp in the Jordan Valley. For a long time I didn't know whether his company was sent to Egypt or Algeria or Libya. He wasn't allowed to disclose his location in the letters he wrote to me. I knew only that he was part of a transport team that drove men and supplies to the front lines, and that this was a disappointment to him. He had wanted to fight. But at least he was a soldier, and in my heart I envied him. Had the kibbutz asked me to join the British army I would have done so. Happily, I would have entrusted my children to the collective and taken up arms. Instead, I joined the refugee absorption committee.

The newspapers were vague, almost secretive, about what exactly was happening to the Jews in Eastern Europe. They had plenty to say about battles fought overseas or new buildings going up in Haifa and Tel Aviv, but reports about what was occurring in the cities and villages we had left behind could only be found in the brief, terse items buried in the inner pages. These reports, which I would read late at night in the *mo'adon* after tucking the children into bed and attending committee meetings, told of things so terrible that we could scarcely believe they were true. Community leaders rounded up and shot, or hanged from street lamps. Innocent people sent to forced labor camps, never to be heard from again. Jews herded together and made to live in ghettos, just like in the Middle Ages.

Yet we knew that at least some of it must be true. We saw it in the faces of the refugees, exhausted and despairing, making their way around the kibbutz. Everyone knew that they had arrived illegally during the night, smuggled in from the sea by the Haganah. Any refugee who came to our gates was given food and shelter, and all we asked in return was that they join us in our labors. We would explain that we were a socialist commune that rejected the notion of private property, and expected all newcomers to put their valuables in safekeeping and donate their garments to the kibbutz clothing pool, which I was put in charge of. As refugees continued to arrive, the racks and shelves of our clothing warehouse filled with dapper suits, stylish dresses, good shoes, warm coats, and all manner of clothes worn by prosperous citizens of modern countries.

— · —

By the middle of July the Vichy regime had finally been defeated in Syria, but what did that matter when the Nazis were moving so quickly across North Africa? Everyone was saying that if they reached Egypt they would continue on to the Sinai Desert and invade Palestine in a matter of months, if not weeks. And the Arabs would be more than happy to help them. Al-Husseini had pledged his support for Hitler; they would welcome Rommel with open arms. There would no doubt be, as happened every time the Arab leaders incited their people, violence in the cities and murderous attacks on Jewish settlements. But this time it would be worse than the massacres in Hebron, worse than the riots in Jerusalem. The attack on Kibbutz Hulda in '29, less than an hour's walk away, was on everyone's mind – how the marauders had come with their wives and their donkeys and camels, the better to load up with whatever they could steal. They burned down the granary and you could see the smoke rising through the night. If the Haganah hadn't sent in reinforcements, Hulda would have been wiped from the face of the earth.

More than once I dreamt that the Nazis stormed the gates of Givat Hadar, killing the guards and rounding up everyone in the dining hall. What would they do after that? Would we have a few minutes' warning to collect the children and hide them somewhere? Perhaps lock them in the kitchen pantry? Or the laundry? Would the Nazis look for them in the laundry? And what then? Would we also be forced into ghettos or loaded onto trucks and taken away? It seemed preposterous, and yet in the towns and cities of our childhood, it was happening. Sometimes at night when terrible thoughts kept me from sleeping, I would put on the light and try to read a little. Alone in my bed, unsure if I would ever see Shimon again, I would turn despairingly to the books my friends and I once considered beacons of humanity and culture: Rolland's *Jean-Christophe*, *Anna Karenina*, the novels of Victor Hugo. They seemed to me relics from a Europe that no longer existed, and had perhaps never existed at all, except in our own romantic, deluded minds.

We are all healthy and well, my mother had written in the summer of '41. *We've been told to pack our bags because very soon we will have to move to a new address, but we still don't know where. Be well, my darling girl, and know that you and Shimon and Yoram and little Dalia are always in our thoughts.* Mama always knew exactly where she was going and what she was doing, and the letter's chipper tone chilled me. Nonetheless, I refused to believe the rumors and continued to send her long, detailed letters filled with cheerful news, like the kibbutz trip to the Dead Sea, and Yoram coming in first place in the children's sports competition, and Dalia's beautiful flute solos that she performed in the dining hall on Friday nights – only to find them again in my mailbox weeks later, stamped in German, *Return To Sender.*

After that I could no longer wait passively for others to carry the burden, and I deliberated about how I could join the only fighting force that might take me – the Haganah. It was an open secret that the kibbutz had various connections with them, but real knowledge about kibbutz ties with the organization was partial and hazy. It was whispered that for years Zorik Kirshenbaum and Lova Schneider had been amassing ammunition from operatives. Before he left, Shimon told me about how he had helped the two of them dig out a weapons cache behind the cowshed. I thought of that cache often and lamented that I didn't even know how to fire a gun.

One rainy night in early fall I knocked on Zorik's door. He is by nature a serious-minded type, a little dry, but sharp as a razor. "I want to contribute," I told him. "I'll do anything that's needed." I feared that he would refuse to take me on, saying that as a mother of two with a husband serving in Africa, I was the last person the Haganah would call upon, and I had prepared several arguments to convince him otherwise.

But he merely nodded, as though filing my offer in a corner of his mind, "Very good," he said in that quiet, laconic tone of his. "If anything suitable comes up I'll let you know."

— . —

I can still see Avner as he was that first day when he came into the laundry: tallish, a little too thin, stoic, self-possessed. Vaguely condescending in his manner. Grumpily he made his way over the wooden planks that lead to the clothes warehouse so as not to tread on the muddy ground. I could tell that he was German even before he opened his mouth – perhaps it was in the cut of his hair, rusty-brown, tidily combed to one side, or the way the sleeves of his shirt were rolled neatly to the elbow, rather than the careless, sloppy style of our men. "I'm looking for Tamar," he said in Hebrew, confirming my suspicions with his stiff, awkward pronunciation. "Are you her?"

I suppressed an urge to laugh, and put on a face that I hoped appeared friendly. "Depends who's asking."

"I am asking." He glanced uneasily over my shoulder at a rack of jackets on the back wall. "A trunk of my clothes is being delivered today, but I was told that it is kibbutz practice to take whatever is brought here."

"That's right," I said brightly. I probably stared at him a little more than I meant to. Despite his grumpy demeanor, something about him, maybe the way his hair fell over his forehead, or the way his pants hung loosely on his narrow frame, reminded me of the boys I once knew in Minsk. In particular, he brought to mind Kiva Zilber, who had laughed at my Zionist friends and my talk of sailing to Palestine.

"But I am not going to become a member. I'm only here for a short time."

"How do you know that?" I smiled again. "You might end up wanting to join us."

"Oh no," he replied quickly. "I'm not…Do you speak any German?"

"A little. I studied it in high school. And I spent some time at a Zionist training farm outside Munich."

"Ah. Good. You see, I'm not suited for kibbutz life," he said, reverting to his traitorous mother tongue.

"What's your name?" I asked him.

"Avner. For as long as I'm here. Avner Fischer."

"Well, Avner Fischer, if you don't plan to stay, you don't have to actually contribute your personal property," I replied in German, making sure to lower my voice, as speaking anything other than Hebrew would bring on a reprimand from anyone who heard me. I was surprised to find, even as I spoke, that I could still put together a half-decent sentence. "But we do ask that you bring it here for safekeeping. If we make an exception for you, we'll have to make it for everyone, and if everyone keeps their own personal property then we won't really be a kibbutz, will we?"

His face fell, and I feared that I had spoken a little too harshly, but his petition for special treatment annoyed me. I knew all about these Germans who showed up at our gates. They weren't interested in joining us. Many of them weren't even Zionists. The only reason they had left their bourgeois lives in Frankfurt or Munich or Berlin was because their beloved Germany had spit in their faces. They had tried so hard to be real Germans. Clothes in the latest fashions. Perfect diction. They could go on and on about German philosophy, literature, music; it would have been comical if they hadn't been reduced to begging the kibbutz to allot them a bed and the chance to earn their keep by harvesting oranges and milking cows. True, some were eager to purge whatever German-ness remained, to contribute what they could. But some, you could tell immediately, would have never set foot on the soil of *Eretz Yisrael* if they had had any choice.

"I mean…" he said, grinning in a way that was slightly ironic – like a schoolboy who thinks he's smarter than the teacher – "I'm an individualist." I responded with a skeptical, inquiring look. "OK, that doesn't sound very good either," he admitted. "Please don't misunderstand me; I think the kibbutz is a wonderful idea. Beautiful even. Everyone according to his ability, each according to his need. So civilized. And what you've accomplished here is admirable. But… what can I say? My parents didn't teach me to share. And I'm too old to change my ways – already thirty! Marx would consider me a stinking capitalist."

Thirty, I mused. A bit younger than I was. "Marx would say that it's never too late to see the light," I said with a wink.

He shrugged. "Who knows? Life is so strange. Who would have thought that I would end up in a socialist collective in the desert?"

Yes, Kiva Zilber, I thought to myself. Earnest. Serious. Restrained. "What would you be doing if you weren't here?" I asked him.

"You mean if Germany hadn't been taken over by a lunatic?" He considered the question. "I suppose I'd be teaching physics in Dusseldorf, probably at one of the better high schools." He stared at me, and with that same slightly ironic smile said, "Frau Tamar, will you please permit me to keep my trunk in my room? I promise never to open it. I understand that you're not supposed to make exceptions, but I'm asking…" He took a moment to collect his thoughts. "I'm asking if you can perhaps make things a little easier for me."

His request was entirely against kibbutz policy, but I was finding it hard to refuse it. Looking at him now, it struck me that it was nothing but fate, random and ruthless, that had brought him here, and that if I could not relent on this small thing, I would be a partner to it. "Wait here," I told him. I went into the back room to a shelf piled with folded tapestries, and pulled out a heavy muslin tablecloth embroidered in a pattern of fish and birds, no doubt the work of some mother or grandmother left behind in Europe. "Take this to your room," I told him, "and spread it over your trunk. Promise me that no one will ever see you open it."

"Of course." He nodded sharply in that way Germans have, but then his look softened. "This is very kind of you." He moved to leave, but then turned back around. "Ah, yes. I almost forgot. There is one more thing." He reached into his satchel, pulled out a small cloth bag and put it on the table. "I was told that valuables can be entrusted to you."

"That's right."

"I would be grateful if you could put this under lock and key."

I picked up the bag, which held something hard with sharp edges inside, and pointed to the metal cabinet behind my table. "It will be right here until the day you leave."

He thanked me again. "Sure," I replied. "Just do me a favor and don't tell anyone about the trunk."

"I won't," he called as he left, and I couldn't tell whether he was sincere or if behind his deferent tone there was an ironic grin.

I unlocked the cabinet with the key that I keep hidden under a pile of winter sweaters. Most of the refugees arrived with little of value. Some had nothing but the clothes on their backs. But over the years there had been a few who managed to escape with pieces of jewelry, a bag of gold coins, or a roll of bills. As I set the bag in the cabinet, it made a strange tapping sound, like two blocks of wood. I opened the drawstring and saw something even more objectionable on a kibbutz than gold or expensive jewelry: two small black wooden boxes and two rolled leather straps. A pair of *tefillin*, for use by religious Jews in prayer. I had not seen such things since leaving home. Even my own father had never used the pair handed down to him by the man who raised him. All of us on the kibbutz had warm, sentimental feelings for the holidays, foods, the music of our childhoods, but no one held the beliefs that went along with them. In our eyes, religion was a means of oppressing people, keeping them ignorant and foolish.

I imagined that what Avner had asked me to lock up was a keepsake, likely given to him by a father or grandfather he had left behind. The thought of him carrying them, alone and homeless, over Europe and across the sea, brought on a sharp pang of melancholy, which I banished as I closed up the warehouse and headed home to change before the children arrived for their afternoon visit.

After that day in the laundry I had little contact with him, though I sometimes saw him pulling weeds or planting flowers with Chaim Richter's team of gardeners. Richter had left Germany while in the midst of an apprenticeship in landscaping, and after being put in charge of the kibbutz grounds he made a point of taking on German refugees to work with him.

It happened occasionally that I would pass Avner on my way to a meeting, or when walking out to the fields with the children. He always seemed to me as I had first seen him that day in the laundry: out of place, pitiable, a victim of circumstance. He would give me a slight nod as if we shared a secret, which I suppose we did, and I noticed that working outdoors had made him somehow ruddier, healthier, more relaxed. One day, leaving the dining hall with Hayale, I saw him playing chess in a corner of the room with Menny Buckstein, who always won the kibbutz tournaments. He waved and I went over to say hello. "Do you play?" he asked me.

"Unfortunately not. I never learned."

"I could teach you."

"Our family is more the backgammon and checkers type," I joked.

"Backgammon and chess," Menny rolled his eyes. "Two different universes. You should take up his offer."

I stared at the board, and for some reason, his *tefillin* boxes with the leather straps came to mind, his keepsake from a father or grandfather, now lying in the cabinet of valuables. I thought to ask him about how he had managed to save them, but his face had taken on a look of thoughtful concentration as he pondered his next move, and I decided to wait for another time.

I didn't see him again until some days later, when I was put on a week of kitchen duty. On the first morning Yehudit Feinstein, who was running the dining hall, sent me to the storeroom to help peel potatoes, and there he was, sitting on a crate amongst two large sacks, peeler in hand. "Good morning, Avner," I greeted him. "Nice to see that you're still with us." The words came out in German, as if we had agreed that it would be our language of conversation – another kibbutz rule broken.

He looked up briefly and then returned his attention to the half-peeled potato in his hand. "Of course I'm still here," he grumbled. "Where else would I be?"

"I thought you were determined not to throw in your lot with us socialists."

"That still holds," he replied. "And anyway," he added with that same ironic smile I had seen that day in the laundry, "I've been thinking lately that your socialism is just a costume. The kibbutz is basically a *shtetl*, just like the ones you left in Russia and Poland."

"A *shtetl*? What a ridiculous thing to say!"

He spun around and grabbed another peeler from the table behind him. "Here," he held it out with a smile. "Each according to his ability."

I seated myself on the crate across from him and pulled a potato from the sack. "You think this kibbutz is like a *shtetl*?"

"I'd say so. You're a bunch of Jews all living together in a small, insular community. You all dress the same. You've made up your own rules and customs. You're practically cut off from the outside world. And you reject every civilized comfort: well-prepared food, nice clothes, good furniture…" He examined the potato he was peeling and added, "Not to mention good manners."

"Is that what bothers you?" I retorted. "That you don't like our manners? That we have more important things to think about than clothes?" I peeled the potato in my hand vigorously. "You see exactly where your manners have gotten you. Germany doesn't want you. Europe doesn't want you. It's not a pleasant thing to accept but it's the truth."

"Germany has been taken over by a gang of thugs. They won't last. There are enough good people in Germany who will run them out."

"Are you crazy?" I laughed bitterly. "What good people? The German people *are* the Nazis. And they're not a 'gang of thugs.' They're the strongest army in the world. Rommel is getting closer every day, and with his Arab friends waiting to welcome him, we're next."

"Oh dear! With that attitude it's a good thing that you aren't Churchill or Stalin. You won't defeat the Nazis by crying and waving a white flag."

"Oh don't you worry. There won't be any white flag, I can promise you that. How can you not see that this is the only place in the world where Jews can live normal lives?"

"Well, I wouldn't exactly say that."

I stared at him, not quite believing what I was hearing. "You would go back?"

"We had a very good life there."

"You were living in a dream."

"Not at all. I had my work. I had…my wife."

This admission came as unexpected news "Oh…I didn't realize…where is she now?"

"It's quite complicated." He looked a little flustered. "She wasn't Jewish but she converted two years ago and we got married. We hoped that things would blow over but they only got worse, and so we decided that given the circumstances, the best thing was for her to renounce her conversion and divorce me, just until this is all over. We talked about leaving the country but her mother is ailing, and she didn't want to leave her knowing that she might never see her again." He said all of this in tones of resignation. "And so we're no longer legally married. For now."

I found his optimism touching. "And you see yourself remarrying her?"

"I don't know," he admitted. "But I can hope. Just like you can hope that you'll see your husband again."

I was about to reply that our situations were in no way similar, but just then Tzvi Gruber appeared in the doorway, saying that Yehudit needed help setting out the dishes. "You've learned to speak your mind like a *sabra*," I remarked.

"I've had many teachers," he said wryly.

That night as I lay in bed my thoughts kept returning to that conversation. It took me back to Minsk, to the discussions we used to have in our youth group, full of impassioned boys and girls who yearned to be a part of the new order, to prove their loyalty, to serve. We would gather in one another's rooms and debate for long hours into the night, waging arguments that pitted Zionism against Communism. Many believed that Zionism was a fantasy and that only Communism could offer the Jews a bright future. Where were they now, those earnest dreaming boys and girls?

The next morning, as I dressed in my shabbiest clothes for kitchen duty, I felt badly about the things I had said. What right did I have to ridicule him? And how could anyone, in these terrible times, deny a hapless refugee his hopes? I decided to apologize. When I spotted him setting out plates of cut vegetables on the tables I went over to him, determined to make amends. But he spoke first. "Please forgive me," he began, "for what I said about your husband. It was callous of me."

"What did you say?" I asked, confused. "You mean that it's not certain that he'll come back?"

"Yes, that. I'm sorry."

"That wasn't callous. It's the plain truth."

My frank response confused him, and a few seconds passed before he said, "Nonetheless, I apologize."

"That's very kind of you. And I...I'm also sorry for the things I said yesterday."

"Don't be. I understand why you said them. And you also spoke the truth. I have no way of knowing what will happen between me and Greta. And I haven't had word from my parents and my brother in months. I ought to be realistic." His tone turned grave. "Where is your husband serving?"

"He's in a transport unit somewhere in North Africa. I don't know much more than that."

He nodded thoughtfully. "Then our situations are similar."

After that it was as if a wall between us had come down. During the break between washing the breakfast dishes and preparations for lunch we shared a cigarette outside behind the kitchen. "So, Frau Tamar," he said with that grin I found so appealing, "How did you come to live in a socialist commune in the backwaters of the Levant?"

"A socialist commune in the backwaters of the Levant has always been my idea of paradise," I laughed. "And at first they didn't even want me. I paid an Arab to drive me to the site – it was basically two tents and a fire pit. They took one look at my big trunk and my dress and fancy boots and told me I wasn't needed."

"Obviously that didn't deter you."

"Just the opposite," I replied with a smile. I was thinking of that first evening: my first sight of the group ascending the hill, hoes and shovels slung over their shoulders, the dusky sky coloring the horizon in orange, purple, and blue, a golden half-moon over the fields, the silhouettes of the tents lit by small lanterns. "I'm Tamar Grupstein," I had announced to the shadows that moved about in the darkness. "I've come to join you. I'll go out to the fields to work with you tomorrow morning."

They ignored my declaration, but they shared their supper of cooked lentils, and afterward I collected their bowls without a word and washed them by candlelight in a pail of water. I could hear them speaking outside the tent; someone read out an article about how the kibbutz was an experiment in social justice, the realization of an economically fair society where everyone was truly equal. One of the men started up a Hebrew song, which I knew. They went on to sing another familiar song, and then another. Someone played a tune on a flute, the high quivering notes of a lullaby that my mother used to sing. Without thinking I began to sing along in Yiddish until someone called out, "Hey, stop that. No Yiddish allowed! Only Hebrew."

"But the singing was tolerable," a voice said, a low, friendly voice that filled me with happiness. I fell asleep that night thinking that I had achieved the most important victory of my life.

"What about your husband?" Avner asked, the next time we went out for a break. "How did you meet him?"

I pictured Shimon as he appeared to me on the day I met him. Dark, wide-set eyes, bushy black hair, a stocky build, and hands so hardened from work in the fields that it was impossible to imagine that he had once been a Talmud scholar, a rabbi's son from Galicia. But he had read all the Zionist writers in secret – Gordon and Ahad Ha'Am, Borochov and Pinsker, and their words had become his bible.

"We talked about you last night," he had whispered to me on that first morning on the hill. "I think you've charmed your way in." After several weeks of evening strolls during which we discussed the advantages of socialism, the future of the Jewish people, and what it meant to devote one's life to Zionism, I decided that this was the man to whom my virginity ought to be lost. When he would speak at meetings, his voice was clear and warm and impassioned. I saw how the others listened, rapt and attentive, and how he was always the first to rise for work and the last to come in from the fields. I fell in love with his seriousness.

Romantic feeling, according to the tenets of the doctrine, was a false concept, a lie people told themselves that gave rise to the bourgeois farce of the family. Free love, on the other hand, was considered a suitable pursuit for the socialist revolutionary. The liberty of it thrilled me. No announcements were necessary. A few months later, we asked a *Keren Kayemet* official who came to check up on the kibbutz to perform a wedding.

—— • ——

"And you?" I asked him the next day. "How did it happen that you fell in love with a German woman?"

He took a long drag on his cigarette. "We met at university. An attraction of opposites. The simplest story in the world."

"I can't imagine that it was simple. Didn't she hear Hitler's speeches? What about Jews being enemies of the people?"

He said nothing, as though the question didn't merit a reply.

"And her parents? What did they think about it?"

"Do you really think that all Germans buy into the garbage they hear on the radio?"

"Apparently enough of them do."

"All evil regimes come to an end."

"True, but the question is when. And in the meantime, your whole life is in upheaval. You've divorced your wife! Changed your name! Left everything behind except your grandfather's *tefillin!*"

A strange, troubled look came over him. I waited for him to speak and when he didn't, I asked, "What is it?"

"They're not my grandfather's," he said quietly, as though confiding a secret. "They're mine."

"Of course. You know what I mean."

"No, they're really mine."

For a moment I was speechless. What he was saying implied something so odd that I wasn't sure I understood. "So you're... religious?"

A pained, perplexed look came over him, as though he was at a loss to explain himself. "My family has always observed *Torah ve'mitzvot.*"

"I don't understand." People were pouring into the dining hall, shouting, laughing, scrambling for places at the tables, and we had to go back to work.

As I pushed the food cart amongst the tables, distributing baked noodle casserole and bowls of cooked vegetables, my head almost hurt with his revelation. How could such a seemingly intelligent man be a believer? I knew that the poor and ignorant masses had a need for such illusions, but Avner had been neither poor nor ignorant.

If he was a religious Jew then what was he doing on a kibbutz – a place which by definition rejected religion and sought to build a society liberated from the fictions that had enslaved people for centuries? How did he agree to refrain from wearing a *kippa*? From praying three times a day? From keeping the Sabbath? From observing the dietary laws? And if it was a kibbutz he was looking for, why didn't he seek out one of the religious kibbutzim that had sprung up in recent years? None of it made sense. I suspected that behind these questions lay something difficult and sensitive, and hesitated to broach the subject.

But the following day, as we lit up cigarettes on the steps behind the kitchen, he himself brought up the topic. "I owe you an explanation," he began.

"You don't owe me anything."

"But I want to tell you."

In a low, terse voice, he told me how he and his wife had been at her brother's house that night in November three years earlier when the Nazis had staged a countrywide pogrom. When the sounds of smashing glass and screams began to reach them, he and his wife hid in the cellar. The next day he went to his parents' house to find his mother and aunt sobbing amongst a scene of overturned bookcases, torn curtains, smashed cabinets. "My mother had suffered for years from a weak heart," he said, "and I could see that she was finished. Completely devastated. When I asked them where my father and brother were, she could barely speak. My Aunt Lotte said that they had both been arrested and no one had any idea what had happened to them." Later, he explained, he received a postcard from his brother saying that they were being held in a camp called Dachau, outside Munich. He heard nothing more. It was decided that his mother would leave their ruined home and go to live with his aunt.

"After that, Greta and I made our plans. We decided that we would divorce. She would renounce Judaism and return to the church, getting all the necessary papers to prove that she was no longer Jewish. And I would leave the country. My father had several business connections in Eastern Europe and I wrote to them, asking if they could help. One of them, a widower in Bucharest with a son who had contracted polio and could no longer go to school, agreed to give me room and board in exchange for tutoring. I was able to make my way to them, and once there I rarely ventured outside the house, as it was dangerous for a Jew to even walk the streets. After Romania entered the war, I used the last of my money to get on a ship headed for Haifa.

The ship was in disastrous condition, and normally I would have refused to set foot onboard. Nonetheless it was packed with Jews fleeing Europe. The journey was horrendous, a nightmare, but somehow the ship made it. The captain waited until the dead of night to approach the coastline and the Haganah came out with some small boats to take us to shore."

He paused, and we watched a group of children chasing a ball down the path that led out to the orchards. "When I arrived I had no money and nothing more than the contents of my trunk. I sought out the community of Germans in Jerusalem and they helped me to find lodging with an elderly couple from Berlin.

"Every evening I would go to the synagogue and open the prayer book, but the words...they no longer...it was as though they had lost their power. I went to the rabbi of the synagogue, hoping that he would give me some guidance. But instead of strengthening me he did the opposite. He said that for one such as I, who had lost everything, the only thing to do was to follow my doubt. He said, 'Go to a kibbutz, live as a man who has no God, no prayer, no belief; only then will you know the kind of Jew you must be.' So you see,

I've taken my rabbi's words to heart. I've come here to live as a Jew who doesn't believe."

I nodded, because words seemed quite useless. But after reflecting on it, I said, "My father is a Jew who doesn't believe."

"I don't understand what that is," he frowned. "What is a Jew who doesn't believe? If he does not believe in the God of Abraham, then how can he call himself a Jew at all?"

"He doesn't believe in a God, but he very much believes that the Jewish people must find a way to survive."

"What if the Jewish people cannot survive without belief?"

"We must. And the only place that can happen is here. If the world has taught us one thing, it is that faith alone cannot save you from your enemies. You, of all people, must surely see that."

He was about to reply, but we were called back from our break. The rest of the kitchen staff were swarming around us, cutting up vegetables, carrying out piles of plates, stirring vats of soup and boiled carrots, and our talk of theology was lost. A moment of truth had appeared and then vanished, like a beautiful bird that flies off the moment you come near. But the conversation had left me with a feeling of happiness. We, the new generation of Jewish socialists, were building a new reality which would be a light to others. We were showing how Jews could live as a modern people, creating a society unburdened by the outdated laws and rules that had kept us in the dark and prevented us from being part of the modern world. The fact that the kibbutz could attract a man like Avner was proof of the rightness of our ways. It gave me hope and filled me with optimism.

Later that day I found out from Hayale, who sat on the cultural events committee, that we were to host a Mozart recital the following week. I was certain that this sort of thing would cheer Avner, and when I came into work the next morning, I gleefully sought him out.

"I also have something to tell you," he replied, "but you go first." I informed him about the recital and suggested that we go together. "I'd be happy to," he replied, "but as it happens, I won't be here. That's what I wanted to tell you. A few weeks ago I put in a request to join the police and yesterday afternoon I received word that it's been approved. I didn't want to say anything until it was final.

I'm to report to the Tel Aviv office next Monday morning. They're putting me up in an apartment, and so I'm leaving tomorrow in order to get settled in."

I was surprised to hear this, but at the same time it made perfect sense. Anyone who could was volunteering to help the British in the war effort. That evening I slipped into the laundry, unlocked the cabinet, and took out the small cloth bag Avner had entrusted to me. I opened the drawstring and drew out the small black boxes, feeling their weight in my hand. The long leather straps were cracked and worn, but the boxes were in fine condition. I knew that each held a small scroll on which were written verses from the Torah. My father had refused to don them in prayer. Instead, he taught us that a Jew must be strong, courageous, open to the world, a champion of what is fair and right. Where was he now? Where were all of them now? All I knew was that he was the reason I was not sharing their fate.

I replaced the *tefillin*, retied the drawstring, and set out for the building known as "The League of Nations," a makeshift dormitory put up in '36 to house the ever-growing stream of refugees.

Avner appeared a little stunned when he opened his door. "I've brought you something," I said, handing him the bag. "I didn't want you to forget these."

"Oh. Thanks. I was going to come by to get them in the morning. He shook his head, as if remembering his manners. "Do you want to come in?"

The room, which he shared with three other men, consisted of four single beds. Two overturned crates had been pushed together to make a table, on which lay a deck of cards, a Russian book, and an old magazine in some unidentifiable language. On the wall above the most disheveled of the beds, the owner had pinned a photo of an American movie star – I wasn't sure who. Over the bed next to it was a photo showing a family – a mother, father, two girls, and an older boy, picnicking in a park. The occupant of the bed opposite had hung a copy of his kibbutz work schedule on the wall. And over the fourth bed, made up with the sheet and blanket tucked neatly under the mattress, hung a colorful painting of a woman, done in a strange modern style. Avner's. A small trunk was open beside it, emitting a scent of cedar and cologne.

"Sorry about the state of the premises," he said. "My roommates don't have much of a taste for housekeeping." But I was looking at the open trunk. With its shiny brass fittings and polished leather, it stood out from its modest surroundings. I stared at the sweaters, the trousers, the vests, the meticulously folded button-down shirts, and in the corner, a physics textbook and a lacquered folding chess set. It seemed an object from another, finer universe, and an odd feeling of longing came over me, a nostalgia for a life that had never been mine. "I'm moving up in the world, trading my kibbutz shorts for a police uniform," he smiled, and gestured to the bed behind me. "Have a seat in our parlor. Sorry I can't offer you anything to drink. The maid is on her day off."

"I'm sure it will be a relief for you to go back to the delights of capitalism," I told him.

He crossed his arms over his chest and smiled. "Oh, I wouldn't say that. Givat Hadar has been good for me. Like a stint in the army."

"Then you're well prepared for your next adventure."

"It's not an adventure I would normally choose," he replied, "but I can't stay here. The only thing any self-respecting man can do right now is join the fight. I imagine that with my German they'll find a way for me to be of service."

It occurred to me then that perhaps joining the police was only a pretense, and that his plans were in fact much more ambitious, and dangerous. I glanced again at the open trunk, which contained everything he had left in the world. And all at once I finally saw it clearly; he was no socialist, no Zionist. He wasn't one of us, and never would be. *I was wrong about you*, I wanted to tell him, but instead I blurted out, "You must take care of yourself."

"There's no reason to worry," he grinned. "I think I've proven that I can take care of myself."

"Well…I am…I'm worried. About all of us. These are terrible times, and who knows – "

Just then the door flew open and a young man burst into the room. "Oh. Sorry," he said, looking from me to Avner and back. "I didn't know you had company."

"That's alright," I said, glancing at my watch and rising. "I have a refugee committee meeting in a few minutes." I held out my hand and wished him good luck with his new job.

He shook it the way a gentleman shakes the hand of a lady, firm but respectful. I thought I would never see him again.

— · —

Suddenly it was spring. Our Passover Seder that year was the largest we had ever had. The days grew longer and the bushes and trees were bursting into bloom, adorning the kibbutz with cascades of purple, yellow, pink, and red. We masked our dread behind the routines of our everyday life. Card games in the afternoons with the children. Pleasant banter as we went about our work. And in the evenings, study sessions, discussion groups, musical concerts given by members or guests.

Two months had passed since I had last had a letter from Shimon. The fighting on the African front was fierce. There were reports of ambushes and surprise attacks on army vehicles and I steeled myself, adopting an attitude of stoicism, an acceptance of whatever fate was going to bring.

I was on my way home after work one afternoon when Zorik appeared, as if out of nowhere. "You told me a while ago that you're prepared to help us," he said, his voice low and even. "Does that offer still stand?"

"Yes. Of course."

"Very good," he said. "I'll visit the laundry tomorrow during lunch."

Hayale and Lili had just left for the dining hall when he came in the next day, holding a work shirt with a missing button. "We have a job we'd like you do," he said. I glanced at the shirt but he shook his head lightly. "You're busy, so I'll be quick. I assume that you're aware that since the riots in '29 the Haganah has helped us to acquire weapons."

"Yes, I've heard."

"The situation is not good. We believe that there is a very real possibility of an assault on Givat Hadar. You can imagine what would happen if we had to repel an attack, like the one at Hulda, with no weapons. And that's not to mention what could happen in a few months if the British can't keep the Nazis out, and nobody is certain that they can." He was saying what everyone was thinking, what everyone knew, yet to hear him speak it now in his quiet, measured tones, was unsettling.

"I want to help."

"Good. We need to acquire as many weapons as we can, but lately it's become more difficult. They must be paying informers because our men are being intercepted. The guns aren't getting here and our helpers are being arrested and thrown in jail. So we've decided to try something different."

"Go on."

"Tomorrow morning you're to put on a respectable dress and take a medium-sized handbag with you, as well as a ladies' scarf or handkerchief. Get on the bus to Tel Aviv and go to Frug Street, building 10, apartment 4. Go upstairs and knock five times on the door, like this." He rapped five times lightly on the table in rapid succession. "You'll be invited in and given something to put in your handbag and bring back to us. Do you have any questions?"

I shook my head.

"We've found that the British are far less suspicious of women. If all goes well you'll be back here in time for tea with Dalia and Yoram."

"And if I'm discovered?"

He smiled amiably. "Use your common sense. I'm sure you'll think of a way to explain yourself." He took a few steps back and regarded me. "You'll be just fine."

At the central bus station in Tel Aviv, I boarded the bus like Zorik had instructed. As we rolled down the colorful, bustling streets, the city seemed unaware that the world was at war. The shops were gay and inviting, pillars were covered in posters for the latest plays and shows, and the cafes were so full that their tables spilled onto the sidewalks. When a policeman held up his hand to halt traffic, I peered out the bus window and watched as two women pushing baby carriages strolled by, absorbed in conversation. A young boy was buying a red-colored soda at a kiosk. Three British officers in short pants crossed the street and went into a flower shop. And the apartment buildings too, with their tidy little balconies and handsome doorways, seemed even more elegant than I remembered. I got off the bus and turned down Frug Street, inhaling the salty air blowing off the sea.

The address Zorik had given me was a pleasant building with a large entry hall. Standing outside the door of the apartment, I put on an appropriately serious demeanor before making a tight fist and rapping as I had been instructed.

There was a soft tap of shoes on a tiled floor. The door opened, and there stood Avner. At first I thought I had the wrong address. "Hello," he said, also confused. It took him a moment to step back and invite me in. "You're not what I was expecting," he said, a little flustered, "but on second thought, it makes perfect sense that it's you."

I too was at a loss for words, but managed to reply, "Zorik certainly is full of surprises."

"Who?" he said, and I understood that it wasn't the Haganah that had set up this encounter, but powers far more random and reckless.

The place was furnished sparsely – a table with two chairs, a bed, and his trunk, now functioning as a nightstand on which stood a lamp and a book. The window shades were half-closed, casting a pleasant cool light on the room. "Can I offer you something to drink?" he said. "I have a bottle of seltzer in the fridge."

"That would be nice."

He pointed to the bed. "Have a seat."

But I could not sit down. I glanced around the room again, and then at the book on the trunk. *Die Sonette an Orpheus.* "Rilke," I murmured aloud. Kiva Zilber had loved that book. He had lent it to me, and in a flicker of memory I saw that same book as it once lay on the nightstand by my bed in my parents' house; and I saw the yellow bedspread, the pile of school notebooks on the shelf over my desk, a picture, sketched by Binyamin of a girl holding a balloon, pinned to the wall. But I quickly shook these thoughts from my mind. "I used to read him. As a girl."

"*You* read poetry?" he called out from the kitchen.

"Believe it or not." I reached over and picked up the book. "Otto Fischer," I read out the name inscribed inside the cover. "Who is Otto Fischer and why do you have his book?"

He came up behind me and handed me a glass of seltzer. "Who do you think he is?"

And then it dawned on me. Avner was the name he had taken on when he arrived, and now he wore it as one wears a costume. I held out the book to him. "Read me something."

"It's in German," he said.

"I know. That's why I want to hear you read it."

He took the book from me and set it down. "*Vor dem Sommerregen*," he began. And then, in a voice that seemed to call up another version of himself, he recited:

> *Auf einmal ist aus allem Grün im Park man weiß nicht was, ein Etwas fortgenommen;*

The words enveloped me with the gentle force of a dream, and quite suddenly I was seeing him through the eyes of the girl I had once been, in my bedroom in my parents' house.

> *The threadbare tapestries glint and play*
> *in the vague light of the afternoon,*
> *when, as a child, you felt so afraid.*

I reached out to stroke away the hair that was falling into his eyes and he touched my face, his fingers running lightly over my cheek, lips, chin. He drew me to him and kissed my mouth, and I was suddenly inside the tight circle of his arms.

What would I remember from those moments? The faint scent of oranges on his fingertips. The warmth of his limbs. The way he held himself, attentive, deliberate, his movements full of care. And the surprise of it, the shock of desire, and the astonishing recognition that I must have wanted this. Thinking back on it all later, I reflected that I could have stopped myself, as one stops oneself from falling over a cliff or tumbling down a waterfall, but it would have taken a resistance far stronger than I could have mustered at that moment. *Accidents will happen,* mother used to say when unlikely things occurred, a reprieve of sorts for unfortunate events that could not be explained. Yet afterward, when he got up from the bed and I watched the slender line of his body as he slipped briskly into his pants, it was not regret that I was feeling, but rather a sense of having fallen into a moment that had no place in the scheme of my life. I rose abruptly, straightened my dress, and quickly drew on my underwear, rough and grey from countless launderings. In the awkwardness of what had just happened, we quickly turned to what were supposed to be the matters at hand.

"So," he said, as he sat down on the bed, "the Haganah has taken to using housewives for gun running."

"And what about you?" I smiled. "A double agent?"

"That sounds sordid. Let's say that I support both sides."

"An opportunist."

"Ach, Tamar, what do these names matter? When the Nazis get here, we'll all be in the same boat. I doubt they'll be interested in my views on Zionism."

Something in his tone unnerved me. "What do you mean, 'when'?"

"Well, I don't have to tell you that the war in Africa is not going well. At the station all the talk is about what the British are going to do when the Nazis cross the Sinai."

"Their defense strategy."

"Not exactly. They're preparing for an evacuation. They all have plans in place to get out and take their families to Iraq and India."

"And leave us here on our own! The Nazis will appreciate that."

"The British are trying to do what they can. They're working with us, with the Haganah. They're giving us military training. They're sending Palmach units to the South."

This was a well-known fact; Palmach fighters often stayed over at the kibbutz on their way down to the Negev. Just a few weeks ago the children had gone to watch them holding drills in the fields, and Yoram and his friends talked about it for days afterward. But the thought of them facing a division of Nazi soldiers on their own was laughable. If the British were going to bolt and leave a few hundred Palmachniks in their place, the battle would be over in about fifteen minutes.

"There's a plan," he said.

"What plan?"

"Have you heard of 'Masada on the Carmel'?"

"No. What's that?"

"It's a civilian defense strategy. The idea is to move the entire Jewish population to the Carmel. The terrain will be difficult for the Nazi army to cross and it will make a good base for guerilla attacks."

"Move us all to the Carmel? We're half-a-million people!"

"I know. It's complicated, but they believe it's our only hope if we want to make a stand. They're still figuring out the particulars. Men from the Haganah are up there working with volunteers. They're digging bunkers and trenches. The British are supervising."

"You're joking!"

"I'm not," he said soberly.

"But that's ridiculous. What will we do for food? For water? Where are we all supposed to live? In the caves?"

"Those are just details; they can be worked out later. The main thing is that with the population protected and a good guerilla force, there's a chance that they'll be able to hold off the Nazis."

I could not believe what I was hearing. "That's insane! If that's the plan then we're doomed. They haven't named it after Masada for nothing."

"Don't be so fatalistic. If I've learned anything in these past few months it's that the *Yishuv* isn't going to go down without a fight. By the way," he added, as though suddenly remembering something, "the bathroom is right through there if you need it."

I nodded. Of course I needed it, assuming I wasn't pregnant already! I washed myself vigorously, as they recommend in manuals for women. I could hear him rummaging around the kitchen and when I emerged he was sitting on the bed, holding a gun. "This," he quipped, "must be the other reason you came here today."

The sight of it startled me, but I quickly regained my senses. "As a matter of fact," I replied, "it's the only reason I came today.

I had no idea that you'd – " He put a finger to my lips and held out the gun.

"Neither did I. But here we are," he smiled. "Comrades."

I took the gun in my hands, surprised by its weight and the way the dark metal gleamed in the light, and then wrapped it carefully in my handkerchief and placed it in my handbag. "It was wonderful to see you," he said as I stood in the small vestibule by the door. "I do hope we'll meet again."

"And what should I expect if that happens?"

He weighed his reply. "That's up to you." His eyes softened and he broke into a thin smile. "More poetry, perhaps."

"No," I said firmly. "This can't happen again." I headed down the stairs, determined to banish every thought but the task at hand.

But moving through the streets of the city, images of what had happened at the apartment flashed through my mind, threatening to overwhelm me with guilt and confusion when I most needed to appear natural and carefree. I determinedly set my sights on the mothers out with their children, buying them ice creams, wiping their mouths, fixing their coats and caps. One day soon I would take Yoram and Yardena out for a day in Tel Aviv. And one day, I had to believe with the most lucid faith I could muster, Shimon would return, and all that went on in these dark days, all the mistakes and momentary failings, the whole nightmare of it, would be over. I had to remind myself that I looked no different from any other woman out that day. If, by some stroke of bad luck, the gun was discovered, I would face arrest, interrogation, and probably imprisonment; the jails were filled with people whose crimes were far less serious. But the ride to the bus station passed uneventfully. Even the policeman who stood by the door of the bus nodded a friendly hello when I climbed aboard. I slid into a seat at the back and felt a heady thrill of exhilaration. It was a small thing, but I had indeed made myself useful.

A week later, Zorik came into the warehouse and asked if I could go to Tel Aviv the next day, following precisely the same instructions as the first time. I immediately agreed, vowing to myself that whatever the circumstances, there would be no repeat performance with Avner.

That night, as I was going through a pile of papers and magazines, I came across an old Yiddish journal that had been sent to me by Gabriel Shulman, a son of my mother's cousin who lived in Vilna. In the years prior to the war, I had written to him numerous times, begging him to find a way to come to Palestine with his family. I had even contacted Nat Wexler, a second cousin of ours who lived in America, asking him to try to help Gabriel to get an entry visa. Nothing had come of either of these efforts. Now, when months had passed since we had received word from anyone left in Europe, I could only pray that he and his family had somehow escaped danger.

In the letter that accompanied the journal, Gabriel mentioned that it contained a Yiddish poem written by a Raizel Shulman, whom he was quite sure was our great-grandmother. It consisted of a few sweet verses about her *shtetl*, nothing of any significance, but I didn't have the heart to throw it away. Now, coming across the journal again, I remembered hearing about a Yiddish library near the central bus station in Tel Aviv that accepted donations of old books and writings, and I slipped it into my handbag.

When the bus pulled into the station my first thought was to look for the library, but I reasoned that if I had trouble finding it, I would be late for the meeting at the apartment, and that it was better to do this errand on my way home.

I had prepared exactly what I was going to say to Avner, a brief speech about fidelity and folly, but when his door opened, I was greeted by a severe-looking young woman with glasses and hair set in a tight bun. "Can I help you?" she asked in a heavy Polish accent. She made no move to invite me in, and so I remained in the vestibule, looking over her shoulder at the state of the room. Everything appeared exactly as it had been a week before, except that Avner's trunk was missing. Was it possible that he was involved with this woman? I glanced at the empty corner of the room where his trunk had stood. "Where is he?"

"Who? The previous tenant? I have no idea. Wait here."

She disappeared into the kitchen and returned with a gun, identical to the one Avner had given me. "Are you also with the police?" I asked as I wrapped the gun in my handkerchief.

"Didn't they tell you not to ask any questions?" She reached into the pocket of her dress and drew out an envelope with the word "Tamar" in stiff Hebrew letters. "This was left for you."

"Left by whom?"

She shrugged. "Read it and you'll know."

Before leaving the building, I opened the envelope and drew out a letter. It was written on lined note paper and dated 28/5/42.

Meine Liebste Tamar, it began.

I'm being sent abroad as part of a unit for German speakers. I'm not sure of the destination, or what my mission will be. Likewise, I cannot say if we will ever meet again. Whatever happens, I want you to know that you have been a single ray of sunlight in the midst of a nightmare. The memory of your visit last week will always be a comfort to me, a reminder of the lovely things that are, in spite of all the ugliness of the world, still possible. Who knows what fate awaits us? Be strong, have faith in the days to come, and know that I will never forget you. With much affection, yours, Avner. (O.F)

As I looked up, two British soldiers were entering the building. I gave them a smile, folded the letter into the envelope, and put it in my purse.

Just as before, I was relieved to find that I could walk the streets of the city lightly, as though I didn't have a care in the world. At the bus station I asked the girl at the ticket counter to point me toward the Yiddish library. I found it tucked away on the third floor of a new building with a young fig tree growing in the yard. The librarian, a bespectacled young man from Warsaw, was pleased to receive my donation.

$$\sim \quad \cdot \quad \sim$$

I reach into my handbag and my fingers brush the edge of the photo. With a heavy heart, I draw it out. "It was taken last month at the beach," I tell Lotte. What I don't tell her, and what she isn't able to see in the black and white photo, is the lovely auburn color of her hair. The mischievous glint in Yardena's eyes reminds me of the elves in the picture books my father once read to me. In her impish little face I can see a reflection of Yehuda, and something of what I remember of my niece Shoshanna, murdered before her seventeenth birthday.

Lotte takes the photo with a controlled urgency and stares at it as though drinking in every detail. I watch her expression carefully, bracing myself for a verdict. "Oh yes," she murmurs. "Of course she's Otto's."

"A week later," I tell her, "Shimon came home on a ten-day leave. His unit had been stationed at some remote place in the Egyptian desert and he had no way to send word." We fell into the bed the minute he walked in the door. He was pulling off my shorts even as I closed the shutters, and I clung to him, inhaling the scent of his skin as though it were oxygen itself. I knew then that he was my only home.

"Later that summer," I continue, "British troops managed to halt Rommel's advance and for the first time in months we could all breathe a little. Of course it was only after El Alamein that we could be sure we were out of danger."

"And you never heard again from Otto?"

I shake my head heavily. "No."

"But you found you were pregnant."

"My husband had come home on leave."

"But you had been with Otto two weeks earlier. Tell me, Frau Sela, was the baby born a little early?"

"Yes," I admit what I have never told anyone. "A little."

"And her weight was normal?"

I say nothing.

"Then it is quite possible that – "

"It's possible," I interrupt, "but I believe that it would be unwise and unnecessary to give the matter much thought. My husband is my daughter's father. There is no reason that anyone should think otherwise."

"Of course," Lotte agrees, but her gaze is triumphant. "Thank you, Frau Sela. This talk has given me a small measure of consolation. You need not worry about my bothering you again."

I sit back, pale and drained. The radio is playing lively band music and the soldiers at the bar are singing along. At the table by the far wall two English women, probably officers' wives, are chatting merrily over their lunch. "What happened to him?" I ask. "After he left?"

"He was given false papers and sent to infiltrate a Nazi government office. We know that he served British intelligence for eighteen months before he was identified by an old classmate. As I mentioned in my letter to you, he was arrested and most likely tortured. He perished in Dachau."

Yes, she had written that in her letter. But hearing it again now makes me almost nauseous. "He was a good man," I say softly. "A very good man."

"They were all good men. All good people. It's a terrible thing that happened to us," and I'm not sure if she means to all the Jews, or to her own husband and sons, or just to the two of us, Lotte and me, who are perhaps the only ones left in the world who hold Avner in memory. "In the end you Zionists had the right idea. Who would have thought? Well, good for you. You'll carry on for the rest of us. What about your own family, dear? Are they here too?"

I stare across the room at the soldiers. There are three of them. One has just made some sort of happy announcement and the other two slap him on the back. "Your family, dear. Are they here with you?"

I can barely speak. "Excuse me," I say, trembling a little, and I get up clumsily, almost toppling my chair.

The ladies' room is sparkling clean, with shiny black tiles on the walls and elegant lights over each of the sinks. Breathless, I collapse into a stall and burst into choking sobs. My hand fumbles in my handbag until I feel the handkerchief, soft white cotton with embroidered blue flowers, faded from years of washings. I squeeze my eyes shut and bury my face in the cloth, gasping for traces of my mother's kitchen.

Tragedy

(Gabriel – Vilna, March 1939)

Like a shooting star in the night sky, Symek Grynberg appeared at the Vilna student writers club one afternoon at the end of winter. Tuvia Ledermen was about to read us his story when there was a light rap on the door, followed by an abrupt turn of the handle. He stood in the doorway in his cap and shabby coat, his gaze conveying something forceful, a challenge, almost a sneer. "Is this the writing group?" he asked in a rather surly voice.

I saw the way the others looked at him, intrigued but wary, but I suspected that despite his working-class demeanor and manners, he was one of them, a teenager with a yearning to put to paper the stories he conjured up in his mind. "That's right," I said feeling an almost fatherly urge to welcome him. "Please. Come in and take a seat." He gave a brisk nod, removed his coat and cap revealing a head of close-cropped hair, and slid his short, sturdy frame awkwardly into the desk closest to the door. I signaled to Tuvia to begin his reading.

Wiry and quick-witted, Tuvia writes in the style of his literary hero, Romain Rolland. His stories are often modeled after *Jean Christophe,* with sensitive young men as their protagonists, and this one too depicted the hero's ruminations on the problem of evil after witnessing some boys stealing apples from a poor woman's stall in the market. I noted that though Tuvia's powers of description are improving, he has difficulty developing new story lines. Nonetheless, his peers adore his work and consider him to be a rising light.

Next up was Fraidel Rozentzvieg, to my mind the prettiest girl of the group, with large blue eyes and Shirley Temple dimples. Her stories, written in a smooth, lively tone, tend to be about amusing incidents at school, parties, picnics, and the like. That day she read out an anecdote about a biking adventure in the country. Subsequently, we heard a poem from Mina Zach, in which she described the *Shulhoyf* on *Shabbes* morning, an essay from Raphael Adler about his days as a young child in *kheyder,* and a ghost story by Daniel Lerner.

All this time, Symek listened restlessly, drumming his fingers on the desktop and jiggling his knee under the table. Now he looked at me, grinning with the pleasure of a child who knows a great secret. "And how about you, Mr…"

"Grynberg."

"Mr. Grynberg. Have you brought something that you'd like to share with us today?"

He jumped to his feet and pulled some folded papers from the pocket of his coat. "Yes, I see you have," I said, "but before you read, why don't you tell us a little about yourself?"

He shrugged sharply. "Like what?"

"What school do you go to?" Tuvia called out.

"None," he answered in his gruff manner. "My father left last year – no one knows where to. My mother is sick and has to stay in bed, and there are six of us at home. I work the lathes down at Zilberman's lumberyard."

They were all staring at him now. "What sort of writing do you do?" Mina asked.

He shrugged again. "I write what I feel like."

"Very well," I said. "Let's hear what you've brought."

He smoothed out his papers and began. His voice had a slight tremor, and he stumbled over the odd word, but no one noticed. They were, from the very start, mesmerized, drawn into the tale, captivated as one always hopes to be. And I too found myself enthralled. The story he read told of a young man who takes to the roads of Poland and Lithuania, travelling on foot, jumping aboard trains, taking rides from anyone he can. He makes no secret of his being a Jew, fends for himself through cunning, or if need be, with his fists, and revels in his encounters with people from all walks of life. He speaks easily with criminals, con men, loose women, but also knows how to make a friend of yeshiva students and rabbis. His quest is to learn through experience whatever he can about life. This protagonist, whom he called Jozef Pozanski, is an orphan, his father unknown, his mother a prostitute. This difficult background serves to make him hardy, resilient, unafraid.

Together with the students I listened to him read, taken in by the rise and fall of his voice, stirred by the restrained style of the writing. His sentences were deceivingly simple, but the language was strong, clean, clear, with not a word wasted. The character of Pozanski is both tough and sensitive, practical and philosophical, charismatic and capable of kindness. But what emerged most strongly from the text was an exhilarating sense of freedom, an attitude of self-sufficiency that lives fully in the moment, without fear. When he was done he eyed us, his audience, with a touch of charming arrogance.

In any group of artists there is always, beneath the surface of the compliments and enthusiasm, a hidden stream of rivalry, and as the others praised the story and the masterful writing, I could sense both their admiration and their envy. "Jozef is such a unique character," Yehiel, the strongest writer of the group, said. "He lives the way we wish we could but would never dare."

"He's a romantic hero," Fraidel added, "like the Count of Monte Cristo, or the Three Musketeers."

"And the way he speaks," her friend Layale Resnick chimed in, "it's like he's simple and deep at the same time. Underneath, he's actually very sensitive."

"It's striking how he knows how to talk to people of all classes," Raphael, a Bundist and impassioned socialist, remarked.

As for myself, I was truly excited about the work he had presented. To instruct a group of would-be writers is one thing, but to discover a true talent, a youth blessed with an inborn ability with language *and* originality of thought is an exceptional thing indeed.

"Sept. 1, 1939," I announced before ending the meeting. "That's the day the winners of the YIVO youth autobiography contest will be announced. I hope you're all hard at work on your essays. Remember, the entries will be judged on sincerity, accuracy, and detail. The essay should show who you really are through the actual details of your life. The deadline is the first of May."

I had been careful not to make too much of Symek and his writing, but after most of the others had left and he was putting on his overcoat, I approached him. "The story you brought in today was impressive," I told him. "Do you have others like it?"

He grinned and tapped his head with a finger. "Sure do. A whole bunch of them about Jozef Pozanski. Right in here."

"Then you must get them out and onto paper. You're a wonderful storyteller. What part of the city are you from?"

"Shnipishok," he replied. "Near the power station."

"Well good for you for coming today. I look forward to seeing you at our next meeting. You must show us another one of those stories you've got."

His face broke into an unguarded grin, and I was already imagining how I might bring him to a real literary event with the most talented writers in the city. How the others would celebrate him and offer to help get his work into print. And how they would appreciate my own role in finding this gem from Shnipishok – like another Sutzkever! That's how much stock I put in the single story he had read to us.

As I walked home that night, the very air seemed charged with the spirit of art. I have been a teacher of literature for fifteen years now, and I well know how infrequently one comes across a true talent. There are quite a few who can write well, and of those perhaps a fraction show mastery, but only the smallest fraction of those have an inborn sense of how to balance the elements into a cohesive, satisfying whole, while disguising the great effort of creation to make it seem simple and natural.

Arriving home, I found Dora preparing dinner while Sophie and Marek, still in their school clothes, were doing their homework at the kitchen table. Dora brought me a cup of tea and I took a seat beside them, watching Sophie, who is already eleven, solve her mathematics equations, her finger curling a strand of hair that had come loose from her braid while, Marek, his small fingers gripping a pencil, was writing out the letters of the Polish alphabet.

I'm very fond of this hour, when the four of us sit in our small kitchen and share the events of the day. Over dinner I told them about Symek and his tale of Jozef Pozanski, and both Sophie and Marek made me promise to tell them what happens next when I find out.

It was only later, when I was helping her with the dishes, that Dora mentioned that another letter had arrived from my cousin Tamar in Palestine. "She just doesn't give up, does she?" Dora laughed.

We both knew what would be in the letter: an impassioned plea to sell our belongings, pack a bag, make our way to the closest seaport, and board a boat setting sail for Palestine. And I have no doubt that she is behind the latest letter I received from Nat Wexler, our mutual cousin in Chicago who kindly sent me the volume of Walt Whitman poetry that I requested. Nat wrote again last month urging me, in spite of the poor likelihood of success, to apply for visas to the United States. "The Zionists are constantly insisting that disaster in Europe is just around the corner," I said to Dora. "It's part of their ideology. Why else would anyone take the trouble to abandon the civilized world and eke out an existence in the desert?"

She rolled her eyes, a gesture which, even to this day I still find fetching. "She's one to talk about danger, living in the wilds and fighting off Arab marauders. Every time we get a letter from her, I'm afraid it's going to contain bad news."

"You mean to say that you would reject her offer to join a socialist collective and live in a hut at the edge of a swamp?" I quipped.

We chuckled, Dora and I, at the thought of it. I opened the envelope, glanced at Tamar's unwieldy handwriting, and put it on my desk, where I would get to it sooner or later.

The following Thursday, I was anticipating seeing Symek again in the writing group. I was curious; was the story he had shown us a singular gem or was he capable of sustaining that same compelling level of plot, characterization, dramatic tension in other work? But to my dismay he failed to show up. Maybe he wasn't feeling well, or he had urgent business to attend to at home. This is what I told the other students, who were also disappointed. "Do any of you know him?" I asked them. "Or someone who might be a friend of his?" A few mentioned names of people they knew from his neighborhood and promised to ask around.

Symek didn't show up the following week, or the week after that. As the days passed, the more I thought about it, the more his disappearance troubled me. It is rare, very rare, to discover a writer who has such an easy, natural way with language, yet is able to infuse his work with depth and distinction. Perhaps he even had it in him to write novels, like Sholem Aleichem or Sholem Asch, but more current, more in tune with the spirit of youth today. What a boon to Yiddish literature that would be!

I decided to seek him out myself. I would simply find him and convince him to return to the group. He had said that he lived in Shnipishok, near the power station. That was all I needed to know.

$\sim$ • $\sim$

On Tuesday afternoons my teaching day finishes early, and when I set out, the pale sun of early spring was still high in the sky. All through the Jewish Quarter, preparations for Passover were underway. The Zawalna market was more crowded than usual, the shoppers more zealous, the quarreling and bargaining more vigorous. All the while I thought about what I was going to say to Symek, what arguments I could make to convince him to come back to the club, and as sometimes happens to me, I was so engrossed in my thoughts that I almost missed the turn down Wilenska Street, which leads to the foot of the Green Bridge.

I seldom have reason to cross the river and venture into the backwater neighborhoods on the other side. The city neglects these places terribly; the roads are unpaved, the houses are decrepit, and many of the roughest elements of society reside there. It was not at all surprising that, growing up in such a place, Symek had intimate knowledge of the lives of the poor and desperate. I crossed the bridge and then turned down Rybaki Street, heading in the direction of the power station, but when I passed the old Jewish cemetery, I stopped for a moment by the gates and gazed in.

In our younger days, before Dora and I were married, we would sometimes meet there and walk amongst the old gravestones, sunk crookedly into the earth like a gathering of swaying mourners. We would pause at the grave of the Gaon, where we would sometimes see a young woman praying silently like the biblical Chana in Shilo, or a Hasid spending a reflective moment after paying his respects at the graves of his grandparents. Thinking back, I'm not sure what drew us, a young couple, to such a place; perhaps we liked the peaceful, weighted atmosphere, suffused as it is with time and memory.

As I turned away, I saw an old woman approaching and I asked her where I could find the home of Symek Grynberg. "Grynberg? With the sick mother? Those poor children..." she murmured, and pointed to a street at the far side of the cemetery.

I followed her directions, and as I started down the road an odd sensation came over me, as though I had gone back in time. The decrepit wooden houses with their rotting roofs and smoking chimneys brought to mind the Belarusian *shtetl* I lived in as a child. There was no one in the street and so the only way to find Symek's house was to knock on doors and ask the inhabitants.

I chose a random yard and was about to head for the door when I saw a youth walking toward me. He asked who I was looking for, and I was suddenly conscious of my clothes and appearance, which marked me as a stranger to the neighborhood. When I mentioned Symek's name he smirked at my predicament. "Symek's place? You'd never find it on your own." He explained that I was to walk to the third last house in the street and then go around the back where I would find a shack, which was where Symek and his family resided. "I don't know if he's back from the lumberyard yet, but the other kids will let you in to wait for him."

Dusk was coming on, and though lamps burned in the windows, the street was still and silent. I found the said house, went around the back as directed, treading carefully so as not to trip in the darkness, and came upon a ramshackle structure of hammered planks of wood, a dim light shining through the cracks between the boards. The chill of night had set in, and as I knocked on the door, I rubbed my hands together to warm them. "Who's there?" I heard a nervous, high-pitched girl's voice call out.

"It's Gabriel Shulman. A teacher at the Tsysho Gymnasium. I'm looking for Symek." The door opened a crack, and then a little wider. Before me stood a girl of about thirteen or fourteen, her eyes narrow like Symek's, wearing a threadbare winter coat. I looked past her into the shack, a miserable room whose sole light was a small kerosene lamp on an overturned crate. "What do you want with him?"

Perhaps my expectations had been naïve, but the scene filled me with dismay. Though he had made it clear that the family was poor, I never imagined that he lived in such abject conditions. "I'd like to speak with him."

"Who's there, Mirle?" A woman's voice, weak and sickly, came from within.

"A man who says he's a teacher. He's looking for Symek."

"Tell him to go away."

"Symek isn't here," the girl said, rather rudely. "And even if you find him, he won't want to speak to you." I stood there, deliberating how to proceed, when I heard the sound of footsteps stepping through the snow. It was Symek, coming from the yard behind the shack, perhaps returning from a visit to the outhouse.

He appeared both surprised and perturbed to see me. "Mr. Shulman. What are you doing here?" He asked in that same hardened voice I remembered.

"Good evening Mr. Grynberg. I want to speak with you."

I feared that he was about to send me on my way, but after a moment's consideration he replied, "Well, you may as well come in then."

I followed him inside and was met by the stares of three younger children, huddled under frayed blankets on an old mattress. On a second mattress beside them lay a woman, presumably Symek's mother. The room was freezing, and reeked strongly of kerosene, onions, and cooked cabbage. All watched as Symek pulled a chair out from under a small table, motioned for me to sit down, and took a seat across from me. "What do you want with me?" he asked.

"Who is this man?" his mother rasped.

"He's a teacher from the Gymnasium, Mama."

"Tell him to go away."

"Don't worry, Mama, I'll handle it."

"Maybe we can talk some other time," I said to Symek quietly, almost whispering.

"You're here now, so you may as well say what you came for."

I glanced around the decrepit room, taking in the sick mother, the children huddling under the blankets, the older girl stirring a pot of potatoes on a hearth warmed with a few burning coals. I realized that my mission to convince Symek to come back to the writing group was practically hopeless. Nonetheless, I had come this far, and so I said what I had come to say. I told him that he was a talented writer, and that his story showed impressive skill and promise. He possessed a gift, I said, and it would be a tragedy for him to neglect it.

"A tragedy?" he said scornfully. "You've got it all wrong, Mr. Shulman. It will be a tragedy if I don't show up for work at the lumberyard. You see these people here? If I don't work, they don't eat. My brothers and sisters will be sent to orphanages. My mother won't live through the winter. How's that for a tragedy?"

"There are services, Jewish welfare organizations – "

He snorted with contempt. "They come around at holiday time bringing us matzos and a few bags of potatoes. But the rest of the year…we could go hungry for all they care." I knew that this simply was not true, but was not about to argue with him. "Look," he continued, his tone softening a little. "I'm glad you liked my story.

And maybe one day I'll be able to write some more. But right now it's impossible."

"I understand. But perhaps you could still come to the writer's club. Just once a week to the meetings."

"Look around, sir," he said in a low, bitter tone. "You see the conditions here. I can barely read a newspaper, let alone write anything."

"You wrote the story you showed us."

"I can't…" he sighed and closed his eyes. "That story was a miracle."

"You told me that you have more."

"I said that I have them in my head. But there's no way I can sit down after a day of work and put them on paper. Maybe one day. Who knows? But right now, it's not possible."

"I'm hungry," a voice whined from under the blanket.

"I'm hungry *and* I'm freezing," another spoke in the semi-darkness.

"Tell your guest to go," his mother groaned. "He's bothered us enough."

It's difficult to describe the despair I felt at that moment. I rose, and despite the black mood that had come over me, I felt compelled to suggest one more idea. "I see how difficult things are," I told him, "but perhaps you can still keep a foot in the world of writing. Tomorrow evening there's going to be a literary gathering in the city. All the best writers in the city will be there: Grade, and Kaczerginski, and Wolf and Sutzkever. You can come as my guest, they're always happy to include talented young people. It's going to be at the home of Pessia Spektor, on Styczinowa Street."

"I don't think so," he said, shaking his head. "That stuff isn't for me."

"I don't agree," I told him.

"We're going to need the table now," the girl snapped as she took the pot of potatoes off of the fire.

"Has he left yet?" The mother said.

I moved toward the door. I had already been there for far too long. "You have the wrong man, Mr. Shulman," Symek said bluntly.

"I apologize," I told him. "It was presumptuous of me to come here. A mistake. I apologize for disturbing you and your family." Without a word he opened the door, and a blast of cold air swept through the little room. "Good evening," I said to the sad, silent children, and went out into the dark night.

As I returned to the more prosperous part of the city, I thought again about the word "tragedy," which I had used to describe Symek's neglect of his talents. I had failed to convey to him what I meant, and it occurred to me that perhaps the notion of tragedy is all a matter of perspective. Perhaps there are certain abilities and qualities whose true value can only be perceived from a distance.

As I expected, Symek didn't appear at Pessia Spektor's literary evening, which was a shame because the event drew a good-sized crowd: writers, artists, journalists, teachers, anyone eager to trade, if for only a few brief hours, the coarse jargon of the market for a Yiddish refined and shaped by poets. Many of us stayed late to chat and gossip, and I was one of the last to leave. Toward midnight, I made my way home with Isaac Schechter, a colleague from work.

The skies were murky and gloomy, with only a distant, fragile moon, yet we were both in high spirits. Grade had read some wonderful new poems. Kaczerginski held a lively recitation and discussion of Leivick. Sutzkever also read new work, continuing in his vein of writing about the natural world. Grossbard presented some of his own writing and a few pieces by Nadir. And then Pessia herself finished off the evening with a reading of Kulbak's *Vilna*. No matter how many times I hear it, I am always moved by the way Kulbak envisioned the streets of the Jewish Quarter so lyrically.

> *Someone in a tallis is walking your rooftops.*
> *Only he is stirring in the city by night.*
> *He listens. Old grey veins quicken – sound*
> *through courtyard and synagogue like a hoarse, dusty heart.*[1]

I deliberated whether to share this with Schechter or to keep it to myself. He was only a teacher of mathematics, not yet out of his twenties, yet I had found him to be a cultured enough fellow with a well-developed literary sensibility. As we neared the end of Miko-laja I instinctively checked the street corners for hooligans from the university. The route down Szawelska Street takes longer than cutting through the side alleys, but one is more likely to avoid trouble. Schechter must have been thinking the same thing. He halted and glanced up and down the street and muttered, "Which way?"

I pointed in the direction of an alley off Straszuna. We headed into the darkness and our conversation turned to Grade's *Yo!*, its strange poetic voice in the Ezekiel cycle an affirmation of the poet's role in difficult times. "I would say that the poem is coming out of Grade's ambivalence about religion," Schechter remarked. "For him, the poet and the prophet are one. The poet – Grade, that is – is struggling with faith. He wants to believe the way Ezekiel believed. But can he? The prophet gives himself to God. But the poet must belong first of all to himself. Do you see the problem?"

"Interesting," I replied. "Theology and poetry. Grade is trying to reconcile two different worlds. But they have a lot in common. The sadness and the idealism. The vision and the self-doubt. It's quite a daring move on Grade's part. It's only when he – " The sharp sound of loud laughter cut the air. We stopped for a moment and glanced up the street but saw nothing. And then a shout flew out of the alley up ahead. With a sinking heart, I deliberated between turning around and making a run for it or continuing on. To be a Jew in Vilna, or Poland, or perhaps anywhere, is to find courage where you thought you had none, to feel it flowing through your veins like blood.

There were three of them. We proceeded, trying to keep our pace easy and regular. To look directly at them was to invite a confrontation, but to shrink from them was worse. They were vodka-faced and crude university students. They swaggered toward us, blocking our way. We stepped off the curb and into the road, attempting to go around them, but they too stepped down, to block us. "Look who's out for the evening," one of them said with a cruel smirk. "Don't you Yids know that it's not so smart for a Yid to be out after dark?"

Schechter and I glanced at each other. They belched their stinking vodka breath in our faces, poking us and laughing. Nu? What was a Jew to do? Try to talk sense to them? Make a run for it? Or wait for it to be over and hope for the best? I no longer knew. I took a small step back but Schechter tried to push his way between them.

In the shadowy darkness I couldn't make out what was happening. I heard shoving, shoes scraping the cobblestones, cursing in Polish. Shadows jumped, their figures traced by the dim light at the end of the alley. There was the sound of a blow and then another. I heard Schechter fall to the ground, cry out in a loud whimper. I should have helped him but I couldn't. I was paralyzed, weak with dread. For the moment the three of them had forgotten about me as they laid into him, kicking him as he covered his head and face. I pictured him calling to me, but all I could hear were his sharp yelps.

It was a matter of no more than five or ten seconds, but it is these seconds that stand out in memory, as real as if they were happening right now, while what came next seems like something I must have imagined. As Schechter lay moaning in the gutter, one of them noticed me, standing frozen as if in a trance. "What are you looking at?" he moved toward me, spat a reeking gob in my face, and sent a ringing slap across my cheek, hurling me to the ground and my eyeglasses off my face into the dark ocean of cobblestones. I watched, almost blind, as he found them and trampled them hard with his boot, grinding their lenses into the ground.

I lay there quite motionless, waiting for further blows, but just then thunder rumbled in the dark sky and a heavy rain began to fall on us all. The two hoodlums who had been pummeling Schechter stood up and motioned to the third, and they all ran off, leaving the two of us lying in the street. I rose slowly, thankful that I had escaped with no more than a ringing face and a burning shoulder. But I could see very little. It was as though the world had gone dark leaving only fuzzy shadows, barely visible through the rain. "Schechter," I called out weakly, and was answered with a groan. "Schechter, they've destroyed my eyeglasses, but I'm going to try and find help."

As I attempted to get to my feet, I heard him groan, and a terrible sense of guilt came over me. Why hadn't I helped Schechter? What a miserable person I was! I hadn't even tried. This knowledge, far more than the ache in my shoulder, was excruciating to me. Slowly and cautiously, I felt my way along the walls of the narrow street as if

I were indeed blind. I forced myself to move forward, stopping only to take shelter in doorways when the downpour grew harder. After some time the rain slowed and I managed to recognize the building where an old friend of Dora's lives. I felt my way up the stairs, two full floors, to the apartment.

I was almost within reach of the door when I somehow lost my footing. The fall was short but my landing was hard. A sharp flash of heat flooded my bones. For the second time that night I lay aching and immobile, but unlike the first fall, the pain I felt was almost unbearable. I heard the door above the stairs open and a woman gasp, after which I blacked out.

— · —

The bells from the cathedral, with their deep musical clang, broke into my dreams. Instinctively I reached for my eyeglasses, which I always put on the nightstand beside my bed before I go to sleep, but when I made the slightest movement, I was struck by a pain so sharp I fell back with a weak whimper. And then I remembered everything and clarity returned like a curse. I saw again the hoodlums, smelt their reeking breath, and saw Schechter lying in the gutter, rain pouring on us both.

I had, until that moment, never appreciated what a blessing it is to breathe naturally, without hesitation, without pain. On that first morning, I would have happily done away with breathing at all if it had been possible, but of course one has no choice, and each breath I drew was an ordeal. These were the things running through my mind when a nurse appeared. "Good morning, Mr. Shulman," she greeted me. "You took a very bad fall last night." I wanted to ask her where Schechter was, but she put a finger to her lips and replied, "Dr. Wasserman is making the rounds; he'll get to this room in due time."

"Schechter," I managed to say.

"Shhh."

I wanted to explain, but again she put a finger to her lips as if I were a troublesome schoolboy. "You've suffered a serious injury,

Mr. Shulman. It's best that you don't exert yourself by speaking." She moved on before I could say anything more, but then returned a few minutes later with some ice packs. "Hold these against your chest," she instructed. "They'll help with the pain."

By the time the good doctor finally arrived at my bedside I had fallen back into a doze, from which he woke me saying, "Mr. Shulman. To what do we owe the honor of your presence here?"

"I was walking home," I began, but seeing my difficulty, he said that the details could wait until it was easier for me to speak. He opened the buttons of my hospital shirt and gently felt my stomach and chest. The moment he touched me I froze, allowing myself only short little breaths like a child who has cried for a long time.

He told me that I had fractured two ribs. Recovery, he said as he wound a bandage tightly around my chest, would take several weeks, but it appeared that I'd suffered no serious damage. Since bed rest was the only cure, I could recover at home. Providing no infection developed, he would release me within a few days.

I motioned for the doctor to draw near. He leaned in close and I asked if they had admitted a patient by the name of Schechter. At first he appeared confused, but then recalled that a patient by that name had indeed been brought in and assured me that he was receiving the best possible care. My wife, he said, had been waiting to see me since 6:00 in the morning and it was best that I see her before thinking about anything else.

He left the room, and a few minutes later Dora came in. "*Oy vey zmir!*" she gasped when she took in my sorry state. She stared at my chest, swathed in bandages. "God in heaven! What is this?"

"We were coming home from the reading at Pessia's," I whispered. "We were attacked. I wasn't hurt, but I lost my glasses."

"But the doctor said that you fell."

"I fell because I no longer had my glasses and I couldn't see properly."

"Nu, Gavril," she stared at me with a look she uses when someone has done something unwise, "You had to take a shortcut home? You were asking for trouble."

"It was foolish," I agreed.

She looked down at me and stroked my brow. "Thank God it's only broken ribs," she murmured. "It could have been far worse."

"I was with Isaac Schechter," I told her. "He really got the worst of it. Maybe even…Dora, please check. I think he's in this hospital." But she shushed me and went off to speak to the doctor.

My voice returned intact on the second day. "At least you had the brains to stay out of the fight," Dora said with a weighty sigh after I had gone over the details of the incident with her. "You could have gotten yourself killed!"

"How is Schechter?" I asked her. "Did you find out if he's here in the hospital?"

"How should I know?" she snapped. "It's enough I have to attend to you!" A stranger would have found nothing in this response that was unusual or suspicious, but I knew my wife well enough to suspect that her irritation was masking something that she wanted to keep from me.

"How is he?" I repeated.

"He's still in a coma. But the doctors are optimistic."

"I feel terrible. I should have helped him."

"I'm glad you didn't. I'm too young to be a widow."

"What about Sophie and Marek?" I asked. "What have you told them?"

"I said that you fell. It's the truth, isn't it?"

"And my father?"

"To him I told the whole truth."

On my third day in the hospital, Dr. Wasserman examined me, and though my bones still burned and ached and cried, he ruled that I could be released to continue my recovery at home, providing that I refrain from physical activity. "Reading, writing, pleasant conversation with friends and family, that's how you ought to pass the time."

For the first time since the incident, I smiled.

Dora hired a droshky to take us home. I was swaddled in wool blankets and helped into my seat. On our way, we drove through the old Jewish Quarter, where during my brief stay in the hospital, preparations for Passover had moved into full force. Blankets were airing from the balconies. Billowing sheets dripped from railings and porches. The alleys ran with rivulets of brown soapy water and from the opened windows, sounds of sweeping, scouring, and scrubbing filled the air. Despite the ache in my bones, the flurry of preholiday commotion cheered me.

Negotiating the stairs to our second-floor apartment was as strenuous as climbing the Alps, but once we arrived and Dora had seated me in my armchair in the sitting room, covered me in a blanket, given me a pillow to hold against my chest when I coughed, brought me a cup of tea, and fetched my book, a Polish story collection entitled *The Cinnamon Shops*, I indeed began to feel better.

Dora returned to her Passover house cleaning. I read and snoozed in my chair, waking only later in the afternoon when Marek arrived home from school.

"Daddy," he shouted when he saw me, and abandoning his satchel by the door, he ran to me, opening his arms for a hug.

"No no no," I cried, wary that his embrace might send me back to the hospital. Dora came running out from the kitchen in time to stop him, and I explained that while I was recovering we would have to make do with a light peck on the cheek. He nodded solemnly and then launched into an animated account of a schoolyard game of tag, his voice rising excitedly, his light lisp made stronger by the gap where a tooth had fallen out several days earlier.

Sophie came in soon afterward. Unlike her brother, she approached me cautiously with great concern. "I was so worried about you, *Tateh*. Does it hurt very much?"

"A little, but every day I get a little better. In a few weeks I'll be back to normal."

"Mama said that you broke two ribs."

"Yes, and that's all. Just two. I had a bad fall. But it wasn't serious."

She stared at me probingly, her hazel eyes clever and alert. "Kids at school were saying that a Jew was beaten up very badly the other night."

One never knows how best to teach children about the evils of the world. It is a question I consider almost daily but now when

I had been, as it were, a victim, I could not bring myself to discuss what happened with her. "Yes, I heard about that," I replied. "A terrible story. But luckily that didn't happen to me, and I'm well on the road to recovery."

"Thank God."

"Tell me what's new in school," I said, determined to change the subject.

"It's been a little dull lately," she mused, and then brightened. "But look what I found in the library." She opened her schoolbag and drew out a book entitled *The Life and Times of Madame Curie, a Woman of Poland.* I had to smile. It seems she has inherited the affinity for mathematics and chemistry that runs in Dora's family.

After dinner, at exactly ten minutes to eight, Meyer and Tziril Rosen from upstairs knocked on the door, punctual as a Swiss watch, in order to hear the news on our wireless. After their youngest daughter got married, they gave her their radio, and now they come over each night to listen with us. "Oy Gavril!" Tziril said as she stood over me with a pained looked on her face. "Everyone is talking about you and the other teacher, but I want to hear it from you."

Making sure that the children were not in hearing distance, I offered a brief description of what had happened. "Animals!" she said. "They'll burn in hell. Are you going to go to the police?"

"That's the last thing he should do," Meyer told her. "They'll arrest him and give those hooligans a medal."

I smiled at Tziril weakly. "Do you really think they'll take an interest? And anyway, I don't have anyone to accuse."

"You didn't see them?"

"It was dark. I would know their voices in a second, but that isn't much help."

"But you can still report what happened. They can't just get away with it." But of course it was exactly the opposite; they could get away with it, and for a moment this unpleasant truth hung over the room like an odor of rot, an apt metaphor for all that is happening in Poland at the moment.

Dora came into the parlor carrying a tray with tea and poppy seed cookies. "The main thing is that Gavril is going to be fine."

"You get yourself in hospital and the world goes crazy," Meyer remarked. "Have you heard the latest?"

"I'm happy to say that I haven't," I replied. "The best thing about being in hospital is that they keep you far from the newspapers. It's a blessing. In fact, I'd be grateful if you allow me stay in this blissful state a little longer."

"No no. That's no good," Tziril said, ignoring my attempt at humor. "Only a fool buries his head in the sand."

I would have replied, but just then the news report began and we all listened closely as if a messenger had appeared to deliver fresh tidings. In a terse, almost morose voice, the announcer read out that Lithuania had capitulated to Hitler's demands to cede and evacuate Memelland. They had simply given in without a fight.

"What's this?" I said, not quite believing what we had all just heard.

"Didn't you hear about Von Ribbentrop's ultimatum? Or was that after you went into hospital?"

"It must have been. What happened?"

"Von Ribbentrop demanded that the Lithuanians hand over Memelland, or else they'll invade."

"But they just annexed Czechoslovakia. Everyone said that would be the very last straw."

"Nu?" Dora said. "That idiot is like a pig that can't eat his fill."

From across the room came a giggle from Marek. I glanced at Sophie, still engrossed in her book. "Just like that?" I asked, trying to keep my voice even for the sake of the children. "But there are treaties. What about the treaties? The League of Nations signed that area over to Lithuania. Where is Britain? Where is France?"

"Italy and Japan are both in bed with Hitler," Tziril reminded us.

"Yes, but where is Britain?" I asked again. "What about France? How could they just stand back and let this happen?"

"They've expressed their sympathy," Meyer said sardonically.

"That's all?"

"They have a very threatening weapon. They call it Appeasement. Nu? What do they care to throw him a bone if it lets them sleep at night?"

"But that's...I just don't understand it. How could they violate their own treaty and abandon an ally?"

"What's a treaty? Words. If their words were sticks you couldn't lean on them," Meyer said, quoting the old proverb.

We fell silent, each of us lost in our own thoughts. I have often been accused of a certain naïveté when it comes to the ways of the world, but I nonetheless found it astonishing that Britain and France, honorable and civilized peoples, would betray their word. "What is this world coming to?" Dora sighed.

"Don't worry," Tziril said loudly, motioning with her eyes toward the children. "The average German doesn't want another war any more than we do." But as she said this I was put in mind of those photographs you see in the newspapers of the Nazi rallies, with their vast seas of enthusiastic supporters, and I wondered where all these Germans who don't want another war might be hiding.

The night passed with much discomfort. Lying down brought on coughing fits that felt as if they might explode my chest from within. When Dora awoke to prepare the children for school, the idea of getting out of bed seemed unbearable and so I slept into the morning.

When I finally rose, the house was empty. Dora had gone off to a meeting of the Jewish Women's Holiday committee. I fixed myself a cup of tea and carried it, very carefully, across the parlor to my desk by the window overlooking the street. I intended to read a little, but as I sat down in my chair my eye fell upon the letter from my cousin Tamar in Palestine, waiting for me on my desk.

Though we have corresponded infrequently over the years, it was only last November, after the terrible events in Germany, that I again began to receive frequent letters from her. Their message is always the same: I must sell my possessions, leave my work, gather up my family, and start anew in *Eretz Yisrael*, as she calls it.

Her language in these letters is blunt. She has no use for formalities. She began with greetings to my family and news of hers, bringing to mind vistas of sunny skies, citrus orchards, and palm trees, but her letter, as always, quickly turned dark.

We are closely following the terrible news from Europe. It sounds as if things are getting worse by the day. I know that I've said this before, but I will say it again: You must leave Poland. I don't believe the comforting words about "peace in our time." I fear that a terrible war is coming, and when it happens no one will move even one finger to protect the Jews. You could move east, perhaps to Minsk. My family there would help you to get settled. But even better would be for you to make your way to Eretz Yisrael. The British would consider you "illegal" but that is irrelevant. The more I think about these things, the more I have come to see that laws, treaties, agreements, and White Papers are nothing but empty words. Have you heard of the "Aliya Bet?" It is our term for "illegal" immigration. Jews make their way to Romania or Greece, and from there they charter boats to bring them here. The boats leave them a short distance from shore and they swim in under cover of darkness or wait to be picked up by the Haganah. Not an easy journey, but once they are here, they build new lives, not as despised strangers, but as masters in their own home.

At the close of the letter, she added, *As you may know, I have written to our cousin Nathan Wexler, Aunt Elkie's son, in Chicago. He is a good, serious man, a journalist who has connections and he may be able to get you a visa to go to America. It is essential that we try all possibilities on all fronts.*

I stood up and went slowly and painfully to the window that overlooks the street. I imagined Dora and me and the children, clutching our suitcases, weary from long days of waiting in the ports of Romania, begging to climb aboard a third-rate ship, and then, after several hellish days, jumping into the waters of the Mediterranean and thrashing, heavy and freezing, through the cold sea in the dead of night.

In the apartment across the way two girls were washing windows. A yeshiva student hurried by, one hand carrying a basket of apples, the other clutching a book. I could hear the hoarse chant of the onion seller, and watched as his cart turned onto our street. Sure enough, not a minute passed before the neighborhood housewives came out to haggle with him. A scene that had been playing out for centuries in villages and cities all over Poland. All was well with the world.

After dinner, the Rosens came down for their nightly encounter with our wireless. As usual, we braced ourselves for the news of the day, but lo and behold, we were finally rewarded with good tidings. Chamberlain had announced in Parliament that Britain and France would lend Poland "all the support in their power" in the face of any threat to Poland's independence. All the support in their power! Even Meyer Rosen agreed that this veiled threat could sway Hitler's thinking about any further belligerence. How good it was to hear, at last, strong words from sane people. After the broadcast we were all in high spirits. I opened the bottle of schnapps I save for special occasions and the four of us drank to the health of Chamberlain and the King of England.

The good news infused us all with hope, but by the time the Rosens left I was exhausted and went straight to bed. Like the night before, my sleep was light and fitful. The smallest sound in the street had the power to rouse me, I could not find a comfortable position in which to settle, and my mind, restless and plagued with dark musings, would not let me rest. As if it had a will of its own, it returned again to those terrible moments in the alley, to Schechter's whimpering, to my own sense of terror. I commanded myself to cease these recollections, to think about something more pleasant and restful. Eventually, as I settled into a state somewhere between wakefulness and dreams, I was again in my classroom. I looked up and there in the doorway stood Symek, returned, holding his folded papers, a new story. "You're back," I exclaimed, feeling a surge of joy, and though he looked at us with that singular keen gaze, in that demeanor of his which seemed to express a dare, I knew that he had taken the words I had spoken to heart. When I woke, late in the morning, I could still see him standing in the doorway in his worn overcoat, a vision so vivid that I was no longer sure whether it had been a dream.

The next day, Marek and I were in the midst of a round of Hearts, his favorite card game, when I received a visit from a delegation of teachers from the school. Like three somber muses they filed into the parlor: Raya Milstein, Boruch Gutman, and Yankev Dalinsky the history teacher, whom, Dora had told me, had been assigned to take on my literature classes. They must have come straight from school, for Boruch and Yankev were in their suits and ties and Raya was wearing a new spring dress. They greeted me solemnly and sat down on the sofa. "What a nice surprise," I said, so as to lighten the atmosphere.

"We've all been so worried about you," Raya said.

"Well, you can see there's no need at all for that. I'm fine. Getting stronger every day. I'm sure I'll be back in the classroom after the Passover break."

"That's good to hear, Gabriel," Boruch said gravely. "We were all very upset when we heard what happened."

"Oh, it isn't as bad as it sounds," I said. "But tell me Yankev, how are you managing with my classes? Teaching literature must be very different from teaching history."

He explained that he had brought in some Peretz stories to read with them, and then launched into a discussion of why literature and history are in fact quite similar, but as he spoke my thoughts drifted to *Ziemia Obiecana,* a novel which I intend to assign the class so they can wrestle with a work in the original Polish.

Dora came in with some tea and carrot cake and more polite conversation ensued. But Yankev's misguided idea of giving the students more Peretz to read had put me in mind again of Symek's story, and how hearing him read it had felt like a wild burst of fresh air. "Say," I said, "do any of you know of a youth by the name of Symek Grynberg? He lives in Shnipishok but he appeared in my student writing club one day, and he showed the most extraordinary talent."

"Who?" Raya asked. I repeated his name, but no one recognized it.

"What else is going on the world?" I asked them, feeling oddly disappointed.

They glanced at one another, and shifted a little. "We've just been to see Isaac Schechter," Yankev said quietly.

"How is he?" I asked, embarrassed that I hadn't asked sooner.

"Not good," Raya said. Boruch gave his head a little shake, as if to silence her.

"No," I said, "tell me. I've been thinking about him constantly."

"He's alive, but unconscious," Raya blurted out. "The doctors can't say if he'll ever wake up. And if he does..." she stopped as though weighing her words, "his mind might not be what it was."

"We saw Rivaleh at the hospital," Yankev added. "She's in a terrible state. They were barely getting by on his salary, and now..."

"I heard that she's applying to *Gemiles Chosodim* for a loan," Boruch said. "It's a real disaster."

For a long moment no one had anything to say, and then suddenly Raya spoke. "I was going to wait, but I might as well tell you all now. For Herschel and me, what happened to you and Isaac was the last straw. We've been talking about going for months, but now we've decided. We're leaving this lousy country. My husband has relatives in Smolensk. We're going to live with them."

"You can't be serious," Boruch said. "You're going to make a life under the Soviets?"

"They say everything is better there. The government makes sure that everyone has work so no one has to starve. And they treat everyone equally. It's easier to be a Jew there."

"I don't care what anyone says," Yankev said. "That Stalin is a nasty character. They say that his secret police are everywhere. One wrong word and you're on a train to Siberia."

"He's a leader," Raya declared, "and that's much more than you can say about our pathetic excuse of a prime minister. He's tough with his enemies. He does whatever needs to be done, for everyone's good. Let's face it, life for a Jew in Poland is miserable. It doesn't matter if you're rich or poor, if you're a millionaire or a beggar."

"What about work?" I asked.

"With my Russian I'll find something, and Herschel is a bookkeeper," she replied. "Our relatives are already looking for jobs for us. If you ask me, anyone who has any chance of leaving this stinking country should get out now."

⁓ • ⁓

Later, after they were gone, Dora came out of the kitchen looking somewhat wilted, her apron damp with soap and water. "I heard Raya say that they're leaving," she said.

"They've been talking about moving to his family in Smolensk for years."

She walked to the window, took a cigarette from the pack on my desk, an indulgence that she rarely allows herself, lit it with my lighter, took a long drag, and stared out at the buildings across the way. "We could go to Minsk," she said quietly, "to your family there."

The words hung in the air and seemed to resonate through the quiet. "Do you mean that, Dora?" It was the first time she had said such a thing, the first time she had voiced the words which had the power to unsettle our lives, to wrench us from the only city she had ever called home.

"No," she said with a sigh. "It's just…good to know that we have options." She came to me and put her arms gently about my shoulders, and we remained that way, in that awkward embrace, for a long moment.

The following day my father came to visit in the early afternoon. He knocked lightly, let himself in, and appeared in the parlor, quite dapper in his spring coat and hat. "You're looking well," he said. "Much better than I expected. Are you able to give your old father a hug?"

"Of course," I replied with a smile and, with a small effort, rose from my chair. "Actually, it wasn't that serious. Just a bad fall really," I told him.

"Ach, Gavril," he sighed, and I at once regretted that Dora had told him about the incident; if only she had spared him the distress of knowing. "I went to the *Shulhoyf* this morning," he told me. "To the Gaon's synagogue. To *bentsh goymel*. To give thanks that you're still here with us."

"Well, that's really overdoing it! I was barely injured. You can see that I'm perfectly fine."

"Thank God," he murmured. "Lately I've been going to the morning minyan. I'm up before sunrise anyway. The old-timers nod at me when I come in. We all sit on the bench by the stove. They ask about my aches and pains. I ask about theirs. But when we all sing the prayers together, we forget our troubles for a while."

My father was once a religious man. As a youth he spent his days studying Talmud in the *Beis Midrash* in his little *shtetl*, and even though he took an interest in what the Socialists and the Zionists had to say, he remained faithful to the Judaism of his childhood. It was only after my brother Elya's death in the war that he stopped going to synagogue.

"Funny things happen to a man's head in old age," he mused. "You know, I used to take Elya with me to the synagogue when he was a little boy, before you were born. He loved to sing and recite the Hebrew prayers. And now, sometimes when I *daven*, I still feel him there at my side." He fell silent, as though staring into Elya's absence, and I too called up an image of my brother, drafted at eighteen into the Russian army, never to return.

"That reminds me," he said, abruptly jolting me out of my memories, "I brought something to show you." He opened his bag, took out what appeared to be a booklet of some kind, and began to leaf through it until he found what he wanted. "You're the expert. Read this and tell me what you think."

It was an old journal, full of poems and stories. Keeping the place he wanted to show me, I glanced at the front cover where the words, *Der Nayer Yiddisher Horizont, Friling 1914* were printed in large, old style Yiddish letters. "Where did you get this?"

"Never mind that. Just read the page."

It was a poem, written in three short verses. *"Drei Gedanken* by Raizel Shulman," I read out and glanced at him. "Wasn't that the name of your Bubbie?"

He smiled like a child caught in the act of tricking his elders. "Exactly. The grandmother I never knew. Have a look. What do you think of it?"

I read it through quickly. "It's very simple," I said, "but it nonetheless has a certain power to it."

"Yes. I knew you would see that," he said happily. "But it's really about my father and his brothers. About her having to split them up. It appears very innocent, almost childlike, but that's what she was really writing about. I'm sure of it."

"Interesting," I mused, rereading the lines. "When you think about it that way, it's actually quite sad. Did she ever write anything else?"

He shrugged. "Who knows? Nothing else survived her. Forty-five years after she wrote it my uncle Itzik had it published in a Yiddish newspaper. And then right before the war, he published it again here, in a proper literary journal."

I leafed through the journal and as I perused the titles of the poems and the stories, it struck me that they were like forgotten snapshots, glimpses into a world that was fading into oblivion.

"I remember when I first saw the poem, the original that my grandmother wrote. It was on a trip to Minsk," he recollected. "My father had sent me there to meet his two long lost brothers, Uncle Itzik, who lived in Minsk and Uncle Avrum who was from Mogilev. That was the first time I met my cousins, Aryeh and Elkie."

"Aryeh Grupstein? Tamar's father? And Elkie…Nat Wexler's mother, the one who went to Chicago?"

"Exactly. You see we all had the same grandmother, but because our fathers had been split up in childhood we had never met before. We had the most wonderful time in Minsk. Those few days were the best of my life." I was surprised, and a little insulted, to hear him say this; it seemed to suggest that all the rest – his years of marriage with my mother, his children, becoming a grandfather, could somehow not compare with whatever had gone on in Minsk. And yet, perhaps it was true, for so much catastrophe was awaiting him.

"The buildings were so tall and the streets were so wide, and the parks were so lovely, and the shops full of astonishing things. Aryeh lived right by the marketplace. It was like a carnival. He was a real Zionist; for him it was like a religion. All he could talk about was how he was going to board a ship and make a life in *Eretz Yisrael*. And then Elkie…well she was something. Beautiful. Spirited. And she was a socialist too, like Elya. She talked on and on about building a new society. That's how they were. They all thought that socialism could turn enemies into friends, Jew haters into brothers and sisters. Each of us was dreaming of a different future. Aryeh went in for Zionism. Elkie got married and after the pogroms in '05 she and her husband gave up socialism and went to America."

"And you?" I asked.

"Me? I went home to Propoisk, to your mother. She was pregnant with Elya. And then came the war, and losing Elya, and the move to Vilna, and your mother dying from a broken heart; all the *drek* that happened to us." He opened his bag and took out two more copies of the journal. "Here," he said. "You take these. A keepsake from your great-grandmother. I have a few more in my cupboard. Ach, Gavril," he sighed, "sometimes I wonder how it is that this world, that I once thought so beautiful and filled with so many astonishing things, turned out to be so terrible."

His visit left me in a melancholy mood, but when Dora and the children came home, their chatter and news of the day filled the house with a liveliness that dispelled it. Dora reported that the women's committee had arranged for five hundred Passover food bags to be distributed in the next two days. Sophie announced at dinner that she planned to follow in Marie Curie's footsteps and become a lady scientist. Marek challenged me to a round of checkers.

Dora, exhausted from the long day of sorting foodstuffs, retired early with the children, but I sat in the parlor late into the night, reading from *Cinnamon Sticks*. Now and then I would raise my eyes from the novel and turn to stare at my bookshelves lining the wall behind me. The books, bound in black, blue, and green cloth like guiding spirits, were a balm for my soul, infused with the quiet power to reassure us that the world is also this – works of imagination that embody the very best of humanity.

At some point I must have dozed off, because I was suddenly awoken by a voice. I opened my eyes and there before me in the dim light of my reading lamp stood Symek, wearing his familiar overcoat, his narrow eyes looking down at me with that same severe gaze I had seen on that day when he first appeared in my classroom. "Sir? Mr. Shulman?" He was saying in a voice a little above a whisper.

"Symek?" I rubbed my eyes, not sure that I wasn't dreaming. "How did you – "

"I let myself in, sir. I knocked, and when no one answered I tried the door, and it was open." He pulled out a chair from the table and settled himself. "Sorry for coming into your home like this, but I have to speak to you...I wanted to come last week, but I heard about what happened and I figured I'd wait a bit. As soon as I heard, I was kicking myself for not coming to that writers' meeting, because if I had been there with you, I would have let those hooligans have it."

"Yes, it's too bad," I smiled. "I could have used the help." Though his sudden presence had startled me, I was, more than anything else, happy to see him again.

"So anyway, the reason I'm here is because I want to say that you shouldn't have come to look for me. You shouldn't have come to where we live."

"I apologize if my visit made trouble for you. It was only that – "

"Mr. Shulman, since you came, I've been like a crazy man; I fought with my sister and my mother, I've made mistakes in the lumberyard. My brain has been in a fit. And it's all because of you. Because of the things you said."

"But that's good, Symek. That's good. Conflict is where writing begins."

"No. That's not how it is. You've got it all wrong."

I shook my head. "No, you have it all wrong. Don't you see, Symek? You must take that feeling and bring it into your stories. You have all of this inside of you. Put it into words."

"No," he said resolutely. "There aren't going to be any stories."

His words stung like a slap. "Why not?"

He glared at me, exasperated. "Do you think that I don't want to be a writer?" he hissed. "That I don't wish every day of my life that I could live like Jozef Pozanski? Do you know how I wrote that story I brought to your class? Late at night, by the light of a candle, my fingers freezing. Each night I forced myself to do as much as I could before one of the kids started crying, or my mother asked me to blow out the light. It's just…impossible. That's it. That's how it is. I have no choice. So what I want to say is, don't do it again. Don't come to bother me and my family. Leave me alone." He rose, glaring at me harshly, filled with the mean spirit of his request. "Promise that you won't bother me again."

The boy was rude, crass, brimming with barely veiled aggression, but I could not be angry with him. On the contrary, I was filled with sorrow for all of the words he would not write. "Alright, Symek," I said quietly. "You won't hear from me again." I would have liked to have spoken with him a little longer, perhaps even tried to help in some way, but he turned and left without another word, the door thudding closed behind him.

And now, in the midst of our fragile, fleeting summer, I am fully recovered and planning my lessons for the upcoming school year. The days are warm and long. Plums and apricots are once more to be found in the markets, and Dora is making pies and preserves. Sophie goes down to the Wilja River to swim each day with her friends. Marek spends long hours with his pals, playing cards, jacks, ball games, all the things that children do. Yet we know that difficult days await us. The army is mobilizing and it seems we will soon again be at war. We've been told to stock up on enough food supplies for two weeks. At night, alone with my thoughts, I am filled with fears.

Though Vilna is a small place where one is always running into friends and acquaintances, I did not see Symek again until last week. I was in the market, browsing through a cart of used books, when I spotted him on the other side of the square, deep in conversation with a pretty girl in a summer dress. She was leaning against a pillar and he stood across from her, his hand resting on the wall by her shoulder. He was grinning, as though telling her an amusing story, and she was gazing at him with adoring eyes. They both laughed out loud, and it was then that he looked up, glanced in my direction, and caught sight of me.

For a fraction of a moment his face clouded over, as though my presence had called up something wild and desperate. He gave me the briefest of nods, then turned away, whispered something to the girl, and led her out of the square.

Theater Tickets

(Nat – Chicago, September 1938)

"Here Natty, look. Yossele Blustein at the Lawndale. With his *gantze* troop. They're putting on *Di Dybbuk*. Frume Ziskind saw them last week and she said they're wonderful. She cried the whole time. Now listen. Here are three tickets. One for me, one for you, and one for that new girl you're too busy to bring home to meet your mother. We'll go the three of us, yes?"

This was on a Sunday after lunch. Nat Wexler was at the kitchen table with his mother, drinking tea and eating stale *rogelach* left over from the Sabbath. She rose and went into the hall, and he could hear her determinedly rummaging through the drawer in the wooden stand by the front door, where she kept an unruly mess of unpaid bills, newspaper clippings, stray buttons, bobby pins, photographs of him and his brothers when they were small, and other items that could not be parted with. When she returned, two envelopes were sticking out of her apron pocket.

Nat tried to keep his tone innocent. "I don't know, Ma. What night is it on?"

"Here." She drew out the tickets and held them in front of his face. "You think I can read such small writing? You tell me."

"*Di Dybbuk*," Nat read out. "Wednesday, November 2, 8:00 p.m." He shook his head in a gesture of regret. "I don't know if she can make it. She works late some nights."

"And she can't change with a friend? Tell her it's for a special night. To meet your mama. Three months you're wining and dining her like a princess! She can at least do you the favor of coming out to the theater with your mother."

The scene played out in his head. His mother in the shapeless green print dress that made her look like a caricature of a Maxwell Street *yente* trying to look like a somebody. Sally Rosenthal, decked out in a classy evening gown and smart hat. And he, Elkie's youngest son, drawing the unabashed stares and whispers of every *yachne* who knew his mother. He tried to imagine Sally who was, truth be told, a south-side snob, weaving herself through the shrill Yiddish clamor, and knew that it could not be.

"What's the matter, Nusseleh? Is your girlfriend too good for such an evening?"

"No, Ma. That's not it at all. I don't think she even understands Yiddish."

"That doesn't matter, I'll explain the story to her. This play is going to be a big deal. Esther Finkelstein is going. And Fania Varshinsky. Even they who sit like queens in big flats on Independence Blvd. are coming to see this play." He would have to think of something. Some way to get out of this. Or at least get Sally out of this. Nat stood up and put the tickets on the table. "He is going already. Where are you going, mister?"

"I have some work to do. Jim assigned me a new piece. Something for Thanksgiving."

"Fine. But you tell your girl of yours that November 2nd she is coming with us to the Lawndale."

"I'll check with her. I don't want to get her in trouble with her boss."

"Good. And now I have something else for you. It also came in the mail. A letter." She pulled the second envelope from her apron pocket and put it ceremoniously on the table.

"A letter from whom?"

"From your own flesh and blood, that's who! From cousin Yoyna's son who lives in Vilna. In Lithuania. Do you even know where that is?"

Nat rolled his eyes. Three years at Northwestern, an honors degree in English, and still his mother spoke to him as though he were an imbecile. "Of course I know where Lithuania is."

"And about cousin Yoyna you remember?"

"Only what you told me, Ma. That you only met him once, but you were great friends."

"No," she said, annoyed but vindicated, as if Nat had just affirmed what she had long suspected. "I talk and talk but I might as well be speaking to the deaf. I said that I met him in Minsk, at the home of another cousin, Aryeh Grupstein. And that night," she smiled wistfully at the recollection, "we went out and didn't get home till morning. Our parents were going crazy, they cursed us and called us Cossacks and hooligans, but we swore that we would never forget each other, and would keep up the letter writing. So for years I would get a letter, once a year, twice a year, from cousin Yoyna in Vilna, and from cousin Aryeh who's still in Minsk, even though his daughter got on a boat to Palestine to make a life with the Zionists."

Nat had heard this story before, but he assumed it to be wildly embellished. Not only could he not picture his mother being called a Cossack or a hooligan, but he couldn't imagine her doing anything to warrant such names. Nevertheless, he knew to save his battles with her for more important things and he let her claims pass unchallenged. "So??" he shot back. He generally tried to cultivate a calm, unruffled demeanor, but his mother had a real knack for getting on his nerves. "I remember all that. So, what's this letter about?"

"Would I open your mail? A letter not addressed to me? What do I care that it's from Europe!"

Actually, she cared plenty, though thirty years had passed since she had slammed the door on the life she'd once had in the place she called "the Black Country." Both of Nat's parents had been born in that fuzzy mass of Eastern European lands with constantly shifting borders: she from somewhere in White Russia, his father from Ukraine.

She disliked talking about her life over there, and Nat knew only the barest facts about it. About the trip over she was more talkative, and when she would tell about the long weeks in the crammed, smelly hold of a ship, Nat envisioned them the way they describe it on the Statue of Liberty – wretched, tempest-tossed, and after six weeks in steerage, yearning to breathe free.

When they first arrived, they had moved in with his mother's sister Sorel and her husband, Abe, and tried to make a go of it in New York. They soon rented a room above a bakery and the owner, a righteous Jew from Galicia, would leave them stale bread by the door. Nat's father, a certified lawyer who once dreamed of opening his own practice, found work as a hospital janitor, while his mother sewed piecework for a sweatshop. Life was dismal, a disaster, but it was still a paradise compared to life in the Black Country. Things improved a little when they moved west to Chicago and found a cheap flat over a secondhand clothes store. And luck intervened when his father met a Jew from his *shtetl* in a local synagogue who gave him a job selling shoes. Within five years Nat's father had learned the ropes well enough to open his own shoe shop.

His mother would mention, when she wanted to goad Nat and his brothers into doing whatever it took to "become a somebody," how she and his father had scraped together every last drop of their savings, *and* sold her golden earrings, *and* the silver candlesticks, *and* used the whole of the five hundred rubles her grandfather had left her in his will in order to pay for "tickets for a place in hell." "But ask me if I would do it again," she would declare, "and I'll tell you, yes! A thousand times I would do it. Because that boat brought us from darkness to light."

His father had also kept silent about his life before America, as if that time hadn't really counted. It was only at his funeral, two years earlier, that his mother had dredged up some old memories, which were new to Nat. "Your father was once a socialist, a real fighter," his mother recounted at the *shiva*, a few days after he died. "When I met him, he was a student, but he spent more time spreading the word of socialism than sitting in a classroom." Nat had tried to imagine his father, grey haired, stoop shouldered, always with a joke that was usually more sad than funny, in the role of Russian revolutionary, but he couldn't conjure it. Even more surprising and disturbing was when his mother revealed to him, together with Frank and Mort (whom his mother still called Feivel and Motele), that his father's entire family had been murdered in a pogrom. "We didn't want to tell you children," she explained, "because it's such a sad story. Your father was away at the time, at St. Vladimir in Kiev, law he was studying. And even though everyone told him that it was doubtful that as a Jew he'd be allowed to practice, he wouldn't give up. We were married by then, but I was still living with my family in Mogilev. As soon as your father got word of the pogroms, he got on a train to his family in Zhitomir, but when he got there, it was too late to do anything. He never told me how they were killed. He said it was too terrible to say it. His parents and his younger brother Motele, after whom Mort was named, and his sisters, Sorke and Mirele. All dead. He came back a different man. I knew then that all his big plans for a new Russia were finished." The next week he sold whatever was worth anything and bought their "tickets for a new life."

She had told all this in Yiddish and they let her talk, telling it her way. "You don't know how lucky you are, living in America," she admonished them, reverting back to English. "America is the best country in the world. What do we lack here? Nothing. Because in America, a Jew can become a somebody." These words were like a family motto, words to inspire, to engrave on one's heart. One could only try to be equal to them.

Nat opened the letter, which was written on thin cheap paper in letters that he knew from the prayer books he opened once a year in synagogue on the High Holidays. "I can't read this," he frowned.

He was conversant in the singular mix of English and Yiddish that his parents spoke, but though he had been sent as a child to learn the Hebrew alphabet with an old-world *melamed,* his reading and writing were poor. "You read it, Ma," he said, handing it back to her.

"Polish paper," she remarked snootily, rubbing the flimsy sheet between her fingers, and read out, her voice warm and fluid, as though embracing the familiar words.

August 16, 1938

Dear Nathan,

My father has assured me that you speak a rudimentary Yiddish, and that even if you don't understand every word, your mother will help to translate if need be. It is strange, I admit, to write to someone one has never met, and yet perhaps because of the stories my father told me about himself and your mother, whom he met but once, I feel as though we already know each other.

My father tells me that you are a journalist working for an important newspaper in Chicago, and that you have in all likelihood studied literature at university. I hope that you are perhaps in a position to assist me. You see, I am a teacher of literature at the Tsysho Gymnasium, and I believe that it is essential that my students be familiar not only with Yiddish literature, and not only with the literature of our region (i.e., Polish, Lithuanian, and of course the great Russians), but also know something of the literature of other peoples. To this end, I've put together a small library of foreign literature, both in translation and in the original languages. Our library of works in their original language now includes Maupassant, some Heine, and even a book of stories by the Irish writer James Joyce. To this collection I would like to add something by an American writer. My knowledge of American literature is limited. When I was a child, in the years before the war, my father managed to secure for me a magnificent Russian translation of Tom Sawyer. *Likewise, a friend of mine lent me his copy, in Polish, of Hawthorne's* The Scarlet Letter, *which, in my humble opinion, can stand proudly beside any work by the Russian Masters.*

But it is not these works that I have in mind for our library. Some years ago while visiting Warsaw, I came across Stefan Napierski's Polish translation of Walt Whitman's poetry, and there was one poem in particular, entitled "Poets to Come," which I found especially moving. I have contributed my own copy to the library, and yet, I would very much like for my students to see the poems in the original English. For this reason, I want to ask if I might trouble you to send me a copy of Whitman's Leaves of Grass. *As you probably know, times are very challenging now, and it is very difficult to find any books in the English language.*

I look forward to receiving a letter from you. Please tell me something about yourself and your life in Chicago.

Sincerely,

Gabriel Shulman

"He is a good boy, Yoyna's son. A teacher," Nat's mother sighed approvingly. "And his father is a good man as well. He was from a religious home, but he used to read the freethinking newspapers. What is this book that he wants? Do you know it?"

"Whitman? Are you kidding? I'll pick up a copy at the bookstore next week." Nat glanced at his watch. He wanted to read another chapter of the Hammett novel he had just started, then shower, dress, and pick up Sally on the way to Lou and Sylvia's place.

"OK, Natty. You go. I'll be fine," his mother said, picking at the last of the *rogelach* crumbs. "I gotta go and see your sister-in-law. I told her I'd come over and teach her to make a borscht like your brother likes it." She put Gabriel's letter back in the envelope and held it out to him.

Nat glanced at the stamps, intricately drawn portraits and landmarks, each topped with the words *Poszta Polska*. "Where is he from? Didn't you say Lithuania? These stamps are Polish."

"Poland, Lithuania what does it matter? They're all *drek*."

"Still, it doesn't make sense. We hardly know anything about what's really going on over there," Nat mused.

"And you don't want to know. Trust me. Their life is no picnic."

Nat put the envelope in the pocket of his jacket. "It doesn't sound so bad in the letter."

"That's because he's hiding how bad it is."

—— • ——

They were outside Lou and Sylvia's door, Nat in his good suit and tie, Sally in an evening dress. He had been dating her for three months now but this was the first time she would meet the Marshall

High bunch, Nat's old gang from high school. He loved those guys, the kind of guys who knew you since you were a kid, knew everything there was to know about you and would never let you down. Though lately, something was changing, a subtle shift of loyalties toward wives, bosses, mortgages, and the looming knowledge that one of these days they would become parents. They still joked around and talked baseball and cars and had poker nights like in the old days, but Nat was aware that as the only one yet to tie the knot, he was falling behind.

The men, Nat was sure, would love Sally. Though she was only twenty-one and barely out of college, her Deanna Durbin looks and warm, witty laugh would win them over. But as for the girls, it was hard to tell. He hadn't been aware of it as a kid, but lately he noticed that they could be as catty as his mother's *yachne* friends.

"Swanky place," Sally remarked with a wink. Nat had to smile. She really was a snob, but it was a subtle, ironic snobbishness, a trait that he liked in men and delighted him in women.

"Yep. Good old Lou's not doing too badly for himself."

"What did you say he does?"

"Lawyer. He's with Alvin Melovsky's dad's firm."

"And he's married to Sylvia, right?"

"You got it, kiddo." She smiled up at him brightly and he wanted to grab her, to take her in his arms and kiss her, just like he did when her parents went out to the symphony on Saturday nights and they could be alone at her place. But just then the door opened and there was Lou, with a chummy slap on the back for him and an admiring grin for Sally.

"Nat, you old Turk!" he exclaimed. "You always pick the lookers, don't you?"

"Nice to meet you, Lou," Sally said, her voice full of that easy confidence that she had with people.

"Same here. Are you the one who's going to make an honest man of him?"

"That's a personal question, I'd say," Sylvia cut in, coming up behind him, holding two martinis with bobbing green olives, which she handed off to each of them. She turned to Sally with a broad grin. "So, are you?"

"I'm giving it my best shot."

She fit right in with them. And why wouldn't she? She was a Chicago girl like the others, except that her family was descended from the German Jews who had settled in the city sixty years earlier. And her parents had been born in America. That, Nat was finding, could make all the difference. "I love your dress," she complimented Betty Melovsky, Alvin's wife. "That bow is awfully cute."

"It's from Uptown Lady," Betty told her, and everyone else. "Do you ever go in there, Sally?"

"Sure. When the sales are on."

"She's a scream, Nat. An absolute scream."

It was Lou and Sylvia, Alvin and Betty, Max and Estelle, and them – perhaps soon to be Nat and Sally Wexler. The connections among them all went wide and deep. They had memorized names and dates in the same American history classes, followed the standings of the Bears, the White Sox, the Cubs, spent warm summer evenings together at Riverview Park, attended the same Jewish community dances, and on the High Holidays made an appearance at services at the same synagogue. Now they were grownups, the men sharp young professionals, and the women full-fledged housewives, not dumpy like their mothers, but modern, gay, and charming. Max had brought along Benny Goodman's latest, and Lou put it on the Victrola. "Hey, don't you have any Bing Crosby?" Betty called out.

"Crosby?" Max cried. "How can you even say that name in the same breath as Goodman?"

"What do you have against Crosby? He's got a terrific voice," Estelle countered.

"Crosby's OK, but he's *just* a voice. Goodman is a musician – a genius. He writes his own solos, he puts together the players, and he's an absolute master of the clarinet. You guys should have seen him when he was here three years ago at the Congress Hotel, with Krupa drumming and them doing the numbers with Fletcher Henderson's band – it would have knocked your socks off."

"Well, I prefer songs with words," Estelle insisted. "A tisket a tasket, a green and yellow basket," she crooned as she grabbed Betty and the two of them started dancing – jitterbug style.

Max rolled his eyes. "I'm tellin ya, jazz is going to overtake classical music. That's why they had to let Goodman play Carnegie Hall last winter. It's like this is a new era and guys like Goodman and Duke Ellington and Fats Waller are the messengers, coming to spread the word."

Betty stopped dancing and broke away from Estelle. "Has anyone heard which band they're getting for the benefit concert at the JPI next week?"

"That benefit for German Jews?"

"Yeah. You going?"

"Of course. We have to do something to help those poor people."

"My whole family is going."

"What are you wearing?"

"I haven't decided yet. You?"

"Probably the same black dress I wore to the Brickman wedding."

"Are you going, Sally?"

"You betcha she's going."

"My grandparents came from Germany," Sally told them. "Thank God they left long ago, before the Germans went crazy. I probably still have distant relatives there, but I don't know them."

"They say it's almost impossible for them to get visas to America. You need money and connections, and if you're anything less than a professor, they won't even look at you."

"Well, that's the point of the benefit. Money. Only money talks. The more we raise, the more we can help them get the hell out of there."

Lou stuck his head in the living room. "The lady of the house says that dinner is served," he announced, and they made their way to the table, Betty and Estelle doing a little dance as they walked.

"So how did you two meet?" Estelle asked as she took a seat beside Sally. Nat grinned sheepishly, remembering how he had once taken Estelle out and told her that he doubted he would marry until he was middle-aged.

"Irv Weingarten introduced us at Abby Silverstone's Fourth of July party."

"Hey, we were at that party," Alvin said. "The one where Solly did his Shirley Temple imitation?"

"And Rosie Feldman sang *The Star-Spangled Banner?*"

"How did *you* get to that party?"

"Abby's my cousin."

"Small world!"

"What do you do with yourself, Sally?" Lou asked, struggling to open a bottle of seltzer.

"I finished my degree at U of Chicago - in education. But there's no work with the school board, so in the meantime I've gotten a job at Chez Helen."

"The French perfume store downtown?"

"Say, that's a swanky place," Estelle nodded, impressed. "I'll bet you get some pretty fancy customers."

"I'll say we do! Even in hard times there are still lots of women whose husbands can afford expensive luxuries. But it's not only rich people. Once in a while a girl comes in and you can tell that she only wants to look around, to see what people buy when they have cash to spare." She smiled slyly, adorably. "Sometimes it can actually be amusing."

"Like what?" Betty asked. "Give an example."

All eyes were upon her but she easily rose to the occasion. "OK. Here's one: the other day this woman comes in with her daughter. It's obvious that they're way out of their league – they're both in these kerchiefs and frumpy house dresses – you know the type, like they just got off the boat. So the daughter says to me, in this thick Yiddish accent, 'I vant to buy my mother a present. Vhat do you have for her?' And I pick up the bottle of Chanel No. 5 that we use for samples and I say, 'Would you like to try some Chanel?' And the mother looks at the bottle and then holds it up to her nose and sniffs at it and says, 'Vhat kind of present is 'dis? Do I need to smell like a French *nafke*?'" Sally had done a perfect imitation of the woman's garble of Yiddish-accented English and everyone responded with terrific laughter. But Nat knew that this laughter was an act, even a sort of a disguise; every one of them had parents who spoke with that accent, whose speech was marked with that cynical, self-pitying Yiddish that was so embarrassing.

"But I'll bet most of the ladies who come in to your store are classy and rich," Estelle mused.

"Of course," Sally said. "After all, the perfume is imported; it's really for high society. But once in a while you see another kind of girl come in — the kind who doesn't have much money, but she's trying to improve herself. You see that she wants to change, to make herself into someone modern and stylish. And sometimes, when I see a girl who was clearly born over there, but she dresses nicely and speaks politely, without embarrassing herself, and really wants to make herself into an American, well, it makes me want to help her out. One time a woman like that came in, and I could see that she didn't have much money, so I asked my boss if we could give her a discount."

"And what did he say?" Sylvia asked eagerly.

"He said I could sell her a cracked bottle at ten-percent off."

"Who wants to help me bring in the pot roast?" Sylvia asked, rising to her feet, and the rest of the women followed her into the kitchen. For a moment the room fell silent.

"Quite a dame," Max said, staring after her.

"Best looking girl I ever took out," Nat grinned. Of course it was more than just her looks. It was everything about her. The way she talked, the way she dressed, the way she always knew the right thing to say. Her father, good-natured but shrewd, her sophisticated mother, their swell house in South Shore. And she was bright, too. Sharp in the way girls could be sharp, noticing everything, understanding things without your having to explain.

"So is she the one? You ready to take the big leap?"

"What are you? My mother?"

"We love you like a son, Natty."

"That's what my boss says whenever he gives me a new assignment." Everyone chuckled and Alvin slapped him hard on the back.

"Say, Natty," Max said in a low voice, his tone suddenly grave. "The news coming out of Europe is pretty grim these days. What do you know that they aren't telling us?"

The others leaned in, eager for anything he could offer. "The sad truth is that basically no one knows what to do. Hitler made his intentions regarding Czechoslovakia clear at the latest rally last week. The pro-German supporters are making trouble and the Czechs had to declare martial law. Now Chamberlain is going to meet with Hitler again."

"To do what?"

"Well, probably to appease him. If you ask me, he'll sacrifice Czechoslovakia if Hitler promises that it ends there."

Alvin shook his head, perturbed. "Chamberlain is an ass."

"He's not alone. I don't see the French lifting a finger for Czechoslovakia or for any other country. The only one with enough gumption to stand up to Hitler is Churchill. Even Roosevelt said that we won't get involved.

"And he's damn right. Why should we jump into a situation that has nothing to do with us?" Lou cut in. "We have troubles enough here at home."

"The thing is that Hitler is crazy. A real madman."

"And that's why he won't get very far."

Nat was about to agree when the women appeared, Sylvia carrying a steaming pot roast, Betty with a green salad, Estelle with a bowl of mashed potatoes, and Sally holding a jar of lemonade.

"Nat, are you talking politics again?" Sylvia asked in a teasing, chiding tone. "A real man of the press. But we have a rule in this house: no politics during dinner." She skipped over to the gramophone, turned the record over to the Gershwin on the other side, and set down the needle. The dramatic opening notes of *Rhapsody in Blue* filled the room.

Nat was sorry to cut short the sort of talk that was most interesting to him, but the dinner was delicious and the company was lively and fun. After dinner Lou passed out cigars while the girls helped Sylvia clear the table. Sally got up too and Nat caught her eye and gave her a wink, to show that she was doing great. Max told everyone about the Ford he was thinking of buying, and Nat was about to say that he'd gotten a look at the new cabriolet models and that they were just beautiful, not practical, but really nice-looking, when Sylvia swung into the dining room followed by the rest of the girls. "Hey," she sang out, "let's have some fun. What should we play?"

"How about charades?" Betty said, and though there were some groans, everyone agreed to take part. The subject was movie and song titles. Betty acted out *My Heart Belongs to Daddy*. Alvin mimed *Nice Work If You Can Get It*. Estelle did a fabulous approximation of *The Lady is a Tramp*. When it was Nat's turn, he got *I've Got My Love to Keep me Warm*, and they were all on the floor. But it was Sally's *Slumming on Park Avenue*, with her rendition of a rich girl trying to behave like a tart that had everyone in stitches.

When the evening ended the girls told Nat that he would absolutely have to bring Sally to Betty and Alvin's Thanksgiving dinner, and Nat knew that she had passed with flying colors.

— · —

It hadn't been an easy climb. Straight out of college he got a job as a copy editor at *The Chicago Daily News*, but management was on the lookout for sharp young newsmen who understood how the business worked, and the promotions started coming. Associate editor in National. Then sent upstairs as a junior writer. And finally, after Christmas last year, his first real break – an investigative piece for the Saturday edition. After that the assignments started to roll in. A series on the city's flophouses. The story about life in the Negro neighborhoods. A feature about the old speakeasies, four years after the end of Prohibition. Hutchinson, the editor in chief of National, noticed his work. Told him he was keeping an eye on him. And then out of the blue, six months ago, Hutchinson took him out for lunch. Gave him gruff but admiring compliments on his "smart, analytical approach" and his "fearless" style, "incisive but evenhanded," and told him he wanted him on his editorial team.

Now Nat was working his way through a piece that one of his top writers, Will Crawly, had brought in on Roosevelt's involvement in the Democratic primaries. He reworded a few sentences, corrected some minor grammar infractions, and cut a sentence at the end in which Crawly, a staunch Roosevelt supporter, had overstepped the limits of journalistic objectivity. That wasn't rare these days; it could be damn hard to keep your own opinions from finding their way into a piece, especially if the topic meant a lot to you. Something about it put him in mind of Gabriel's letter, which was still in his jacket pocket. Funny, getting a letter all the way from Lithuania. And such an odd request, asking for the Whitman as if that was what people over there would have on their minds right now; as if his school library was a burning issue.

He pulled the letter from the pocket of his jacket and studied the stamps. *Posczta Polska*. So what was it, Lithuania or Poland? All those funny little Eastern European countries that didn't know who they belonged to, didn't know if they were coming or going. And those Hebrew-Yiddish letters, as tough to crack as a code. Only the English words, *Leaves of Grass*, were clear, an island in a sea of swirling lines. It was a missive from another world, no less.

Nat had always dreamed of going to see Europe firsthand, but now with Hitler threatening to take over the continent, who knew when he would get there. Of course he could still go. He could get on a boat and visit Gabriel in Vilna and maybe come up with an article about what it was like to live so close to the border of a place gone insane. He stared at the cryptic letters and wished that he could read them, but as it were he would have to ask his mother to read it to him again, complete with a heavy dose of sighs and nostalgia.

At noon a colleague stuck his head in and asked if he wanted to come with the guys to grab some lunch. But he had started going over a big story for the Saturday edition about the effects of the new minimum wage laws on factory workers' households that had to be ready at the end of the day. The office emptied out and as always, he did his best work when he was alone, following the progression of the sentences and working instinctively with his red pen in hand. He was interrupted when Frieda from the typing pool came in to pick up the work that was ready for final copy. "Hiya, Mr. Wexler. Is this all?" she asked, rummaging through the wire basket on his desk.

"That's it for now, Frieda." Nat glanced up at her. Not exactly the type of dame a man wanted to see when he needed a distraction from work. Her hair, dark and frizzy, was pinned back off her face, the look in her large solemn eyes was grave and a little anxious, and she was dressed, as always, in a plain brown skirt and starched blouse. When she had first started at the newspaper, several months earlier, he and Jim had snidely speculated on how she got her job

– her Polish accent and thick figure were a steep departure from the cute typing pool girls. Jim, with his dirty mind, was sure that Dawson, the head of Administrative Personnel, was being, as he liked to put it, *compensated.*

But Nat knew a straitlaced Maxwell Street immigrant when he saw one, and he found it hard to believe that this was the case. The first time Irma, the head of the typing pool, brought her upstairs to show her the ropes, she had told him, straight out, "My neighbor got me this job. My English is not so great, but I type 150 words a minute."

Still, Nat was curious about her. "Hey, Frieda, how's about you get me a coffee and make one for yourself too?" he said congenially the next time she came up.

"I must work," she answered, in a way that was deferential, but mildly scolding.

"Your work can wait," Nat told her in Yiddish.

She stared at him, startled. "*Du bist a Yid?*"

Nat grinned. "What did you think? I'm Irish?"

"I think I don't wanna get fired."

"You won't get fired. Making coffee for the editors is part of your job. Didn't Mr. Dawson mention that?"

"He did not."

"Alright, kid," he said, rising from his desk. "Then I'll make the coffee."

She frowned as if he had performed a sly trick of rhetoric. "No, Sir. You sit. I'll make coffee."

After some long minutes, she returned with a coffee for him. None for herself. Apparently, she adhered to some European work ethic that forbade informal staff fraternizing. Still, something about her appealed to Nat: her seriousness, her ant-like industriousness, efficient and correct. Whenever she came in to collect the articles, he liked to make a point of chatting it up with her.

"Where are you from, kid?" he had asked her.

"From a place you don't know."

"Russia? Poland?"

"What does it matter?"

In time, he learned that she had come to the US with her mother in '32 with the help of an uncle in Chicago who agreed to sponsor them. But the uncle died two months after they arrived and her mother, apparently a difficult woman by Frieda's description, didn't get along with her sister-in-law. Now, as far as Nat could gather, they lived on Frieda's salary. "That typing class I took in New York was the smartest thing I ever did," she told him. "Only in America can a girl make a living from her ten fingers."

Nat suppressed a grin and nodded sympathetically.

"My mama said, 'What does a smart girl like you need to learn to press keys on a typewriter?' But I knew that typing was what would save us. Typing was our ticket up."

Nat suspected that Frieda might be in love with him. She never said anything, but one day he caught her staring at him with an oddly dreamy look on her face. "Can I ask you something, Mr. Wexler?"

"Sure."

"Do you have a sweetheart?"

The way she said sweetheart amused him, as if the word felt exciting in her mouth. She caught his smile and began to apologize. "Sorry, Mr. Wexler," she looked away, flustered. "It's not my business."

"That's OK, Frieda. I don't mind telling you that I do."

A look of resigned disappointment crossed her face. "She's a lucky girl, Mr. Wexler."

"Actually, I'm the one who's lucky."

After that, she never asked again. She seemed to him a strange combination of severe and shy, familiar yet decidedly distant. But he didn't think about her much these days, or at least not as anything more than a distraction.

"You all done with these, Mr. Wexler?"

"Yep. They're all yours."

She gathered up the morning's work from the wire basket. "I'll take care of them by the end of the day."

He stared at her, wondering why she didn't doll herself up a little. Get her hair styled. Invest in some prettier skirts. "Say, Frieda," he began suddenly, "You read Yiddish, right?"

"You know that I do. Why are you asking me that?"

"See, I have this letter, in Yiddish, and I was wondering if you might read it out for me."

She stared at the envelope on his desk. "It is from the old country?"

"Yep. From a cousin. Well, sort of a cousin."

"Where does he live?"

"In Lithuania. Or maybe it's actually Poland," he corrected himself, glancing at the stamp. "Vilnius. Or should I say Vilna?"

She heaved a sigh full of emotion. "Vilna."

"You know it?"

"My father's family is there. It's a special place."

"Really? Why is that?"

"The Jews there are Litvaks. Very proud, with their noses in the air," she demonstrated lifting her finger to her nose, "but they are also serious scholars who follow the traditions of the Gaon of Vilna. He was the most brilliant of them all. And there are some very old important synagogues, right in the middle of the Jewish Quarter called the *Shulhoyf*. They're built deep into the ground, because it was not allowed that a synagogue should stand high."

"You've been there?"

"Just once. When I was a child. We went to Vilna for *Yontif*. It was Rosh HaShana, and we all went to the great synagogue to hear the *shofar*. I was just a little girl but I remember the synagogue court-yard was packed. We were many people all standing together. It had rained that morning and I could smell the wet wool from the coats.

Nat was not a synagogue-goer but he would accompany his mother to *shul* on the High Holidays. He mostly daydreamed through the service; the thought of the holiday *Kiddush,* with its plates of sweet herring and *teiglach* was what usually got him through.

"When we heard the *shofar*, it frightened me and made me cry. Everyone around me was giving my mother dirty looks, and someone put a candy in my hand so that I would eat it and be quiet. But a woman who was standing beside me said to me, 'Go ahead and cry, little girl. Cry for the Jews who suffer so much in this world. Cry so that God will have pity on us and show us some mercy.' You see, there had been a terrible pogrom a few years earlier, it was still in everyone's head."

"A pogrom? In Vilna?"

"Nu? Is this a surprise? Your cousin is still writing you letters, thank God, so he is fine. Give me the letter. I'll read it for you." As she read, Nat stared out his window. Frieda's voice was full of pathos. It made the language sound somehow different. More weighty. "So he is a teacher at the Tsysho Gymnasium," she remarked when she was done.

"You know of it?"

"Everybody knows it. The teachers are of the highest quality. Intellectuals, all of them. Like university professors. Have you heard of the writer, Moshe Kulbak? He once taught there. He was the star of the school. All of the girls were in love with him. It is so sad, what happened to him."

"Why? What happened to him?"

"He returned to Russia, to Minsk several years ago. And then we heard that he was arrested."

"For what?"

"Do they need a reason? It's not like in America where they have to have a reason. There, they can arrest you if they don't like the color of your eyes."

Though Nat was familiar with such stories, the way she told it was like hearing it for the first time. "Unbelievable."

"But your cousin, may he live long, is doing OK. Are you going to send him that book?"

"Yes, of course I will. I want to write to him. Do you think he understands English?"

"What a question! If he can read poetry in English, he must be able to read your letter too, no? But I'll tell you what. If you write it in English, I'll translate it into Yiddish for you, just to be sure."

Before going home that day, Nat went up to see Fred Anderson at World Affairs. They had started at the paper around the same time and Fred was considered a rising star among the foreign correspondents. The paper had sent him to Vienna in March to cover the *Anschluss*, and he had returned full of awful stories about how the Austrians were over the moon when Hitler came, and how they were beating up Jews and communists in the streets. He had returned home after his dad passed away, but now with everything that was going on with Czechoslovakia, it looked like they were going to send him over again. Nat told Fred about Gabriel's letter and showed him the envelope with the *Posczta Polska* stamp. "I don't get it. Isn't Vilnius in Lithuania?"

"Depends what day you ask," Fred told him. "The Poles annexed the city and the surrounding region back in '22. Now they call it Wilno. The majority of the citizens are Polish, so it sort of makes sense, but they're on shaky ground. Just like all the Baltic states. Hitler and Stalin both have their eyes on them. Maybe not yet, but give them a year, two years…"

"Really?" Nat had heard such opinions from others, but coming from Fred they had more weight. "You think in two years Hitler will still be making trouble?"

"Well, he does have a plan. He's set on the Sudeten in Czechoslovakia. And so far, he seems dead serious."

"What about the rest of Lithuania?"

"They're basically a sitting duck. Back in March when everyone was getting all upset about Austria, Poland used the "opportunity" to force Lithuania to normalize relations with them, which in effect meant agreeing that the Vilnius region would be internationally recognized as part of Poland. The Lithuanians didn't have much choice; if they refused the ultimatum, it would look like they wanted conflict. And of course there was the usual pressure from the other European countries. If you ask me, they saw what Hitler was getting away with in Austria, and figured this was a good time to get a piece of the action."

"So Vilnius is now in Poland."

"Well, legally speaking, yes. But it's still pretty complicated. The Lithuanians hate the Poles. Some of them are in cahoots with the Russians."

That afternoon on his way home from work, Nat stopped by a bookstore and picked up a copy of *Leaves of Grass*. He had read Whitman both in high school and at college, and after dinner he opened the book and revisited some of the familiar poems. Later that night after his mother had gone out to the pictures, Nat sat down at the kitchen table and wrote a letter to Gabriel, first in English and then in his broken Yiddish, thinking that rather than involve his mother, he would bring it to the office and take Frieda's offer to tidy it up.

— · —

"So when am I going to meet your mother?"

They were sitting at a booth in Kranz's. Nat shifted a little as he reached across the table and took Sally's hands in his own. "And why would you want to do that?"

"Well…we've been going together for a while now and I think it's time I met your family. Unless, of course, you don't *want* me to meet them," she said, her eyes wide and amused.

He sat back and smiled, a little too stiffly. The previous Sunday, Sally's mother had invited him for afternoon tea. Sarah and Isaac Rosenthal were part of the old German-Jewish community that had settled in Chicago two generations ago, which was practically like saying they were among the founding fathers of the city. Along with the tea, fancy sandwiches had been served in the elegant living room that overlooked their well-tended garden. When Sally's father asked the usual questions about what Nat did for a living, he watched their faces carefully, trying to gauge what they thought about a newspaperman dating their daughter. Sarah had frowned when he described his work, but Isaac seemed to approve. "No doubt about it; a newspaper is where the action is. Shaping public opinion. Deciding what goes in and what stays out. Essential to any democracy."

"She does want to meet me, doesn't she?"

Nat recalled the theater tickets his mother had stashed in her drawer. "Oh, she wants to meet you. She even wants to have you over."

"Swell."

"I just need to check when would be a good time for her."

Sally smiled winningly. "Then check." The day was cold but sunny. Nat held Sally's hand tightly and they walked under the trees, bright with red and orange foliage, in a close, comfortable silence. They went as far as Buckingham Fountain, and as they watched the glimmering streams shooting into the air and then falling like diamonds, the world seemed just about perfect.

They had just stepped out of the park when a young child came careening down the street and smashed into Sally. His mother, a haggard-looking woman pushing a little girl in a dilapidated baby carriage, came running after him screaming in Yiddish that he was a stupid mule and he should watch where he was going. "I'm sorry, Miss," she said to Sally in heavily accented English.

"Oh, that's alright," Sally replied gallantly, brushing off her coat.

"*Vilde chaya,*" Nat heard the mother mutter in Yiddish.

"Come on Mama, you have to catch him," the little girl cried, wiping her nose on her sleeve.

Sally watched coolly as the woman slapped the child's hand. "What did she just say?" Sally asked. "I didn't understand a word."

"She said her son is like a wild animal."

"Well at least she's got that right. How she's ever going to make her children into proper Americans I can't imagine." A vision of the theater tickets flashed again in Nat's mind. He saw the crowds pushing their way through the overcrowded lobby, the tearful audience, the Yiddish actors, crying and gesticulating on the stage. There was no way he could take Sally to such a production.

He didn't think of the tickets again until several weeks later. Hutchinson had asked him to run down to Photography to choose the pictures for a follow-up piece to the minimum wage story, but as he headed down the stairs, he heard the choked sound of weeping. After a moment's deliberation, he continued down to the very bottom of the stairwell where he found Frieda, wiping her eyes and sniffing. "Hey, what's the matter?" he asked, reaching into his pocket to offer her his handkerchief.

She took it from him and blew her nose with a loud, wet noise. "I just heard something terrible," she wailed. "The Germans have expelled all the Polish Jews living in Germany. My brother and his wife are in Germany. They have two small children. They have nowhere to go."

"That's awful. But can't they just go back to Poland?"

"The Polish government has said that they won't allow them back," she said tearfully. "Nobody wants them. Nobody will help.

We told them, come with us to America. Uncle Zalman has a connection. He can get you visas. That was in '35." She sniffed and blew her nose again. "When everyone still thought Hitler was a big joke."

Nat sighed in commiseration. It really did sound terrible, but his instinct was to try to cheer her up nonetheless. "Listen, Frieda. You mustn't worry about them. You're here and they're there, and the truth is that there isn't that much you can do for them. But I'm sure they'll find a solution. Hitler is a temporary problem. The man is insane and everyone knows it. He'll be finished within the year. So if your brother can just sit tight and wait it out, things will sort themselves out."

"No," she sobbed. "Nothing will sort out. You have no idea what it's like there. They hate us. They make laws so that we can't make a living. They blame us for everything bad that happens. And now Hitler comes and says that he wants to get rid of us. And so many people agree with him. The people there, they are crazy. And dangerous. You don't know."

He nodded sympathetically, and as he watched her blow her nose again, an idea came to him. "Say Frieda, do you like to go to the theater?"

"Why do you ask?" she sniffed.

"Because I have a spare ticket to see *The Dybbuk*. It's a Yiddish production. This Wednesday night. At the Lawndale."

She sniffed again, wiped her nose, and looked up at him in surprise. "You're asking me to go to the theater with you?"

"With me and my mother."

"Your mother? Why? Do you need a chaperone?"

"What? No. No no. I didn't mean…of course not."

"I'm just joking, Mr. Wexler," Frieda looked up at him with a smile. "It would be an honor to go to the theater with you and your mother."

——— • ———

A new dress, matching shoes from the same store, and a trip to the hairdresser. Nat hadn't seen his mother so excited to go out in a long time. In the year after his father died, she had refrained from going to family celebrations out of respect for his memory, but she had always loved the theater and once the year of mourning had passed, she made a point of going to every Yiddish show that came to town.

"I hope your girl doesn't think your mother is a schlepalong," she said, standing before the mirror in the front hall, fixing her hat with hairpins. "I was young once. I remember what it's like to want to be alone with your sweetheart."

He had put off telling his mother that he was bringing Frieda to the show, but now, seeing her excitement, he knew that he could delay the disappointment no longer. "Actually," he admitted, "she's not my sweetheart. She's not Sally. Sally really wanted to come but just like I thought, she had to work late at the store. So I asked someone else. A very nice girl I know from work. I have a feeling you're going to like her."

She stared at him, perplexed. "What is this? A trick? So I'm not going to meet your Sally?"

"Not tonight. But soon. I promise, Ma."

She stared at him, disbelieving. "And this girl from your work – she knows Yiddish?"

"Yes. Absolutely. It's her mother tongue. She just came over on the boat from Warsaw a few years ago."

"So I'm inviting a girl from Warsaw to see Yiddish theater in Chicago! Nu? She's probably seen *The Dybbuk* a million times."

"I'll pay you for the ticket."

"Ach, Natty," she sighed and waved away his offer with her hand. "That's OK. Even if it's not Sally, I'll treat your friend. You enjoy with her."

The Lawndale Theater was packed, just as Nat knew it would be, with mostly elderly and middle-aged Jews. He had read somewhere that the Yiddish theater was losing its audience, that the old generation of native Yiddish speakers was ageing and that the younger, American-born Jews could not be counted on to support it. Nonetheless, as they maneuvered their way through the crowds, it was clear that productions in Yiddish were still in terrific demand.

They found Frieda standing by the box office. Though she had worn her hair down, she was dressed in the same boxy skirt and jacket that she wore to work. Nat introduced her to his mother and before he knew it the two of them were chatting away in Yiddish. "So what do you do at the newspaper?"

"Nothing. I'm just a typist. Not very smart work. I want to be a journalist, to write articles for the paper, but my English isn't good enough. I'm going to English classes at night, but it's very hard. I'm too old to learn another language."

"That might be true," his mother agreed. "But thank God, at least you have a job."

Yes, Nat ruminated. This was much, much better than bringing Sally. When they took their seats, Nat's mother took the place in the middle, between him and Frieda. The play, a supernatural tale about a bride possessed by the spirit of her true love, exemplified, in Nat's opinion, *shtetl* culture at its most superstitious and sentimental. The scenes where the spirit of the beloved invades the bride's body and speaks through her appalled him. When Chanaleh, the bride, cried out in a man's voice, "I am the dybbuk," he winced, almost in pain.

Frieda and his mother, however, were enthralled. Both sat spellbound, giving themselves over to the melodrama. When the dybbuk spoke his absurd lines, he saw Frieda grip his mother's arm in terror.

As the curtain came down and the audience clapped wildly and shouted their approval, Nat imagined that his were the only dry eyes in the house. After the play, Nat wanted to take Frieda home and then, as an antidote, settle down with something hard and unrelentingly real, *The Bridge of San Luis Rey*, for example, or some Steinbeck.

"It was just like in Warsaw. Better than in Warsaw," Frieda enthused. "The actors know how to make you cry like a child."

"We all need a good cry sometimes," his mother agreed, "and nothing makes you cry like hearing your *mamaloshen*. Isn't that right, Frieda?"

"Oh yes, Mrs. Wexler. There is nothing like our Yiddish." He was helping his mother on with her coat when Frieda said, "I have an idea. Why don't you come back to my house for a nice cup of tea?"

He was about to make a polite excuse when his mother said, "Wonderful. A cup of tea is exactly what I need right now."

Nat tried to remain even-tempered, but this was really too much. It occurred to him to bow out, but nonetheless, he soon found himself helping his mother onto the streetcar with Frieda, headed toward the old neighborhood. They got down smack in what was, during the day, the middle of the market, and followed Frieda past the peddlers' wagons, fruit stalls, and shops, all closed for the night.

Everything about the third-floor walk-up that Frieda shared with her mother was exactly as Nat knew it would be. The smell of fried onions on the stairway. The dingy wallpaper in the hall. The peeling linoleum of the kitchen floor. And the grimy walls of the tiny kitchen, threatening to close in on them as they sipped tea in chipped tea cups.

"That Ansky was a genius," Nat's mother said. "A man with a brain, but also with a heart. How did he know to make a play out of that old folktale?"

"I'll tell you how he knew," Frieda replied. "Ansky saw that Jews were leaving the *shtetls* and moving to the cities, and he wanted to write down all the special stories and songs before everyone forgot them. So he got some money together and hired some helpers and told them to go to all the little *shtetls* in Poland and Russia, to ask people about what they still remembered. He used some of those stories when he wrote *The Dybbuk*."

Nat's mother considered this. "Do you think he got to Mogilev?"

"Probably. He went everywhere."

Nat's mother sighed heavily, but didn't say anything. Nat waited for her to offer a comment or a remark, but she seemed to withdraw into her own thoughts.

"You are from Mogilev, Mrs. Wexler?" Frieda asked her.

"Ach what do you know, you young people?" This, Nat knew, was directed at him. "We used to get all the best theater there. Do you know what was the very first play I ever saw?" Nat yawned and checked his watch. "It was *Mirile Efros*."

"I know it," Frieda cried. "Such a beautiful story."

"Well, I saw it in Mogilev. I went with Dovid Frankel. A troupe of Yiddish actors came to town to give three shows. Of course the theater wasn't a big fancy building like the Lawndale. Who in Mogilev knew of such luxury? But did this bother us? Not in the least. We were happy just to see the play."

"Sure you were," Frieda agreed knowingly.

"Who was Dovid Frankel?" Nat asked.

"Not that we had any money for plays in those days. Dovid was a real revolutionary. He spent his days writing flyers, he didn't have a kopek to his name. I remember how I got dressed up for that night. My best dress. My hair done up on my head. As if I was a woman of the world, not a little nothing from Mogilev."

Nat stared questioningly, waiting for an answer to his question. She seemed to gather herself together, readying for a confession. "While your father was alive, I tried not to think about him, but now that your father is dead he comes to my mind sometimes."

"Who was he?" Nat asked again.

"Only the first man I ever fell in love with. If things had gone a little differently, he would have been my husband, and you, young man, would have been someone else."

Frieda leaned in, rapt and concerned, and took his mother's hand. "What happened to him?"

"What happened to him? The same thing that happened to all the dreamers who didn't know how to keep their heads down and their mouths shut. About a week after we saw *Mirele Efros*, he was arrested. Some people, friends of his, tried to blow up the Police Commissioner's carriage and they arrested anyone connected to the Jewish socialists. They broke into his house and searched his room and of course they found the flyers and the pamphlets, so they arrested his brother and sister too. Sent the whole lot of them to Siberia. That's how it was in those days. And that was the end. He wrote me two letters but I never saw him again. At first I swore that I would wait for him, however long it took, but a year later his mother received a letter telling her that he had gotten tuberculosis and died."

Frieda gripped his mother's hand hard and Nat saw that her eyes were red. "People are so cruel…" she whispered.

"In the last letter that he sent me from the prison camp, he wrote that to keep his spirits up he would imagine the two of us married.

He imagined how we would have a son, and how he would teach that son to fight against everything that was wrong in the world. Right to the end he believed that the only way that there would be fairness and justice was if good people worked to change the system from top to bottom." She let out a long sigh. "What did he know? What did I know? When you're young, you think you can do anything. So many people ended up dead or rotting away in Siberia. And those who stayed, their lives were *drek* as well. Russia, Poland, and now Germany – black places for Jews."

For a moment the only sound in the room was that of Frieda, softly sniffing. "I'm sorry I'm crying, Mrs. Wexler," she said, wiping her eyes with her handkerchief, "but your story makes me think about my brother. He was living in Germany, in Berlin, but now Hitler kicked out all of the Polish Jews and Poland won't take them back. He has nowhere to go. I don't know what he's going to do. And he's got two little boys. They have to find somewhere to go but no one wants to help them."

"Have you tried to get visas to bring them here?" Nat's mother asked.

"Of course we have. But who's giving Jews a visa these days? It's like all the doors in the world are locked and no one anywhere will let them in." Nat's mother put her arm around Frieda, who sobbed into her shoulder, and they stayed like that for a while, Frieda sobbing and Nat's mother rocking her back and forth.

How had it come to this, Nat brooded. How had what was supposed to be a pleasant night at the theater ended in the two of them bawling in the miserable little kitchen? It was as though just beneath the happy façade of the special outfit and the excitement of going out on the town lay a gaping abyss of sorrow and horror. A feeling of claustrophobia came over him. He was drowning in a sea of misery, he needed air. "We should be going, Ma," he said, trying to keep his voice even. "It's been a long night."

Somehow he got his mother to part from Frieda, say a tearful goodbye, and descend the two flights of stairs. The street was eerily quiet, and they too walked silently, as if what Nat's mother had confessed was too troubling to discuss any further. "Here, Natty. Here's the house you were born in," his mother told him as they passed the familiar secondhand clothing store. "We lived right above the street, five people in two rooms, and I had to boil water for your bath on the same stove where I cooked, and your father worked for allrightniks selling shoes ten hours a day. Those were black years. You think it was a life? It was slavery."

Nat shuddered. It was all weighing down on him, as oppressive as a life sentence. "It's a good thing that you brought Frieda to the theater tonight instead of your American girl," his mother told him.

"Yeah. I'm glad you see it that way, Mama."

"What does your American girl know of demons?"

"You're right, Ma. That stuff's not for her."

"Better to take her to some cheery American show."

"Well, yes. Something that's not so…so Yiddish."

As soon as they walked in the door Nat's mother said goodnight and went off to her room, but Nat felt as restless as a teenager. He slipped out the door, went down into the street, and hailed a taxi. The roads were quiet and clear but the streetlights shone bright, lighting the way for the couples on their way home and cars cruising through the night.

What power had ruled that Dovid Frankel and Frieda's brother and his cousin Gabriel and his father's murdered family and so many other doomed Jews of the world had to suffer homelessness, exile, and hatred, while he was destined to live his life carefree and safe? There was no logic to such a thing. The randomness of it was brutal.

Sally always said empty streets made her feel lonely, but as he rode through Hyde Park with its big houses and wide, green lawns, all Nat felt was a comforting calm.

He had only seen her bedroom once. It was after one of their first dates, when her parents and older brother were out. They had been kissing on her bed and he sensed that she trusted him somehow, with the instinctive understanding that he would not let things get too far. He had asked her, jokingly, if her past boyfriends had climbed up the tree to get to her window. "Up till now they've always used the front door," she quipped, "but maybe you'd like to try it some time."

He could still recall her bedroom, painted pink and decorated with a wallpaper print of delicate red roses. The large picture window over her desk looked out on an expanse of the yard with a big old apple tree and a wooden swing. A French style dressing table held her perfumes and make up, and in the corner opposite her bed a white bookshelf neatly displayed the novels she loved, a few stuffed animals from childhood, and a souvenir pennant from a trip to Niagara Falls.

How good it would be to climb through that window into that room with the rose wallpaper. How good to lie down beside her, to hear the soft rhythm of her breath, and inhale the clean scent of soap on her skin. How good to fall asleep in that pink room and then to wake at her side, the sun casting a warm light across the roses on her walls.

Separation

(Yoyna – Propoisk, Belarus, 1896)

Any fool can read from the Talmud and understand what is written there, black on white, but to pry out the essence of a passage, to follow the thoughts of the great scholars as they trace the finer points of their arguments, this is the difficulty. Today, for example, we were reading from Ketubot, specifically the passage concerning a man's marital duties. Zelig Feld, my study partner, was fascinated by the debate regarding how often one is obliged to unite with one's wife. Zelig is not yet married, and the interest he took in this particular question showed on his face. But I, already nineteen years old and a husband of six months, know that he has little to look forward to.

Chana-Sheindel is not an ugly girl. Tall and long-faced, she's beautiful in her own way, as my mother said to me the night before I was to marry, and indeed everyone agrees that she has an attractive smile. Though she is childlike and tends to chatter incessantly about matters of little importance, I believe that as a wife, she is as worthy as any girl. In those moments when I go to her bed, I find that my body responds to her with little urging from my mind. Yet if one is supposed to feel the deep and mysterious feelings described in the Song of Songs, well, I have not been blessed. And now that, praise God, Chana-Sheindel is pregnant, and complains of all manner of aches and pains, I suppose that I will not be visiting her bed for many months.

More interesting to me is the tale of Rav Rahumi, a student who lived at the academy of Raba in Babylonia, while his wife remained at home in their village. Each year when the holy fast of Yom Kippur approached, he traveled home to undertake the fast with his wife. But one year, the legend tells us, he failed to make the journey. The reason given by the text is *mashcha oto ha sugia*. He was drawn by forces stronger than he could resist into the holy books, enthralled by the question, the dilemma, the problem. His wife waited for him in vain and in her disappointment, she cried bitter tears. Rav Rahumi, alone and far from home, went up to the roof, perhaps to be closer to the heavens. Yet at the exact moment that his wife wept, the roof suddenly collapsed under him, bringing about his demise.

It is more than clear why the Rabbis included this story in the Talmud. Study must be balanced with the baser demands of life. To deny them is to court death. Clearly one cannot live by study alone. Yet though I am a married man, soon to be a father, I am sometimes troubled by the notion that I have, in truth, lived by study alone.

— . —

One evening last spring, after a long day of learning at the *Beis Midrash*, I was about to go home to my wife when I was given a note calling me to my father's bedside. As I put on my coat and hat, I braced myself for bad news; several weeks earlier, while taking a shortcut over the town's half-frozen river, my father had fallen through the thinning ice and caught a chill, from which he had not yet recovered.

I entered my childhood home, fearing that I would see my mother and sisters weeping at his bedside, but instead found the girls making a soup in the corner beside the fire, my mother going over the accounts from her store, and my father sitting in bed, sipping a glass of warm tea.

"Yoyna," he called to me in a weak voice, as I entered his room and sat down at his bedside. "Do you remember the small leather pouch with the verse that my mother wrote?" He pointed to the chest opposite the bed. "Bring it to me. It should be at the back, under the socks your sister knitted last year." I did as he said and came upon a pouch of hard, cracked leather.

His fingers pried it open and gingerly drew out a torn, yellowed piece of paper, with a few lines of script. Squinting into the light, he read it to himself, leaned back into his pillow, and shut his eyes. "Do you remember the poem, Yoyne'le?" he murmured, and held it out to me. "Look. My mother's handwriting. Simple as a little girl's."

He had shown it to me once before, on the day of my bar mitzva. After we returned home from the synagogue, he had retrieved the pouch and together we read the words of the little verse. "My mother has been dead for so many years that I can scarcely recall her face," he told me then, "but when you were called to read from the Torah today, I felt her there, in the synagogue, watching over us."

"Why do you want to see it?" I asked him.

He reached under his pillow and pulled out an envelope. It was addressed *To Yankel Shulman, Propoisk*, in a heavy hand. "I received this last week, but only today did I have the strength to open it. Read it aloud," he told me, his expression alert and impatient. I took the letter in hand and read:

My dear dear brothers,

For so many years my heart has cried for you. Together we came into this world, triplets from a single seed, but alas, we were torn from each other at a young age and the years have passed and now we are old men.

Avramele, I have made many enquiries and have learned that you are living in Mogilev. Yankele, I know you are still in Propoisk, perhaps still living in the very house where we all were born. I am writing this to both of you, in two identical copies, to ask you to come to me in Minsk, and bring with you the little wallet that holds a verse that Mama gave to each of us. I pray that like me, you have kept it in your possession.

For years I have dreamt that one day we and the three verses would be together again. I want to show the whole poem to the editor of Der Layt, *so that he can publish it in our paper, in memory of our dear, unfortunate mother, may she rest in peace.*

To this end, I propose that you travel to my home in Minsk on the second Shabbes following the festival of Shavuos, on the 17th of Sivan, 5656. And if, God willing, you still have in your possession your part of the poem you must bring it with you.

My brothers, let us reunite, not after our deaths but now, when we are all still alive and with God's help, in good health. It is almost summer and the roads to Minsk are good.

Your long-lost brother,
Itzik Grupstein
Alley of the Butchers, behind Teitlboim's dry goods store,
Minsk

My father was gazing at me, his eyes wet. "For years I dreamed that I would one day see my brothers again. After my father remarried, he never spoke of them. The days and years passed and I too became caught up in the troubles of life, a wife, children, *parnoseh*. And now, when God in heaven finally sees fit to bring us together, I'm as sick as a good-for-nothing invalid. "And here, as if to emphasize his point, he broke into a terrible fit of coughing.

I watched him gasp and writhe as if the devil himself were inside of him, struggling to get out, until finally he coughed some phlegm into his handkerchief and fell back onto his pillow. "I've written to them," he said in a hoarse voice, "to say that my health will not permit the journey, but that I will send you in my place. Go to Minsk and take them the poem your Bubbie wrote. You too have always loved the written word. Perhaps things have turned out as they should be."

These remarks, though uttered innocently, made me ashamed. I thought of the papers, forbidden writings concealed in the pocket of my coat, and averted my eyes from him. "What? Will Chana-Sheindel make faces?"

"I don't know…probably not. She has her mother to help her."

"Good," he said conclusively. "So you will go. According to what is written here, you should be in Minsk this coming *Shabbes*. You will meet my brothers and see their families and when you return you will tell me what has become of them." He tucked the leather pouch into my hand. "Keep this close as though it holds a thousand rubles. If Avrum wants to copy out what is written there, so be it, but don't let him keep it. It's the only thing that I still have from my mother."

"You're going to leave a pregnant wife!?" My mother-in-law lamented when I told her and Chana-Sheindel that my father was sending me to Minsk. The two of them were sitting by the fire and knitting, not baby clothes – that would be bad luck, but shawls and blankets.

"I'm only going to spend a *Shabbes* with them. It's for my father. He's asked me to go in his place."

"When a man's wife is carrying his child, his place is by her side," she remarked. I glanced at my wife and her small, rounded belly. She was only three months pregnant but the two of them behaved as if the world had stopped the moment her pregnancy began and nothing of significance existed beyond the four walls of the house. Later, when we were together in our room, Chana-Sheindel looked at me with her large, imploring eyes. Her eyes have always looked this way to me, from the first moment I saw her, anxious, doubting, afraid of the world. "Do you really have to go? Minsk is so far…and dangerous. They say the roads are full of bandits and criminals."

"Don't be ridiculous," I told her. "Plenty of Jews live in Minsk, and they seem to be doing just fine."

"But they're not like us. They're used to living side by side with goyim. They know where it's safe to go and where it's dangerous. And there are so many stories about swindlers. Baila's brother went to Minsk and lost all his money in a game of cards."

"Is that what you think will happen to me?" I asked, making sure she could feel my annoyance.

"Heaven forbid! It's just that you are good, and…pure. And the city is full of wicked people. You don't even know these relatives of yours."

"They're my father's family. His brothers."

"You know nothing about them. What if they're revolutionaries…or freethinkers?"

I regarded her sternly. "Are you telling me to refuse my father's request?" Chana-Sheindel looked away but I saw that there were tears in her eyes and as always, her tears had the effect of softening my anger, arousing my pity and making me feel more like her father than her husband. "I don't really want to go either," I admitted. "But you have no reason to worry. I'm the kind of man who, even when he comes across something indecent and sinful, can stare it in the face and refuse it."

Though I said this with conviction I happen to know that it is not entirely true because I am no stranger to the indecent and the sinful, not in the sense of temptations of the flesh, God forbid, but in the form of Yehiel Jakubovitz, the pharmacist. It is a secret that no one, not my mother and father, not my friends, and certainly not my wife, is aware of. For in meeting with him I violate everything I have been raised to be, and were my parents to hear of it, it would break their hearts.

It began two years ago, and it was not he who sought me out, but I him. Yehiel is known in town as a freethinker – one who has cast off the weight of Torah and *mitzvos* to seek out foreign ideas and invite them into his mind. It was no secret that he had ceased to observe the Sabbath, and his neighbor, old Dvoireh Vitkin, who can see clear into his window, swears that he fails to wait the prescribed time between eating *fleishigs* and *milchiks*. But most telling is the matter of his dress – he shaves his *payos*, and dons high boots and a thick leather belt as if he were a goy. The righteous people of the town avoid him. When I was young my mother would give me strict warnings about looking the other way whenever I passed his house.

Perhaps it was those warnings that made me steal quick, furtive glances through his window on my way home from the Talmud Torah. I would see him sitting at his table, reading from a book or a Hebrew newspaper or a pamphlet the likes of which I would never see in my own home.

There came a day I could no longer contain my curiosity. After sundown I went to Yehiel's house and knocked on his door. When he invited me in and pulled a Russian school book from his shelf, I did not flee as my parents would have hoped, but on the contrary, I followed his lesson closely. Ah, Beh, Veh, Geh…He made me recite the letters, the same way that my father taught us Hebrew in *kheyder*. And just as the study of Talmud comes easily to me, the Russian language fell upon my ears like a bright, colorful tune.

It did not stop there. I got into the habit of visiting Yehiel on Saturday afternoons when my parents lay down for their *Shabbes* nap. On the pretext of getting out for some air, I would visit him and together we would read the Russian newspapers, learning of all that was happening in Russia, and even outside of Russia – in England and France and America. In this way I became an educated man, a man who knows something about the world, even though I've scarcely seen any of it.

But this too is not all. If I were merely reading the news and discussing the events of the day, my activities would have perhaps been forgivable. But with Yehiel's guidance, I have done worse. In those Russian newspapers one finds not only news items and reports on the events of the day, but sometimes there are also made-up stories. At first, he would read them aloud to me, explaining the passages that I couldn't understand, but in time my Russian improved so that not only could I understand every word, but I was even reading to him. We read stories by men whose skill with words can bring tears to your eyes: Gogol, Leskov, Shcheglov, Turgenev, and the greatest of them all, Tolstoy and Dostoevsky. When Yehiel had finished with his newspapers and was about to throw them on the fire, he would allow me to tear out the parts with the stories and keep them. The tales they tell are wonderful – all about goyim, both good and wicked, peasants and noblemen, drunkards and beggars, servant girls and fine ladies, people with whom I can scarcely expect to exchange a word. Yet these stories captivate me; even if they tell of a godless scoundrel, I avidly follow his adventures and pray that things will turn out well for him.

It is one of these stories that lies folded now in the pocket of my coat. It's called *A Little Joke*, written by the great Chekhov, and though I have read it so many times that the paper is worn and the ink is smudged, I still don't know what to make of it. The story itself is simple. A boy and girl, neighbors, live beside a great hill. It is winter, and the boy convinces the girl to slide down the hill with him on a device called a toboggan. (There are no hills in Propoisk, and no place to do such a thing). She is frightened but agrees. As they slide down the hill together, with the wind rushing in their faces he whispers into her ear, "I love you."

Such a thing seems impossible to me. How does he know he loves her? And if he does, how can he be so forward as to say such a thing to her? If he really does love her, why not ask her father for her hand – to show his respect for her? The way he behaves is practically an insult. And yet Maryushka, the girl in the story, is not insulted. Puzzled, yes, but not insulted. In fact, she is overjoyed. Were I to say such a thing to my wife, she would look at me with her big, child-like eyes in confusion. Or she would laugh out loud, as if I had said something so odd as to be amusing.

Chana-Sheindel said nothing more, and that was how we left it. I could see that she was vexed, but she nonetheless packed a small bag for me the night before I left, adding some apples and carrot cake for the journey. I rose early, said the morning prayers at home as the sun was rising, and then headed out on the road that leads west, to Bobroisk.

I had never ventured further than the small towns around Propoisk, and this trip was my first foray into the world beyond. I had made light of my wife's anxiety, but that morning I prayed that God would keep me far from harm and deliver me to my destination without testing me along the way. Soon after I started on the road out of town, Shmiel Freidman, who delivers wood from the lumberyards, stopped his wagon and gave me a ride all the way to Bobroisk. He left me in the corner of the market where the drivers congregate, and a sturdy Jew who spoke in the accent of the Litvaks agreed to take me and three other passengers to Minsk. In the evening we stopped at an inn owned by Jews, where for a small sum they give you boiled potatoes, kasha, and a plate of herring. Altogether the journey passed without incident.

We arrived in the city late in the afternoon, just before the onset of *Shabbes*. I was on edge to find Itzik Grupstein's house, so much so that I scarcely had a chance to mark the amazing things that were appearing before my eyes. The spires of the church towers, for example, stood so high that I could not even conceive how they had been constructed. As we rode onto a wonderfully handsome bridge over a wide river, I struggled to take in both the finely wrought iron railings and the multitudes of people strolling along the water below. The broad clean roads, the giant buildings, the miracle of trains travelling down the tracks into the enormous station, the elegant droshkies in the streets, I saw it all but saw nothing. And then, without warning we turned into a vast, chaotic market. I have witnessed many market days, both in Propoisk and even in Gomel, but this was something else entirely. The rush of people reminded me of ants in a panic. Everywhere one looked there was haggling, waving hands, vendors hollering, children dashing amongst the carts and stalls. The very air reeked of fish, damp hay, overripe fruit, and challah bread just out of the oven. Our wagon came to a jerky stop. "Everybody out. Let's go." The driver cried, "A Jew has to get home in time for *Shabbes*."

I collected my bag and gazed around me, dumb as a stick of wood. I had thought to ask the driver to help me find my uncle's house, but before I knew it, he had driven off and disappeared. *Alley of the Butchers, behind Teitlboim's dry goods store,* I repeated the address I had memorized, but as I stood there in the swirling chaos, I felt like a lost child. On an impulse I stopped two yeshiva *bochers* as they walked toward me and asked them, "Is this Alley of the Butchers?"

"No. It's the Alley of the Unlucky," they answered, snickering.

Hoping for a kinder response, I approached two old women selling apples on a street, and though I was not at all hungry, I drew a few kopeks from my pocket and bought a fruit while asking for their help. One of them screwed up her eyes and looked at me as if I were a lunatic. "This is the Alley of the Butchers," she gazed warily at her crony, "because they'll butcher you before you can collect a few coins to make *Shabbes*."

"What are you complaining about?" the second gawked at her companion. "You've sold at least five today."

"It could have been ten if not for you parking your fat *tuchus* on my corner."

I was beginning to feel like the town fool, whom everyone uses as the butt of their jokes. "Where can I find Teitlboim's dry goods store?" I tried again.

A bell rang out and a loud voice boomed, "Yidden! *Shabbes!*" Evening was upon us and an air of urgency filled the marketplace. Shutters and doors were closing. Vendors were packing up and people were gathering their things and heading home. "It's down there," I heard the woman who sold me the apple call out. "Right after the Synagogue of the Tailors. Teitlboim's store is on the other side."

I found the synagogue and Teitleboim's. "I'm looking for the Grupstein family," I told a young man who was locking up.

"Do I look like I know every Jew in Minsk?" he replied with a shrug. "But it so happens that I do know them." He pointed to a long alley that ran behind the store. "Their building is down there." Perhaps this was the Alley of the Butchers? I started down the narrow walkway, the walls of the buildings enveloping me like a dark forest. A small boy passed me and two more chased after him, almost knocking me down. *Shabbes* candles glowed from the windows, and the smells of chicken, fish, and sweet *kugel* pervaded the houses that ran along the alley. I stopped at a gated courtyard, empty of people save for two young men conferring in a corner by a staircase. I reckoned, judging from the style of their clothing, that they were students or intellectuals. Neither had sidelocks, and my first thought was that the two might be *Shabbes* goyim. They noticed me and stared a moment before one of them asked, "Are you Yoyna Shulman?"

"Yes, I am," I said, bewildered that someone in this foreign city knew of me.

"Cousin," he cried and threw his arms around me in a hearty embrace. "You're here! Just yesterday we received the letter from your father saying that you're coming." He parted from his friend and led me into a dark stairwell and up to the first floor. "How is your father? How is his health?" he asked excitedly. Before I could answer he added, "Uncle Avrum and Elkie already arrived this morning. She's still getting ready for dinner, so you'll meet her later."

"Yoyna's here," he cried as he burst in the door, and in an instant I acquired a second family. A room full of people was upon me, embracing me, kissing me, staring at me as if I had come back from the dead. I easily identified my uncles; in spite of some differences in dress and appearance (Uncle Itzik had no beard; Uncle Avrum had the belly of a man who has eaten well all his life), they were precise replicas of my father. I tried to recall what blessing one must say when coming across such a wonder.

"Look at him! Who would have believed!" one cried in a voice so like my father's that I glanced about the room to see if he had somehow joined us. And even more oddly, he was answered by the second man, in that same voice again. "Look how pale he is! You can see he's a scholar. And so handsome. His mother must be a fine woman."

Slowly all became clear. Aryeh's parents were Uncle Itzik and Aunt Zusa, and Uncle Avrum had traveled here from Mogilev. They asked for news of my father and I was about to reply when I heard a low, mournful groan. With a start, I saw that from behind Aunt Zusa, a boy of perhaps twelve with the dim expression of an imbecile was staring at me.

"Leibele, do you know who this is?" Uncle Itzik said in a voice one uses with a small child. "He's my brother's son, Yoyna."

"Yoyna," the boy repeated in a thick, slurred voice, and said again, "Yoyna." At this, a girl came into the room and ran to the boy. I was startled to see that her face was terribly deformed – her nose appeared to be squashed flat like a damp rag, and a long, deep scar ran down the left side of her face. God knows what she had endured. I struggled to conceal my horror.

"Leibele and Rivke, my adopted children," Uncle Itzik explained. "Zusa's relatives. A few years ago there was a pogrom in their village. Their father was murdered and their mother died a few weeks later. We've taken them in."

The hour was late and we soon left for evening prayers. As we emerged from the alley the street was filling with Jews dressed in their *Shabbes* finery, hurrying to *shul*. Uncle Itzik was a regular at the Three Trade Synagogue where the cobblers, the tailors, and the printers all pray. Before the service he had a word with the cantor, telling him of our family reunion and explaining that he wanted to chant the *She'hechiyanu* blessing. And indeed, at the close of the Maariv service,

I stood together with my uncles and cousin and recited, *"Blessed are you Lord, our God, Ruler of the Universe that has given us life and sustained us and allowed us to reach this day."*

Afterward the men crowded around us, but Uncle Itzik whisked me away, calling out to them that he would tell them the whole story after *Shabbes*. We started home as two couples, Uncle Itzik and Uncle Avrum in front, and Aryeh and I following behind. I learned that he was sixteen years old, a student at a trade school where he was in training to work a printing press. On school holidays he apprenticed with a neighbor who had a workshop near the market. He gave three-quarters of his salary to his mother and the rest he kept for himself. It all sounded very exciting, and it made me feel a little badly about my own life, which is quite dull compared to his. "What about you?" he asked. "You live off of money from your in-laws, right?"

"Not exactly," I explained. "We live with them and they look after everything we need. I study from morning till night. My wife helps her mother – they have a dry goods store."

"Is there a Zionist group in the town?" he asked abruptly.

"I should say not," I laughed at the thought. "Many of us are followers of Rebbe Meyer Sondheim. A true *tzaddik*. There are no freethinkers in Propoisk…. except for one man who reads the newspapers." I paused, deliberating whether to say more about my own heretical activities, but decided against it.

"And this man, is he familiar with the works of Pinsker? Has he read Lilienblum? Ahad Ha'am? Does he know about the *Hovevei Tziyon*?"

I know these names. Rebbe Meyer speaks of them often, calling them Satans, servants of the devil, and heretics. But Yehiel got hold of some Zionist pamphlet or other, and we read through it together one *Shabbes* afternoon, astonished by the ideas about the Jews forming an independent state in the Land of Israel. Yehiel had also mentioned these *Hovevei Tziyon* groups, who speak of packing up and leaving for *Eretz Yisrael*. We had a good laugh about it, envisioning our Propoisk Jews living in tents and bargaining with Turks in the markets of the Levant. "Of course," I replied.

"And what do you think about their ideas?" he continued, and I knew that my answer to this question would shape his opinion of me. Nonetheless, I was not about to lie to him.

"They are…interesting," I said cautiously, "but they sound more like fantasies than real plans."

"You don't believe in the words of the prophets about the return of the Jews to Zion?" he asked sardonically. "What would your Rebbe say?" His tone annoyed me. It's ugly the way freethinkers are so eager to mock God-fearing Jews. "Or is your Rebbe waiting for God to send the Messiah, who'll lead the Jews to Jerusalem, raising the dead as he goes?"

The last thing I wanted was to get into an argument with him, not only because I dislike arguments, but because the things he was saying echoed thoughts which trouble me, problems which I have not yet been able to resolve. I was going to tell him that we must wait, that we Jews have always waited, and that if we become impatient and try to change things on our own then we will no longer be Jews but heretics who consider themselves exempt from God's laws. But he went on, "I used to be like you. I don't mean that I was a scholar; it was torture for me to sit in the *kheyder* and read from the holy books – but I was a believing Jew."

I was not surprised to hear this, for my parents and teachers have often remarked that in that until recent times, there was no such thing as unbelieving Jews. But the irreverent way he told me this, as though proud of it, was shocking. "What made you into a heretic?" I asked, dismayed, but burning with curiosity.

He stopped and turned to me. "Did you see those two orphans we adopted? The girl with the funny nose and the boy who can't talk?" I nodded. "They're from my mother's village, her cousin's kids. Their parents were murdered in a pogrom five years ago. Rivke, the girl, was attacked by drunken peasants who cut off a piece of her nose, and Leibel, the boy, was whacked in the head with an axe."

"God preserve us!" I exclaimed.

"No. Not God preserve us," he said emphatically. "We cannot just sit and wait for disaster to arrive. We have to preserve ourselves!" He put a heavy hand on my shoulder. "When Rivke and Leibel came to us and I saw how these two children had been turned into a freak and an idiot, whatever faith I might have once had flew out the window. But it was more than that. For a long time I've been thinking about this whole business of being a Jew. What good is it? What's the point? It only makes sense if we can be free men, living in a land of our own, with no goyim to tell us what we can't do, where we can't live, what we can't study. One day, my friend Dov Spector – you saw him tonight when you arrived – gave me a copy of Pinsker's *Auto-Emancipation*. I read the whole thing in an hour. Every word was like a voice speaking directly to me. From that day on I became a Zionist. I joined a Zionist youth group, sort of a *Hovevei Tziyon* for young people. Every week we hold meetings where we read the Zionist newspapers and plan what we can do to further the cause. Hey," he grabbed my sleeve excitedly, "tomorrow night we're meeting with one of the real *Hovevei Tziyoniks*. It's going to be brilliant. You have to come and hear him."

The idea of attending such a meeting did not appeal to me and I tried to think of a way to avoid it. "After *Shabbes*?" I asked, hoping that it was to be held during the day, and that I could use this as an excuse not to go.

"Of course after *Shabbes*! Will you come? Elkie is coming too."

"Who?" We had reached the courtyard. The *Shabbes* candles burning in the windows shone a warm light over the cobblestones.

"Oh, right, you haven't met her yet. Well, you'll meet her now. I'm not your only long-lost cousin, you know."

As we entered the flat, I saw a young woman braiding Rivke's hair into a long, golden strand. In the dim light of the lantern, I couldn't see her nose, so for an instant she appeared a pretty little girl. But a moment later she turned her face and I was horrified anew to see her deformity. "*Gut Shabbes*," the young woman said to us, and then, staring intently into my face, she asked, "Yoyna?"

"Look at that!" Uncle Avrum exclaimed. "Cousins who don't even know each other. Of course he's Yoyna. My brother's son! A smart boy, a torah scholar. Yoyna, this is my daughter Elkie."

Naturally, I'm not in the habit of speaking with women I don't know, and for a moment I wasn't sure what I was to do. She appeared to me as beautiful as a nobleman's daughter. Her dress was of fine green fabric and her hair was done up in a way that framed her face and seemed to add sparkle to her greenish-brown eyes. She held out a bold hand, and though the gesture was awkward to me, I shook it. "My father told me you're married," she said admiringly. "Was it recently?"

"Elkie!" her father admonished her. "You don't have to start up with your questions right away. You barely know each other."

"How can he know who I am if I don't speak with him?"

"Yes," I couldn't help grinning. "A few months ago."

"What's your wife's name?"

"Chana-Sheindel."

"Do you live with her parents?"

"Yes."

"Nice. Is she pregnant yet?"

"She's expecting around *Sukkos*."

"Mazel tov. God keep her well."

"Amen," my aunt nodded.

"Are you a socialist?"

"Him?" Aryeh laughed. "Does he look like a socialist?"

"He's a scholar," Uncle Avrum repeated.

"He comes from Propoisk," Aryeh added, as if this explained everything.

"Then we'll have to take him out and show him the city, won't we?"

"He's going to come to the Youth for *Hovevei Tziyon* meeting after *Shabbes*."

Elkie frowned. "That's a start, but he should see more than that, don't you think?"

"It won't be necessary," I told them. "Don't trouble yourselves."

"What trouble? It will be the best part of the trip," Elkie declared. "I've already told my father that I plan to go for a long stroll with my cousins after *Shabbes*."

I imagined that her father would object, but he smiled approvingly. "Mogilev has become too small for her. You should go too, Yoyna. Sitting in the yeshiva all day you forget that there's a big world out there." I thought then of Chana-Sheindel's warnings, yet it seemed foolish to object, and so it was decided. I would see Minsk.

We welcomed the Sabbath with *Kiddush* and the *Sholem Aleichem*, after which my aunt served a meal fit for a king. Over dinner my uncle spoke about a local newspaper, *Der Layt,* published by the workers' organization. "Mostly they just publish news about Minsk – who's getting married, who's lost a relative, whose son got into a government school, things like that. But there's also a section where they publish little poems and stories. Mama's poem would be perfect for it." He looked up from his soup and asked me, "Did your father send his part of the poem with you?"

"It's in my bag."

"Wonderful. You must show it to me. Avrum's already given me his verse. I'll put the three parts together and send it to them next week."

"What made you remember the poem?" Elkie asked.

Uncle Itzik smiled wistfully. "The truth is that I've never forgotten it. I've always kept the part that Mama gave me at the bottom of our chest of drawers in the bedroom. Zusa was cleaning out the drawers for Passover and she put it on the bed. I walked in and saw it there. I hadn't looked at it in years, but something made me take the little paper out of the pouch. As I read my verse, I remembered Mama saying that she had given a part to each of us. And then I had an idea – if I could somehow put it together with the other verses, then I could have the whole poem published in the paper. What an honor that would be for Mama, may she rest in peace."

It had been arranged that I would board with Gitta Grossman, an elderly widow who lived in a ground floor apartment on the other side of the courtyard. Aryeh showed me to her flat, carrying with him a pot of cholent, which I understood to be payment for giving me a bed for the night. She lived modestly in a single room, but her kitchen led out to a small shack behind the building. Gitta made her living selling old hinges and nails and the shack was filled with her rusty wares, but a bed with clean linen was made up for me in the corner. As I lay down to sleep that night I said a special prayer, thanking God for bringing me safely to Minsk, and for allowing me to meet my miraculous uncles and my remarkable cousins.

The next morning we all rose early and set out for *shul*. After prayers, Aryeh headed for the far end of the courtyard where Dov Spector, whom I recalled from the evening before, was speaking to someone in low tones. "The meetings are secret, so we never know the address until the last minute," Aryeh told me, "but I'll get it now." As we approached, I saw Dov give Aryeh a discreet nod, and when we drew closer Dov muttered an address under his breath.

Aryeh frowned. "That's the worst neighborhood in the city."

"It's Kaplansky's grandfather's house. We'll start at 10:00 sharp. A representative from the Odessa group is coming to speak to us. He's just returned from *Eretz Yisrael*." I stared at him, startled by his Hebrew pronunciation, and he returned my gaze coolly. "Are you bringing your cousin?"

"I'm bringing two," Aryeh grinned. "My long-lost relatives."

Dov looked me over with a critical eye. "Just make sure they know to keep quiet. Last week the police broke into Mishkin's meeting and arrested them for revolutionary activity. Half of them are still in jail."

"God protect us!" I couldn't help but blurt out, and the two of them glared at me as though I were a troublesome child.

When we returned home we found my uncles, my aunt, Elkie, and Rivke gathered around the kitchen table. "Yoyna," Uncle Itzik cried, "it's good you're back. Go and get your verse of the poem. We'll put it here beside ours and see the entire thing in one piece."

"It's in my bag. At Gitta's place," I told them. "I'll get it right now."

"At Gitta's?" Uncle Itzik exclaimed. "But she goes every *Shabbes* afternoon to her sister's house. Aryeh, go check if she's at home." He ran out to the courtyard but instead of following him, I stared at the two yellowing papers laid side by side on the kitchen table.

The writing had faded, but the letters had been formed with a firm hand and I could easily make them out. I read the verses and found them strange, even cryptic, as if my grandmother had written them in code. "We're not sure what they mean," Uncle Avrum said despairingly. "That's why we want to see your verse. Maybe it will explain it all."

But it was not to be. Aryeh returned reporting that Gitta had indeed gone and taken the key with her. "She'll only be back tonight, after *Shabbes*," Uncle Itzik lamented.

"Can I serve lunch now?" my aunt asked, as if she was done with indulging my uncles in their games. "Elkie, come with me to the ovens, they're at the bakery around the corner." I watched Elkie as she followed my aunt outside. She was wearing a white blouse that framed her collarbones and had pinned her hair up in the style of an aristocratic *shikse*. Rebbe Meyer says that Jewish women must dress like Jewish women, but I had to admit, my cousin looked very pretty.

Over lunch, Uncle Arvam told us about the day his older daughter Soreleh left for America. "We took her to the station, and my wife was crying and Elkie was crying and do you think I wasn't crying too? Who knows when we'll see her again? But she has a good head on her shoulders," he added, as if to comfort himself. "And Abrasha, her husband, he's no fool. They're only six months there, and already they're real Americans. As soon as they arrived Abrasha shaved his beard and *payos*; he says that's what all the Jews do when they come to America. And Soreleh says she can speak enough English to chat with the landlord. Can you believe it!?"

My aunt looked across the table to Elkie. "And what about your young man? The one you were telling me about? Does he also want to go to America?"

I looked up sharply. What was this? Elkie had a young man? Was she engaged? Who had arranged it? Her father, apparently, was also taken by surprise. "You don't mean that troublemaker Dovid Frankel?"

"Of course not. Dovid is a socialist and so am I," Elkie replied, ignoring her father. "Our place is here in Russia. And," she turned to her father, "he's not a troublemaker. He's a fine and noble person who thinks of nothing but how we can improve the lives of the workers and the peasants."

"Your place, *meidele*," he said, wagging a finger at her, "is with a good upstanding boy. Over my dead body you'll marry a revolutionary."

Elkie said nothing and everyone avoided looking at her, for it was clear that this was a sore point between them. After lunch Uncle Avrum returned to his lodgings in a nearby boarding house for Jewish travelers. Uncle Itzik and Aunt Zusa retired to their bedroom. Leibele and Rivke went out to join the neighborhood children in the courtyard and Aryeh invited Elkie and me to take a walk.

The day was warm and it was wonderfully pleasant to stroll through the wide streets of the city. I could have sat down and just watched the people as they went about their business, but Aryeh insisted that we continue down to the river that runs through the center of town, and then into a large, beautiful expanse called Governor's Garden. Just being in such a lovely place put me in high spirits, but my cousins seemed almost oblivious to our surroundings, conversing instead about serious matters of the day. Aryeh, for instance, expressed doubt about Elkie's belief in socialism. "How is it that a nice, clever girl like you has become a socialist?"

"The question you should be asking is how can any fair-minded person *not* be a socialist!"

"Socialism is a dream," Aryeh countered. "Do you really think that a workers' movement could topple the czar?"

"Dreams begin with people, people who join together and build something new. Imagine if all the socialists in Russia, or even in all of Europe, could come together and unite into a single entity. We would be stronger than an army. In a socialist society Jews would have the same rights as everyone. There would be no more quotas, no more 'Pale of Settlement.' It would be paradise."

"You're really dreaming!" he exclaimed. "Do you really believe the Russians would ever call you sister? You think they would let you live in peace? I wish that I could agree with you, but the worst thing for a Jew today is to be naïve."

"You have to have hope, Aryeh. Without hope, nothing will ever be achieved." Elkie turned to me, her eyes impassioned and serious. "What do you say, Yoyna? You should speak up. What are your opinions about the Jewish question?"

She was so pretty and her eyes were so earnest. I felt a despair rise in me, for I had nothing to reply, not even a clever question of my own. In the yeshiva we often debate questions of a philosophical nature. Where does the Almighty dwell? What will happen when the Messiah comes? How is a Jew to refrain from resisting the temptations of this world? But these questions seemed to belong to a different order.

"What opinion can a Jew have?" I shrugged. I was thinking of the expression that Rebbe Meyer often says, *Man plans and God laughs, and the only thing a Jew can do is trust in His mercy.* "I believe as my Rabbi does," I told her. "Only God in Heaven knows when we'll be redeemed."

"Nu? He's waiting for the Messiah," Aryeh said sarcastically. "You think he's going to come down from the sky and lead us all to the Land of Israel! And until that day?"

"We must have faith in God. We must study Torah and keep his *mitzvos.*"

Aryeh broke into a scornful laugh. "Pinsker says that it is that same faith in the Messiah that has kept the Jews from trying to better their miserable situation. But I've had enough with stories and prayers. Salvation isn't going to come from above any more than Rivke will get her old face back, or Leibel will get his brain back." He shot a critical look at Elkie. "Or that the Russians will give equal rights to the Jews. And even if it were to happen, they'll always hate us in their hearts. Look at Dreyfus in France. Or do you Propoisk Jews not read newspapers?"

"Of course we read newspapers. Our *maskil,* Yehiel, has a subscription. As soon as he gets his paper people gather in his yard to hear him read it out. We don't miss one word."

"And what have the good Jews of Propoisk decided about the case? Is he innocent or guilty?"

I shrugged. "Who knows? Even the noblemen of France are divided."

Aryeh stared at me in exasperation. "You're even worse than the mobs that cry 'Death to the Jews' in the streets. Dreyfus is an innocent man!"

"How do you know that?"

"You can see it. He's the victim of someone else's crime. An innocent man, rotting in jail; that's French justice for you."

Well I was not about to defend the French. If Aryeh had decided that Dreyfus was innocent, so be it.

"My sister says that in America the judges treat everyone the same," Elkie cut in. "No one gets special treatment or favors. Not even if you're an officer or a nobleman. That's why the judges are heroes in America."

Aryeh considered this, and then asked her, "Have you read Pinsker? Do you know his pamphlet, *Auto-Emancipation*?

"Auto what?" she laughed, and the trickle of her laugher shot through me like hot tea.

"*Auto-Emancipation*," Aryeh said slowly, grinning at her, and all at once I was struck with the oddest feeling of envy. Aryeh was only a trade school student, but he was quick-witted and full of character. I imagined how he must attract the attention of the girls, how they must whisper about him, just as they whisper about the yeshiva students when they come out of *shul* on Shabbat mornings.

"And what does it say in this Autoeman…" she burst out laughing again.

"It asks a simple question: Why do the nations of the world hate us? The answer is that we don't fit in. Wherever we find ourselves, we take on the features of the country that hosts us, but we can never succeed in truly assimilating and we end up looking ridiculous. And as a result, we have no national character of our own. The goyim see us as aliens, dependent on the good will of others. Because we belong nowhere, they don't respect us. And without respect, without a land of our own, there can never be equality."

"You want to talk about respect? About equality?" Elkie cried. "You don't need a fatherland; you need to join the socialists. Socialism insists that all men are equal, and that every man deserves to hold his head high. The ruling classes will never agree to that because they are the ones who benefit from inequality. And they benefit most from anti-Semitism. Whenever the czar fears an uprising, he turns the anger of the masses on the Jews."

I must admit that Elkie's speech impressed me. Not so much for her arguments, which I was familiar with from my talks with Yehiel, but for the way she stated them. My own wife would never voice opinions about world affairs with such confidence. In fact, I doubt that she would have been able to partake in this conversation at all.

"So now you blame the czar!" Aryeh countered. "Of course he is to be blamed, but a pogrom cannot take place without the cooperation of every level of society – the czar, his ministers, the police, and the so-called 'masses' who take axes and pitchforks in hand to attack defenseless people."

"The masses are ignorant, but once they're educated, once they have their rights and their self-respect, they won't agree to be mere tools of the czar."

We had been walking as we spoke, but now Aryeh stopped in his tracks and looked at me with fire in his eyes. "*Petach Tikvah. Rishon LeTzion. Rehovot. Hadera. Mishmar HaYarden.* Twenty years ago they didn't exist, but they are all real places now. Places that you can find on a map, where we can build a new homeland, without pogroms, without fear. Places where a Jew can hold his head up high and live like a Russian in Russia, like a Frenchman in France."

I saw Elkie's expression of amusement and I sent her a smile. But Aryeh had excited himself with his own words and he regarded us with bright, glistening eyes. "Tonight, at the meeting, you'll see and hear for yourselves."

Elkie nodded happily. "Can we pass through the fancy parts of town?"

"I don't know if that's possible. My friend Dov gave me the address. It's in a neighborhood on the other side of the river. I just need to figure out the best way to get there."

"I can't come," I told them. "Dov said that the meeting starts at 10:00 but *Shabbes* ends right around then."

"There's no law against walking on *Shabbes*," Elkie said.

"But what about *Havdala*?" I reminded them.

"We'll say it in our hearts."

I looked at him as if he were mad. "The whole point of the ceremony is the separation of *Shabbes* from the rest of the week. You can't just say it in your heart."

"Look," Elkie said. "What do you need? A little wine? A candle? A little bit of cinnamon? We can take those things with us and make a proper *Havdala* on the way."

The idea sounded wrong to me and I tried to recall the laws pertaining to when and how one should make *Havdala*. "We can't carry – " I tried to tell them.

"Elkie and I will carry everything." Aryeh laughed. "We'll be the *Shabbes* goyim."

"You'll be sinning. And it will be on my head."

"No. It will be on our heads," he insisted. "You'll remain holy and pure."

I was not deaf to his mocking words, and I could have simply told them to go to the meeting without me. So why didn't I? I believe the reason is this: though I am a God-fearing Jew, there is a small part of me that is curious about the very things that the Rabbis warn against. I reasoned that if I did not satisfy that curiosity, it would grow and overtake the parts of me that are righteous. It seems almost blasphemous to say so, but I believed that hearing the arguments of heretics would make my faith stronger, not weaker.

In short, I wanted to go. I wanted to meet these *Hovevei Tziyoniks*, to listen to their speeches and hear their crazy ideas. How could one *not* be curious about these Jews, against whom Rebbe Meyer speaks so vehemently, and whose arguments Yehiel reads with such interest. There is something in my mind that yearns to see these things, as surely as my lungs need air and my body needs sustenance.

But my consent was not only due to curiosity. I had so enjoyed myself that given the chance to walk the wide streets, to see the fine buildings and observe the city people, I wanted to do these things one more time. As we stood at the edge of the park, a couple passed us, a young man and woman walking hand in hand, absorbed in a conversation of their own. I followed them with my eyes as they stopped by a garden of rose bushes, and watched, spellbound, as the man gave the woman a lengthy kiss, in full view of all the passersby. The woman was clearly not a whore, and I scarcely knew what to make of such a display.

Where but in the city of Minsk would I ever see such things?

～ • ～

We set out at dusk. Aryeh packed a sack with a bottle of wine, a candle, a couple of matches, and a few cloves for scent. He led us down the darkening alleys of the Jewish Quarter and out onto the Street of the Butchers. All through the quarter I could sense a quickening, a quiet stirring. Very soon the Sabbath would depart and the warm light of lanterns would be seen in the windows.

Only when a Jew has seen three stars in the night sky can he decree that the holy Sabbath is over and the new week has begun. The moon was almost full that night, and the sky over us was a milky bright grey, as if the day refused to make way for the night. We scanned the heavens, trying to discern points of gold in the twilight sky, until finally we could count three distinct glimmers.

Aryeh took us through the market square where the Gentile peddlers were closing their stalls, to a grassy spot by the river. He asked if I would say the ritual benedictions and, resigned to the fact that we had already transgressed by carrying the *Havdala* implements before the close of the Sabbath, I agreed to chant the blessings over the wine, which he poured into a small cup he had taken from his mother's kitchen, a handful of cloves, and the braided candle, which Elkie lit.

"Blessed are You, our Lord, King of the universe," I chanted the concluding blessing, *"who separates between the holy and the profane, between light and dark, between Israel and other nations, between the seventh day and the six days of the week."*

As I recited these words, I could feel the *Shabbes* ebbing away, leaving us in the world of the wicked where there is no holiness but only hard labor and strife and struggle and longings which cannot find peace. Yet strangely, my heart was filled not with regret but with happiness, and not only with happiness, but with anticipation. At home, because I must gather strength to study the holy books, I usually retire early. But on this night, in this city, with this bright sky and my two cousins who were to me as two new worlds, I felt a readiness to meet the city in all its profanity.

174

"We had better hurry," Aryeh said. "Dov told me about a shortcut through the side streets. If we go quickly, we won't be late." He led us away from the river and into the city. We passed through narrow alleys with buildings so high that they blocked the moonlight. Just as I was despairing that we were lost, we turned onto a wide, handsome square, which appeared extraordinarily bright. I saw that this was because it was lined with high poles holding lanterns which seemed to burn from within.

Though the hour was late (surely everyone in Propoisk was already in bed), the square was full of people. Smartly dressed men and women strolled leisurely by, while carriages fit for princes drove up and down the wide street at the edge of the square. I watched, rapt, as an ornate coach pulled up beside us and three young women in colorful dresses stepped down, the sweet lilt of their voices tinkling in the air. Elkie stared after them, captivated, her ideas about class equality forgotten. The buildings, with their large windows, smart iron railings, and prominent doorways, seemed built not only to put a roof over one's head, but to enhance the city with their charm. "What a beautiful street," Elkie cried, and like a vista opening before me, I too could see it. The street *was* beautiful. The lights were beautiful and the trees that lined the walkways were beautiful, and the fine men and women were beautiful, and even the milky grey sky with its coy golden moon was enchanting. All of it had come together in a vision that felt to me like a dream. What if it *was* a dream? Would I soon wake in my bed in Propoisk, Chana-Sheindel snoring beside me?

"Come," Aryeh said, impatiently. "The meeting has probably begun by now and I'm not sure where…." His voice trailed off and we followed him reluctantly away from the enchanted square and into the darkness of the alleys. After some time, as we turned onto a street of small houses, Aryeh came to a halt, glanced this way and that, and admitted, "I think we're lost."

Though this predicament would normally have made me anxious, I felt, on this night, strangely calm and even excited about what was going to happen next. Aryeh glanced about, looking for someone who could help us, but Elkie pointed to a small house lit up from inside. "You wait here…" Aryeh was saying, but she put a finger to her lips, and said. "Listen."

In the quiet we could hear the sound of faint, impassioned voices, and as though pulled by an invisible force, Elkie advanced in the direction of the house. Aryeh muttered some objection under his breath but started after her, and I followed close behind.

As we drew nearer, we heard the sounds of a man and woman arguing in Yiddish. The man was shouting in harsh, angry tones, and the female voice seemed to be begging. I thought it unwise to intrude on such a scene. Who knew what was going on in that house, and how the dismal couple would react to our intrusion? But when we came closer, we saw that the doors were open and that the house was in fact filled with people seated on benches and small stools. All eyes were on the center of the room, where a man and woman stood before them in bed sheets tied with belts of rope, their feet bare. A small group of people, also in sheets, were standing around the pair. We were just in time to see the man storm off stage and the woman rise from her kneeling position on the floor. All of a sudden a piano started up, and the woman, rather than speaking or crying, began to sing.

I realized that we had come upon some sort of drama, a play, as is put on by actors on the festival of Purim. Aryeh appeared as bewildered as I, but Elkie was swaying to the music, mouthing the words of the song, her face animated as if she too were feeling the sadness of a woman cast out, pleading with the man who shunned her. I could hear Elkie's voice rising together with the desolate, heartbreaking tones of the singer, and at that moment she appeared to me as a figure from one of Yehiel's books – a goddess, pagan, immodest, indecent – yet the sight struck me with more force than I have ever felt while praying to the God of Israel. The Rabbis teach that a woman's voice has the power to induce desire. True, she is my cousin and I am a married man, but I sensed at that moment that the Rabbis know of what they speak. *Shame on you,* I rebuked myself, *she is your cousin.* The song ended and everyone applauded the singer, Elkie as enthusiastically as any of them. "I just love the theater," she told us. "I'm going to speak with them."

She headed toward the actors, and Aryeh stared after her, irate and exasperated. "We're definitely going to be late."

I went to retrieve Elkie, who had not managed to cut through the small crowd surrounding the singer. Reluctantly she followed us outside and again we were in the street, as lost as we had been before. Yet something was different. The sky had finally darkened and the moon hung like a bright beacon in the night sky. Was it the play that gave the night such a strange, unreal quality, or was it the moonlight over the silent streets, or was it just the feeling that we had somehow stepped outside of our lives and come to a strange in-between place where anything could happen?

All was quiet and very still. We passed the sleeping houses like spirits or angels, the only sound the treading of our feet on the cobblestones. It seemed that rather than leading us back to the center of town, Aryeh was taking us further away, into distant neighborhoods where no Jew ever set foot. But I no longer cared. The warm night air, the lovely moon and the soft fall of my feet on the earth seemed to lull me into a dream of lightness and carelessness.

I was lost in this sweet, happy state, when we heard a sound that brought me back to myself. It was a child, a little boy of about five or six, coming toward us down the dark alley, weeping softly.

"Look," Elkie whispered, "the poor thing," and with the maternal instincts of the female, she went to him. "Where's your mother and father?" she asked him in Yiddish. They say that half of the inhabitants of Minsk are Jews, yet it was clear that he belonged to the other half. "Are you lost?" she said kindly. The boy stared at her, frozen with fear. I glanced at Aryeh and realized that he, like her, spoke no Russian. And so I too approached the child and asked him the same question in my faltering Russian, a Russian that I know only from books.

He stared at me, wide-eyed, and began crying again, louder, and I was filled with foreboding. For we were in a Gentile neighborhood, and if anyone were to see us with the crying boy, who knows what accusations they would make. Everyone well knows the dreadful stories of innocent Jews who have the misfortune to be accused of murdering a Christian child. But Elkie's pity for the boy must have been stronger than fear. She took his hand in her own, grasping it tightly. "Over there," the boy whimpered. We looked where he was pointing and saw no one. "My mama is over there."

We were at a loss for what to do. While we were wary of being seen with the boy, none of us had the heart to leave him there all alone. Aryeh glanced up and down the empty street. The shutters over the high windows of the alley were locked shut, and the only sound was the soft squeal of mice. "I'll go and see if there's anyone out looking for him," he said.

"He's going to look for your mama and your papa," I told him. To my surprise, he broke into a smile. Clearly his parents had not yet instilled in him a fear of Jews. I watched as Elkie began to sing softly while she played a little finger game with him, a game that all of the Jewish mothers play with their children. The boy could not understand her words, but he warmed to her attempts and was soon imitating the movements of her fingers. By the time Aryeh returned we were all as old friends.

"I think they're down there," he reported. "Right through the square, behind the houses. There's a bunch of peasants having a party of some sort." The boy peered down the length of the dark alley, still gripping Elkie's hand.

"Let's take him there," she said. "At least part of the way." We made our way carefully over the cobblestones, regretting that we had no lantern in hand. I followed my cousins and the boy with a feeling of dread, certain that we were losing ourselves in the neighborhood of the Gentiles and that no good would come of it. As we neared the square, we could hear the faint sounds of an accordion.

"Come. They're over there," the boy cried impatiently, dragging Elkie by the hand. We crossed the square in the direction of the music and continued down a dirt path that led to a clearing where a large gathering of peasants were drinking and reveling in the field. "Come," the boy said again, and as we neared the group a young woman broke away and came running toward us.

"Yuri! Where have you been, you scoundrel?" She smacked him even as she picked him up and clasped him tightly to her. "We've been looking for you everywhere."

"This good lady helped me," he told her, rubbing his face.

"God bless you," she cried to us. "God bless you, good people! Good people have found Yuri," she cried out joyfully to everyone.

"Please," she demanded, pulling Elkie affectionately by the arm. "You must come and have a drink with us. My cousin has just married and we are all very happy tonight." Several more of the group came toward us and the young mother cried out, "These good people have found Yuri and brought him back. Bring them each a drink." The peasants raised their cups to us, grinning their drunken but welcoming grins, and two women came forward, holding out tin cups brimming with dark wine.

I looked anxiously to Elkie and Aryeh, worried that they really were going to drink the wine of the goyim, and sure enough, Aryeh was raising a cup with the men, and Elkie was shyly accepting a cup as well. When a full-faced, blond woman handed a cup to me, I found myself smiling like a fool, touching my cup to hers and gulping down the *goyishe* wine along with her. On this night, it seemed the world had been turned upside down, and all the laws by which we Jews have always lived seemed unnecessarily strict.

A pretty peasant girl, cheerful and drunk, swept over to Aryeh and held out her arms in invitation. "You," she cried. "Come and dance with me," and he allowed himself to be led to a circle of young people, where men and women were dancing with each other to the music of the accordion. *He will make a fool of himself, aping the goyim*, I thought, but I was wrong, for Aryeh put his arm around the girl's waist and she put her arms around him as well, and they danced together with the peasants as if he himself were one of them. Had this night not already been so strange and full of upside-down occurrences, I would have turned my eyes from the sight of them, so as to avoid sinful musings.

I turned to see what Elkie was making of it all, and saw that she was staring, enraptured, at the dancers as though she too was hoping that a young man would take her in his arms and whirl her around the moonlit field. And suddenly, gazing at her pure and lovely face, I imagined that I myself could be that young man, that I could take my lovely cousin and dance with her with the abandon of the goyim. Just as I was thinking these unseemly thoughts, I saw a young man, utterly drunk, with outstretched arms and burning eyes moving toward her. She had, as it is written, found favor in his eyes, and I realized with some alarm that he was about to invite her to dance.

In the seconds that passed, my mind whirled in panic; for Elkie to dance with a strange man, a goy, was absolutely unthinkable. But what could I do? On a mad impulse, most likely under the influence of the drink, I grabbed Elkie's arm, pulled her toward the dancers, encircled my arm around her waist and began to whirl her in careful circles so as not to collide with the others. I had never done anything of this sort before; never before had I held a woman's waist and moved with her in time to music. But somehow, as if Satan himself had wished it, my feet found their place, and my hands held her as though conducting myself in this manner was entirely natural to me.

What were her thoughts in those moments? Had she seen the drunk peasant approaching and understood, as I did, that something had to be done? I don't know. For as we danced to the music of the accordion, I caught a glance of her face, lit with delight. When the last notes of the song rang out everyone clapped and cheered. Cups were filled and we drank again, and the soft, dreamlike quality of the night pervaded everything like a warm and tumultuous sea, a sight which I myself have never seen, but have read of in Yehiel's books.

A young boy brought us yet another cup of wine and, past all thought for what is proper and seemly, we drank it down like demons. Someone began to play a fiddle and another a flute, and the dancing started up, and Elkie grabbed me and led me off to dance with her again.

I don't know how long we stayed with the peasants. The wine pervaded my limbs with a lazy, hazy joy, and the moonlight seemed to embrace us all so that we were not flesh and blood, but silvery ghosts dancing through the fields, coloring the night with something that was not real, but as I have said, like a dream. After some time, I cannot say how long, the music became slow and sweet and melancholy, and Elkie and I collapsed onto a blanket that someone had spread over the thick grasses. We lay down and gazed up at the moon and stars and soon fell asleep, side by side like tired children.

The sky was still black when Aryeh woke us. All around lay people dozing in the fields. The air was chilly and my head ached but the memory of the strange and wondrous things that had happened lingered in my mind.

It was that hour just before sunrise, when the world is dark but tidings of the dawn to come are already in the air. We went slowly down the still streets past the shuttered windows, each of us lost not in thought but in a private fog, not unlike the state of a fetus before coming into the world and becoming a person with definite features, ideas, opinions. We walked for some time, hoping that Aryeh would come upon a familiar sight or street, until fatigue threatened to overtake us and put us to sleep on our feet. "Is there somewhere we can rest?" Elkie murmured.

And then, just as she spoke those words, we came upon a synagogue, not a grand one, but a modest synagogue for modest Jews, small, airless, and dark, where the benches are worn with use, the walls are unadorned, and the only light is the lantern of the *ner tamid*. We wandered inside and found that it was empty, save for an old man sitting by the stove in the corner. "*Sholem Aleichem*," he called to us. "Have you come for morning prayers?"

Aryeh shook his head. "We just want to rest a moment."

"A Jew comes to the synagogue to rest?" he asked, his tone a rebuke. "What is this world coming to? Nu, dawn has broken, and the regulars will soon be coming to pray *shacharis*.

"You *daven shacharis* with them," Aryeh said to me. "Elkie and I will wait on the bench outside the door."

I readily agreed. What better way to cure my sinning soul than to pray with other Jews. But instead of rejoicing in the opportunity to beg forgiveness for all the transgressions of the night, I found myself troubled, almost annoyed by the idea. Indeed, men were starting to wander into the synagogue, prayer books in hand, to take up their places, some in a coveted place by the eastern wall and others in less auspicious seats, to recite the prayers which speak of God and his glory, his laws, ordinances, and traditions. And his mercy.

I of course had no *tallis* or *tefillin,* and to say the morning prayers without them was like praying without shoes on my feet, but the *shames* tapped me on the shoulder and handed me what I required. As I wound the leather straps around my arm and wrapped myself in the frayed folds of the *tallis* my lips began to move in unison with the others. But even as I chanted the words I perceived that something had changed in me, something had broken away, so that those very words, which I had always loved and trusted with all my heart now seemed distant, weak, and tired like an old grandmother whom one respects, but only out of duty.

As I stood there amongst the men in the synagogue, my heart was not with the ancient prayers, but with the scent of the fields, the taste of the wine as it pervaded my blood, Elkie's beaming eyes while I whirled her about, the laughter of the peasants, and the warm earth as I lay upon it like a welcoming bed, gazing up at the stars.

We walked home in silence, but the silence was not empty; it was full of all that we had seen and heard and done but did not know how to put into words. "What is your greatest secret?" Elkie asked suddenly, her voice cutting the chilled morning air like the sweet song of a bird.

"What is yours?" Aryeh grinned at her.

"You tell me yours first."

Aryeh's expression turned grave. "I'll tell, but you have to swear you won't tell anyone."

"Of course we won't, right Yoyna?"

"Of course not."

"Alright then. My greatest secret is that I plan to go to the Land of Israel to join the *Biluim*."

"What?" Elkie exclaimed, shaking her head. "You're insane!"

"It's my dream, and it's going to happen. I don't know how, but it will. Now you tell me your greatest secret."

Elkie stopped in her tracks. "You can't tell *anyone*."

"We won't," Aryeh said impatiently.

She glanced around, as if an informer might be lurking in our midst, and then said soberly, "My secret is that Dovid Frankel and I are in love, and we're going to elope. He's the leader of our group, a true socialist, and a revolutionary. I'm going to marry him."

I stared at her in dismay, though I had no right to feel such a thing. "You're going to marry a socialist?"

"A socialist and a revolutionary. He's the finest man I've ever met."

"He'll end up in prison, or in Siberia," Aryeh warned her.

"I'll go with him. Where he goes, I'll go." She smiled to herself and then turned to me. "Now you, Yoyna. Tell us your greatest secret."

Aryeh had spoken of moving to the Land of Israel. Elkie had spoken of eloping with a revolutionary. Though the conversation had taken this strange turn without warning, there was no doubt in my mind as to my own greatest secret, yet I was reluctant to share it with them. My secret, which I had always considered terribly daring and defiant, suddenly seemed laughably childish and simpleminded. But since they had spoken truthfully, I felt bound to do so as well. "I…I read books," I told them. "Forbidden books. With a freethinker. Maybe to people like you that doesn't sound like anything at all, but if my parents knew they would tear their clothes and mourn me as if I were dead – or had married a Gentile." This was, of course, a great exaggeration; for reading books is not the same as marrying a Gentile. But I wanted them to understand why my meetings with Yehiel were something I had to hide.

I expected the two of them to laugh at this confession, but Aryeh put a brotherly hand on my shoulder and said, "That's very good, Yoyna. Sometimes I think that our parents don't understand anything about how the world really works. We have no choice but to educate ourselves."

Elkie too was gazing at me with wide, serious eyes. "My father said that you're a brilliant scholar. But a modern Jew must open his mind to the world as well."

I nodded wordlessly, and my heart was full of gratitude. Not just for their kind words, but for the fact that I now knew that I had two cousins, fine and good people who were setting out on paths far more exciting than my own. The sad thought struck me then that I had no idea when I would see them again. "What a shame that it has taken us so long to meet," I said, "and that we cannot say when we'll have occasion to meet again."

"But we will," Elkie said firmly. "I'm sure of it. After all, we're family. And until then, we will write letters to each other. We'll tell each other all that happens with our secret plans."

"Let's swear on it," Aryeh said. "Let's make a pact." And right there, in the middle of the street, as the orange light of the sun broke over the city, we swore that we would write to each other and follow each other's plans from afar.

By the time the sun rose in the sky we had turned onto the Alley of the Butchers. We found my uncles and my aunt asleep at the kitchen table, but though we tried not to disturb them, they woke, startled, and then fell upon us, embracing us and screaming at us at the same time. "Where were you hooligans? We waited up all night for you to come home. Your mother was sick with worry. We were going to go out and search the streets."

Aryeh said words to calm their anger. We apologized for causing them worry, but we did not tell them the truth of where we had been and all that had happened. "We got lost," we explained, "and afterward we spent the night at one of Aryeh's friends who gave us a place to sleep." This story sounded so convincing that I wondered if I had only imagined that Elkie had sung with the Yiddish actors, and that we had danced with peasants and drunk their wine and fallen asleep alongside them in the high grasses, and that as I chanted the morning prayers in the little synagogue, my head was full, not with thoughts of the almighty, but with all that goes on in the world while I sit in the *Beis Midrash*. And that we had shared our greatest secrets with one another. It seemed like a dream, yet my soul felt these things with a certainty that told me that they were real.

As my uncles and aunt continued to shower curses on my cousins, I was grateful that my own parents were far away, asleep in their beds. I turned away from the commotion and my eyes fell on the kitchen table. Three pieces of yellowing paper lay side by side, their rough edges matching and completing one another, and attesting to the fact that they had indeed been torn from the same page.

Uncle Itzik saw me staring at the table and he began to explain. "When Gitta came home I went to her and asked for your bag. I apologize for going through your things, but I couldn't wait to see that third verse."

"We're all family," Uncle Avrum added, as if this were reason enough. "We were certain you wouldn't mind."

I nodded, glad that they had been distracted from their anger, and leaned over to read what were quite obviously three verses of a single poem. The lines written by my grandmother were charming, and I could envision her looking down on us from heaven, delighting in seeing her sons reunited, together with her grandchildren.

"When we weren't imagining the three of you dead somewhere we were trying to figure out what it means," Uncle Itzik said.

"God forbid!" my aunt murmured.

"What it means?" I stared at the three of them. "But the meaning is completely clear."

"You see? It takes a Talmud scholar to figure it out," Uncle Avrum said admiringly.

"Well? Tell us then," Uncle Itzik demanded.

"She wrote it about you," I replied. "The three of you. You, and you," I said, with a nod to each of my uncles, and my father. "It was her way of saying goodbye. And asking…" I stopped myself a moment, and then decided to say it anyway, "for your forgiveness."

They all stared at me with varying expressions of confusion. "How do you know this?" Uncle Itzik demanded.

"I…it's obvious to me; the words are shouting it, loud and clear from the pages."

"It does make some sense," Uncle Avrum admitted. "Perhaps that is the explanation."

"I agree!" my aunt declared. "The woman wouldn't have just sat down and written nonsense."

"But why couldn't she just write what she felt in plain Yiddish?" Uncle Itzik mused.

"No," Elkie said, "this is much better. It has so much more feeling."

"Will you really send it to your newspaper?" I asked my uncle.

But at that moment Leibel woke with a loud sob and Rivke ran in crying that he had fallen from his bed and that she needed help getting him off the floor, and that was the end of our talk about my grandmother's poem.

The new week, with the rush and strife of this world, was upon us. Later that morning I took leave of my uncles, my aunt, their adopted children, and my cousins, Aryeh the Zionist, and Elkie the Socialist. Aryeh left for his carpentry school. Elkie went to pack her bags. Uncle Avrum insisted on giving me money for a train ticket to Bobroisk, which would get me halfway home, and found a driver to take me to the train station. Thankfully, he also explained the required steps to buying a ticket, locating the right platform, and finding my seat. Without these instructions I would have surely been as bewildered as a child.

What can I say of that trip home? I traveled as a prince, in a seat as soft and comfortable as a bed, amongst ladies and gentlemen who are accustomed to such fine things. Yet what I remember most clearly is the astonishing speed of the train as the wheels spun beneath us, and how I stared, rapt, out the wide window. Like the gods in Yehiel's books we flew over the world, past green fields flush with the grasses of spring, villages of tidy cottages lined with vegetable gardens, cows grazing contentedly in the pastures, clusters of workers tilling their lands, lovely peasant girls heading home in the glow of the afternoon sun.

Tradition teaches us that when we witness a miracle, we should recite a blessing thanking God for what we have seen. But as the wheels rolled under me and I pressed my face to the window, it was not a prayer or a blessing that I murmured but the words that came to me from the strange story nestled in my coat pocket. *I love you*, I whispered to the green fields and the trees and the peasants and the little houses. *I love you.*

With the remainder of the coins in my pocket, I bought a seat in a wagon heading east. The driver left me off at the road that leads into Propoisk, and flinging my bag over my shoulder, I started home to my parents, to Chana-Sheindel, to our child-to-be, to my mother-in-law, to the *Beis Midrash*. In short, to my life.

Three Fathers

(Raizel – Propoisk, Belarus, 1850)

Every year, right around the short, dark days leading up to Hanukka, the boys of Propoisk become scarce. Suddenly there are empty seats in the synagogue. Boys are no longer seen skating on the river or throwing snowballs in the town square. Sisters report to the *melamed* that their brothers have fallen ill and can't come to *kheyder*. On the snowy road leading out of the village, strange leavings appear: a single woolen scarf, frozen apple cores, a rotting mess of chicken bones. And in the forests one sometimes comes across the smoldering ashes of crudely built fires. The boys are gone for weeks, or even months at a time, and when they resurface, they are often found to be irrevocably altered; some are missing a pinky finger or a toe, others have gone deaf or blind in one eye. Still others return clutching hastily drawn marriage certificates linking them to wives several years older than themselves, as if they've decided to play a joke on the town.

But these disappearances and strange occurrences are no mystery to the Jews of Propoisk. Isser, the deputy appointed by the town *kahal*, has his quota to fill, and he won't rest until he has delivered exactly twenty boys to be taken as soldiers for the czar's army. When recruitment season comes around, everyone lies low and lets Isser do his job because for every boy he fails to deliver, the army will demand three Jews in his place. The official age for the draft is twelve, but when Isser can't find enough twelve-year-olds he goes after the eleven-year-olds, the ten-year-olds, even nine-year-olds. When he gets really desperate and even the bounty hunters can't come up with enough boys, he has been known to take eight-year-olds as well.

Raizel Shulman has three boys, identical triplets born on the feast of Purim. Since her own father's name was Avraham, and her husband Anshel's father had been Yakov, it was only natural to call the third Yitzhak, thus naming the three boys after the three patriarchs. Of course the whole town calls them by their Yiddish names, Avrum, Itzik, and Yankel. Everyone has delighted in them since they were babies: perfect, wide-eyed, completely identical infants who have grown into three little boys with curly dark hair and laughing eyes. If Raizel were rich, she would pay any price for Isser and his men to turn a blind eye, to look through them as if they were air. But Raizel and Anshel are both orphans, pauper's paupers, and as the old proverb says, a poor man is as good as dead.

Since the week after Purim, right around the time of the boys' eighth birthday, Raizel has forgotten what it's like to sleep peacefully. In the dead of night, when the soft sounds of the boys' breathing mix with Bubbie Hudis's snoring, she envisions Isser breaking into the house, snatching the boys from their beds, and throwing them in the storeroom of the *Beis Midrash*, which he locks with an iron key. The soldiers roll into town on their wagon with the huge wheels that sit high above the street, and Isser's men load it with tearful boys. When Raizel finally does fall asleep, she dreams of the wagon rolling out of town and her running after it while a merciless soldier hollers at her and cuts her down with his whip.

Whenever Raizel spies Isser passing her house on his way to the synagogue or talking with the town elders, her heart starts to pound. One time she caught him eyeing the boys as they skipped home from *kheyder*. He stared after them the way a wolf stares at newly hatched chicks, and Raizel could swear she saw his eyes narrow and flash red. He appears to her as fearsome as the demons that the peasant women curse whenever a harvest is ruined or a goat falls ill and dies. The women have a set of secret magic spells to be invoked against such demons, and even though Rabbi Yehezkel has said that Jews are absolutely forbidden to use spells, she is powerfully tempted to find out what needs to be done.

Some whisper that Isser is the devil himself. Others say that he has no choice, that if he doesn't do the czar's dirty work, someone else will. Isser has no children of his own. The czar pays him a pittance but most of the year he lives off of the blood money that families of rich boys give him in exchange for leaving their sons alone. Raizel has no means for such a scheme. She has made inquiries with Manya Bronsky, who sometimes hires her before Passover to help with house cleaning, and Henia, the butcher's wife. Their sons are safe because they've slipped a purse full of bills to Isser and he has promised to pass over their houses, just as God passed over the Israelites' houses in Egypt. Exorbitant sums they whispered into her ear, sums equal to half a year's worth of flour and potatoes.

All week long Anshel travels on foot from village to village, lugging his sewing machine and also a sack of the dolls that Raizel and Bubbie Hudis make from old socks. When he returns home for *Shabbes*, she waits until they are in their bed at night to whisper her fears to him: Isser has put his evil eye on them. He'll soon come to snatch two of the boys away. Two, because the *kahal* has ruled that each family must be left with at least one son. Which two will he take? Avrum and Itzik? Itzik and Yankel? Yankel and Avrum? Raizel would not wish such a question on her worst enemies. But Anshel scolds her for such thoughts. "Who is to say how the will of God will play out?" he replies in a tone that always exasperates her. "We must trust in Him. Only He decides the fates of all things."

But not all the Jews of Propoisk are content to leave things up to God. Faigle, for example, the shoemaker's wife, sends her son Motke to hide out at her uncle's place on the far side of the forest. She packs him a loaf of bread and a pouch of raisins to keep up his strength on the long walk through the deep snow. As long as Motke is missing, Isser will have to find another boy to take his place in the wagon.

Soon the czar's soldiers will roll into town again. Isser's men will go from house to house, snatching boys from their beds and throwing them in the storeroom of the *Beis Midrash* until it's time to load them onto the wagon. Each year when the wagon parks in the center of town, Raizel can't bear to even look at it. It's enough to hear the wretched mothers and fathers screaming, crying, fainting, and tearing at their hair, to make her sick and give her nightmares for weeks. Raizel imagines Avrum, Itzik, and Yankel holding out their arms to her as the wagon drives out of the square and into the terrible cruelty of the world forever.

It was Bubbie Hudis who taught Raizel how to make a doll from an old sock. First you wash the sock and mend the holes, and then you soften two half acorn shells in boiling water so that they're soft enough for a needle to go through. Then you sew the shells where the doll's eyes should be. The mouth is easy – it's made from a small piece of wool dyed in beet or raspberry juice. But the most important part is the hair. Little girls love to play with a doll's hair, and Raizel knows that it's the long strands of yarn dyed yellow or brown or red that beckon them to the worn blanket she spreads on the ground at the market. Wide-eyed with delight they gaze upon her wares as if all the enchantment of the world can be found in the embroidered smile of a little sock doll.

Bubbie Hudis isn't Raizel's real mother. She isn't even Raizel's grandmother, just her grandmother's sister. But what does that matter when she is the only mother Raizel's ever known? Though years have passed, Bubbie Hudis can still remember the horrible mess, the jug of milk strewn in pieces on the floor, the cupboard hurled on its side, pieces of crockery scattered everywhere, feathers from slashed pillows floating in the air. She can hear the cries and shouting, the sound of doors being kicked in and windows shattered, Avraham yelping as he was beaten to a bloody pulp just outside their doorstep. She can see her niece Sheyna, Raizel's mother, putting her infant into a drawer just before three drunken peasants pound open the door with a hammer, stab at the blankets ripping them to long jagged pieces, and turn the pot of beans that was simmering on the stove over Sheyna's head. She well remembers running out the back to hide in the outhouse, and how two of them followed her and held her down as they had at her. And how afterward, with so many dead and so much devastation there was no reason to tell anyone what had happened to her. It happened to lots of women. She knew from the stories, and from the children born nine months after disasters like this one. Everyone knew to seal their lips and to keep whatever vile things they suspected locked in their hearts.

Nine months later Moushka was born with a squat body, a pug nose and a wide peasant face, just like the ones Bubbie Hudis would spend a lifetime trying to forget. But Moushka was like a sister to Raizel, the little orphan whom God had somehow spared, and when she died of fever eight years later, no one had cried over her open grave like Raizel did. Or perhaps Raizel had shed those tears for her mother, her father, and all the other holy Jews who had died for the sanctity of His name.

Yet in spite of the tears, in spite of all of the reasons that Raizel had to be sad and fearful, she had grown up as sturdy and cheerful as a peasant herself, her lively hazel eyes as alert and clever as her father's. As a young child she learned to sweep out the dust and shine the windows and scrub the floors, to kosher a chicken and make challah. Had her parents lived, she would have been considered a fine match for a scholar; after all, Avraham's father had been a Torah scribe. But as an orphan with no dowry and no home that could support a man who devoted himself to study, the best she could hope for was a boy who, like herself, was healthy and capable of hard work.

When the town beadle, who dealt in matchmaking, suggested that Anshel, the orphan who had lost his parents in the same pogrom, marry Raizel, everyone said that the match was fitting. An orphan with an orphan. Together the two youngsters would raise a new family. Just the thought of it put a smile on people's faces. Anshel was already nineteen, and Raizel was fifteen, a perfect age for marriage. And the groom even had a profession; his uncle, a tailor, had taken him out of *kheyder* at the age of ten and taught him to sew. Anshel had no shop, and so he would walk from village to village, offering his services to the peasants.

When Raizel was growing up, she and Bubbie Hudis lived off whatever they could make from the billy goat they kept in the backyard that earned them a coin or two whenever he was needed to mate with a she-goat, from the onions and beets they grew in the garden, and from the little sock dolls that they made. Every second Tuesday they would load the vegetables and the dolls into cloth sacks and set out for the market in Gomel. In those days Bubbie Hudis was full of hope that Raizel would one day marry a shopkeeper or a tradesman so that she wouldn't have to make sock dolls anymore. But once the engagement to Anshel was final, it was clear that she would be making dolls until she dropped dead.

The few coins that Anshel brings home every week are barely enough to clothe and feed three little boys, let alone Raizel and Bubbie Hudis, and so even though her eyes are going bad and her fingers are no longer nimble, Bubbie Hudis still sits by the fire in winter, and on the front stoop in summer, making dolls for Raizel to schlep to the Gomel market every second Tuesday.

The sky is grey this morning, and the air is very cold. Raizel would have been happy to stay at home where she could keep an eye on what was going on in the town, but she owes the dairyman payment for two weeks' worth of milk, and the sacks of barley and kasha are almost empty. If she doesn't sell at least two dolls there will be no chicken on Friday night, and no money for flour to make challah bread.

The day begins well. Shaike the Fatty sees Raizel walking along and offers her a ride to the market. He raises chickens in his yard at the edge of the village, and his cart is so full with crates of eggs that there is no room for the Edelstein sisters whom they pass on the road, making their way with sacks of goose feathers on their backs. When they reach the market women are already setting out their merchandise on wooden stands or old blankets.

Raizel always sets out her wares beside the Widow Frumke's fruit stand, where she sells apples in winter and plums and cherries in summer. "Good people, buy from a poor widow," Frumke calls out to the passersby. "I have six hungry children at home. My husband is dead. Do a mitzva and God will reward you." Frumke's cries bring people to her stand and once there, they always cast an eye on whatever Raizel is selling as well. Frumke is not blind to what goes on. On days when Raizel sells a few dolls, Frumke glares at her and complains, "I holler my throat raw and you collect the reward."

"And what about the people who come to see my dolls and end up buying your fruit?" Raizel answers her. "And besides, just because you're a widow it doesn't mean no one else should get any business."

The cold weather makes people crabby and sour. The women glance at the sock dolls on Raizel's threadbare blanket and then look away, as if the very sight of them is a reminder of their empty purses. And even when little girls draw near, their eyes wide with delight, their mothers and fathers pull them away before they can beg for a doll that must be refused. But the Gentiles' Christmas is coming and that means that the peasants are on the lookout for gifts. Raizel knows only a few words of Russian, enough to entice the children and hold her own when their mothers try to bargain her down. If not this week then they will be back next time, she mutters to herself. And then she sees the two little red-haired Jewish girls with long braids.

The first time they pass she can already tell from their wistful gazes that they'll be back. Sizing up the holes in their heavy woolen shawls, their worn mittens and their faces, pale with cold, Raizel knows that the love affair won't end in a sale. Only two types of customers actually open their purses and buy: those with a few extra coins to spare, and those who can't refuse the light in their child's eyes. Raizel always hopes for the first type, from whom she can take money easily and with a clear conscience, but she won't lower her price for the second. Her children need to eat as much as anyone's.

Sure enough, the girls soon return with their mother, a short, round woman with strands of red hair falling from her kerchief, and wide, freckled cheeks. She is carrying a young child in her arms while her older daughter has slung a sack of barley over her shoulder. "This is the nonsense you're excited about?" she says. "From an old rag I could make a better doll."

"But look how pretty her hair is," the younger coos like a small bird. Raizel smiles sweetly, recalling how she dyed the strands of yarn in onion skins so as to give them a special rust-colored tint, just like the girls' own hair. "Please, Mama," the older one says. "I'll never ask for anything else as long as I live."

The mother rolls her eyes. "Until the next time she sees some foolishness." She shakes her head and glares at Raizel. "You see what girls are? A well with no bottom, that's what they are. Do you have boys or girls?"

"Just boys. Three. But your little girls are sweet. God willing they'll bring you grandsons."

"Grandsons would be nice. But until then who's going to feed them? A plague on all of them! Thank God that you have sons who'll take care of you in your old age, instead of draining you dry." She spins around and glares at her daughters. "The two of you made a promise that if I took you with me to the market you wouldn't ask for anything. Four girls I have," she tells Raizel. "Four girls and not one boy. Do you know how much we need to save for their dowries?"

"Toys are for rich children," the oldest girl scolds her sister and pulls her by the arm. "Let's go. We have to start back before it gets dark."

The little girls reluctantly follow their mother away when suddenly a voice calls out, "Wait a minute." Everyone turns to see who has spoken.

Raizel glances up and sees that it is Rich Gittel, whose widowed father used to run the tavern on the edge of town. Though the tavern put bread on their table, it had been no life for a girl. Each night the peasants would come to drink wine and settle scores. The next morning Gittel could be seen sweeping up the broken glass, driving nails into the wooden fences, and repairing the smashed chairs. In those days, everyone called her Big Gittel, because there was another Gittel in town who was small and delicate, whereas this Gittel was large boned and tall. But after her father married her to Lazer Rudensky, a grain merchant from Mogilev, people took to calling her Rich Gittel instead.

Gittel had returned to Propoisk some months before to care for her father on his deathbed, and then stayed on in order to sell the house and tavern. After he passed, Gittel had commissioned a scribe to write a Torah scroll in his memory. The Jews of Propoisk, who scarcely had enough money for an extra sack of beans, were impressed that she could endow her father with such an honor. But no one truly envied her, for all of her children had been stillborn. Gittel gazes at the girls and asks, "How much for two dolls?"

Raizel normally charges five kopeks apiece, but she's no fool. She looks Gittel in the eye and tells her, "Ten. Ten kopeks a doll, so two would cost you twenty, but from you, Gittel, I'll only take eighteen."

Gittel stares again at the little girls and Raizel imagines that she is thinking about her own babies, all born dead. "Give me two," she says. "Or better yet, why don't you choose, girls? That way they'll be like your own children."

"Absolutely not," their mother steps forward. "What's your name? Gittel? You have a good heart, Gittel, but I don't need anyone to buy my children presents."

"Please. It gives me pleasure."

"Then buy them for your own children."

Raizel winces. "I have none," Gittel sighs. "God chose not to bless me. So allow a barren old woman to do a mitzva."

The mother casts a skeptical eye over Gittel's smooth face and brown hair. "You're not that old. And if you really want to help out, my oldest is already sixteen and we have no money for a dowry. My husband, may he live and be healthy, is a water carrier. From schlepping water you can't marry off a daughter."

"No," Gittel corrects her in a sad and wistful voice. "It's just the opposite. A family always finds money for a dowry. It's little things, like a doll, that have to be foregone." She opens her purse, counts the coins, and holds them out to Raizel. Astonished, the girls look hopefully to their mother and she pushes the hand with the coins away. But Gittel motions for the girls to choose a doll. Raizel holds her breath and God, in his greatness, softens the mother's heart.

At the end of the day, when the peasants pack up their wagons and the vendors lower their prices, Raizel makes her way around the squashed vegetables and refuse to the far side of the square to buy flour, beets, butter, pickled herring, a sack of barley, raisins, and three poppy seed cookies – one for each of the boys. She would have liked to get a ride home on Shaike's wagon but he's long gone. As she walks home under the darkening winter sky snow begins to fall, the flakes dancing around her in the bright moonlight. The forest at the edge of the road beckons to her; she well knows the way, and if she cuts through, she'll get home in half the time. It is a legend amongst the Jews of Propoisk that when their ancestors first arrived in the town, they carved the names of the tractates of Talmud into the trunk of the oldest tree in the forest as a charm against the evil eye. But now, as she peers into the foreboding darkness, she thinks only of the demons and evil spirits that Bubbie Hudis warns against. It's enough to make her consider taking the long road around the forest, but on the other hand, the thought of Avrum, Itzik, and Yankele sprawled out on the rug by the fire, playing with the toy soldiers that Anshel made from pinecones, makes her impatient to get home.

When the boys were newborn babies, tiny and shriveled like little chicks, they looked so similar that Raizel had trouble keeping track of who was who. It was only when they had grown a little that she learned the differences in their temperaments, and from then on it seemed to her that they were as different as people could be. Avrum was bold and quick-witted – the first to sit, the first to talk, the first to say the *Shema Yisrael* by heart. He was the natural leader of the three, the one who invented their games and decided who the winner was. Itzik was bright and feisty, prone to get into fights, quick to forgive. But Yankele was different. Even as a baby he would look at everyone with a curious gaze, as if the world were a place where everything deserved one's solemn attention. When he was only three, he had taken his father's prayer book from the shelf and tried to learn the letters. And when, at four, he had asked Anshel why all the letters wore crowns, they were certain that he had been blessed by angels. It hadn't come as a great surprise when, the previous spring, Zecharia the *melamed* had paid her and Anshel a visit. He could be a scholar, an *ilui,* Zecharia told them. With a mind like his, his place was not in Propoisk but at the famous yeshiva in *Volozhin.* That day Raizel went to the synagogue and offered up her own prayer of gratitude.

Raizel knew that she had been lucky, lucky in a way that was a little uncanny. She had been lucky that the Cossacks never discovered her as she whimpered inside the drawer. She had been lucky that Bubbie Hudis had survived the pogrom and was able to raise her to be a righteous girl. She had been lucky that God had given her Anshel as a husband, and that she was strong enough to keep house and tend the garden and make her sock dolls to sell at the fair.

When she became pregnant and the old women told her that she was big enough to be carrying twins, she was certain that God must be shining his light over her and granting her far more than she deserved. And when her time came and she lay writhing in her bed with labor pains the midwife whispered to Bubbie Hudis that when it came to multiple births only one baby usually survived, and that a triple birth was beyond the strength of most women. Yet, Raizel had not given birth, as it is written, in travail, but in joy, each pain sending surges of jubilation through her, every ache filling her with happiness. Such a thing was abnormal, against the very words of the Torah. And then, for not one or two, but three of the babies, all boys, to live, to grow into children – such a blessing was beyond all understanding. All of this was a miracle, but it also filled her with foreboding; that one woman might be the recipient of so many blessings was unnatural, and she was always fearful that the sum of her present luck might well be equal to the measure of her future grief

She steps into the forest like a child stepping into a vast, silent room. As she makes her way amongst the trees the winds die down and the cold night air becomes quiet and still. A ray of moonlight shines down through the bare branches, casting a pale light on the snowy forest floor. She walks briskly, trying to think pleasant and happy thoughts. How she will open her door and find the three of them playing their imaginary games. How Bubbie Hudis will have a hot soup cooking over the fire. And how, when she gives them the poppy seed cookies, they'll practically topple her over with hugs and kisses.

And then she sees something that makes her heart stop. It is a seated figure wrapped in a blanket, wearing a boy's hat and leaning upright against a tree. A ghost! Right before her eyes! A ghost that looks exactly like Motke Shapiro! When the women of Propoisk tell tales about the ghosts and demons of the forest she laughs at their foolishness. But what if those stories are true? Though she's shaking now, truly trembling with terror, she has to know for sure. She drops her sacks, falls to her knees, grasps his thin shoulders, and shakes him. Her frozen fingers try to open one of his eyelids, and she catches a glimpse of a dull, glassy eye. "Motke!" she screams, and smacks his cold, hardened face. "You can't die here in the forest. Wake up! Wake up!" She pinches his nose and pulls his ears. An image of Motke, his dark hair falling over his eyes, a smiling scarecrow of a boy who just last week was teaching her own Itzik to skate on the river, flashes in her mind. She clasps him roughly, as roughly as she would her own sons. His cold, stiff body sends a tremor of horror through her, but still she holds him tight, as if the fervor of her embrace might revive him.

When she draws away from him and sees that he is still cold and stiff, his eyes still closed, she breaks out into a long wail of despair. "Motke," she cries, over and over, "you must wake up. Your poor mother is waiting for you at home." Finally she rises to her feet, gathers up her sacks, and trudges on to Propoisk. All the way home hot tears fall down her cheeks. What will she tell Faigle, the boy's mother? When she tries to imagine herself saying the words, she knows that she can't do it. She'll tell someone else and they'll do it. She'll tell Shmiel Zusman, Faigle's cousin. She'll go straight to his house and tell him that Motke is dead in the forest and that he should harness his wagon and ride out to collect him and bring him home. Yes. Shmiel Zusman will break the terrible news to Faigle.

Raizel barely feels the icy winds and the wet snow that collects on her shawl. "Poor Motke!" She wails as she walks down the frozen roads. Though she is wearing the thickest woolen socks that Bubbie Hudis knitted last winter, they chill her feet as the cold and the wet penetrate the worn soles of her old boots.

When she at last sees the lighted windows of Propoisk she forgets her decision to tell Shmiel, and a powerful wail rises in her again, and she cries out, "*Yidden!* A terrible catastrophe has occurred… in the forest. Motke!" She screams like a mad woman. People come rushing out into the street, their eyes full of panic. "What? What happened? What happened to Motke? Which Motke? Not little Motke Shapiro! Ayyyyyyyy." A high-pitched scream soars over the noise. It's Faigle, scratching her face and tearing her hair. "Where's Motke? Where is he?" she screams. Her face is white with terror, and her lips quiver wildly. "Take me to my son!" she commands. "I want to see him right now!"

"He's dead. Frozen to death in the forest." Raizel cries out to the crowd. Faigle lets out a high-pitched yelp and sinks to the ground. The men in the *Beis Midrash* hear the screams and come running into the street. "God help us," the men cry. "Where is Velvel? Go and find him. But he's at home! He's sick with a fever! Oy, Poor Velvel! What a catastrophe! A disaster! Frozen to death in the forest!"

""I tried to wake him up," Raizel cries again, "but he was stone dead."

"Poor thing," the women whisper fearfully to each other. "She's in shock. Probably thinking about her own boys."

Shmiel sets off for the forest and the *hevra kaddisha* are summoned to prepare the body for burial. The women crowd around Faigle, who's wailing into the snow, and Bluma, who lives in the house next to Raizel's, puts an arm around her and leads her home. When Raizel sees her own house, she breaks into tears again. If she were Faigle right now, she could not bear to go on living.

"Come," Bluma beckons her. "You must try to forget what has happened and what you saw in the forest. The little ones are waiting for you." Raizel nods and allows herself to be led up the porch stairs.

"Mama! The boys cry when they see her, abandoning their games and rushing to her. "Mama where were you? It's so late!" Itzik cries.

"Bubbie Hudis gave us beans and potatoes but they were cold."

"And then she fell asleep!" Raizel falls on them with hugs and kisses as she glances despairingly at the old woman, snoring in her chair in the corner. Lately, Bubbie Hudis's mind seems to be failing her. She forgets Raizel's instructions about what to give the boys to eat, and just last week Raizel came home to find the window open to the cold night air, the boys jumping on her bed like hooligans.

That night, as she tucks the boys into bed, she hugs them so hard that they yelp and push her away. First Avrum, then Itzik, and then Yankel, and then back to Avrum again, over and over. The boys join in Mama's funny game, and no sooner has she embraced one, the next in line calls, "Mama, come to me. It's my turn." This goes on for a long while until one by one the boys close their eyes and settle into sleep.

It's only then that she wakes Bubbie Hudis and helps her to her bed by the fire. For a while, Raizel is able to forget the way Motke's glassy eyes looked into her own. But when she finally lies down in the bed beside the children the terrible sight returns and chills her blood. She thinks not only about what can happen to boys who hide, but also about what can happen to boys asleep in their own beds. Nowhere is safe, she concludes. Catastrophe lies in wait at every turn.

In the stillness of the night, she thinks of Berl Davidovitch. Berl was a boy her own age, the youngest son in a family of bakers. No one knew exactly when Isser came for Berl. Nothing was heard about him for three or four years, until one day he appeared in the *Beis Midrash* dressed in the torn, dirty garb of a military school boy.

The tales he told broke everyone's heart. He recalled how as soon as the wagon left the village, the soldier in charge pocketed the money for the trip and sent the driver and his wagon home. The long weeks of trudging through mud, snow, and ice had been too much for some of the children to bear. They were given so little food that many collapsed and died while they were still on the way. When they finally reached the military school, the priests who ran the place did everything they could to make Jewish boys into Christians. For days they would be given nothing but fried pig meat. If they refused to eat it, they were made to swear that they loved Jesus and say that he had died and returned to life and other such nonsense as the Christians believe. But what the priests really wanted was for the Jewish children to be baptized. The younger children often gave in quickly, but the older ones who refused were beaten, denied water to drink, or forced to kneel for hours on dried peas.

It was almost too awful to be believed, except that there were others who told of the same things. Mendel Sagorsky, for example, had recently returned after fifteen years of army service. The only reason they had released him was that he had become ill with a disease that made him cough up blood as if the devil himself were strangling him. Mendel had once been the prize scholar of the town, and he had kept his wits by reciting to himself as many tractates of Talmud as he could remember. It was the magic powers of the Talmud, he told everyone before he died, that had given him strength to survive the cold, the beatings, and the cruelty of the priests.

All night long these memories mix with the image of Motke in the snow. She longs for daylight to come, for the relief she'll feel in the morning when she can laugh at her nightmares and know that it was she, and not the world, that is going mad.

"You must pray," Rebbe Pesach tells the distraught collection of men and women, the parents of boys whose age has marked them for recruitment. "Pray and fast. That is what Jews have always done when faced with a calamity." The next day Raizel begins her fast. She will refrain from eating all day and only after the sun has gone down will she put a few crumbs of bread in her mouth. She spends her days in the synagogue with the other mothers of young boys who, like her, are weak with horror at the thought of Isser and his wagon, all of them weeping and praying like mad women before the holy Ark.

Anshel is a follower of Rebbe Pesach, a disciple of the hasidic Rabbi of Belz. He reveres every word that Rebbe Pesach says and never makes a decision without consulting him first. Raizel likes Rebbe Pesach. His round, almost childlike face and smiling eyes fit her idea of what a true, good-hearted *tzaddik* should look like. She likes to hear him talk about how it is a mitzva to live in joy, to be happy, to sing and dance and praise God whenever the urge arises in the soul. But she has never forgotten that her own father had not been a Hasid. In fact, he belonged to those Jews called *misnagdim*, who dismissed the singing and dancing of the Hasidim as mindless nonsense and even heresy. Bubbie Hudis told Raizel that her father's rabbi was Rabbi Yehezkel Lerner, a renowned Talmud scholar who lives on the other side of town. When Raizel was a girl Rabbi Yehezkel would pinch her cheeks and tell Bubbie Hudis to spoil her with raisin cookies. Now that Raizel has thrown in her lot with the Hasidim, she rarely has the opportunity to speak with Rabbi Yehezkel.

But she thinks of him now. Bubbie Hudis had always said that he is not only learned, but also wise. It's known that he has read from the forbidden books of the Gentiles, just like the *maskilim* – the Jews who no longer want to be Jews, whom Rebbe Pesach scorns and mocks. One night as she's reading psalms in the synagogue, Rabbi Yehezkel's spirit comes to her. She sees his kindly face, fatherly and full of pity. *Rav Yehezkel,* she whispers to him tearfully, *what will become of my boys? What can I do to save them?* She feels an overpowering urge to go to him, to fall at his feet and hear his wise words.

Under cover of darkness, Raizel sets out for Rabbi Yehezkel's house. Should she be seen, she'll have to explain herself to Rebbe Pesach and his followers. But Raizel is feverish with despair. She's full of black thoughts and horrible visions. If only someone would tell her what has to be done. Maybe she ought to undertake a full fast. Maybe she needs to perform seven difficult good deeds for seven consecutive days. Or maybe her prayers, fervent and desperate as they are, are not fervent enough. Prayer that is truly humble and sincere has been known to induce miracles.

Rabbi Yehezkel lives in the old neighborhood on the other side of town. His house is in poor repair. The walls appear to be sinking into the snow and the rotting shingles on the roof are as old as Rabbi Yehezkel himself. Raizel makes her way up the icy steps and knocks on the door. When the rabbi opens it, he looks a little surprised. "Raizele? It's been years since you've come to visit me. Isn't Rebbe Pesach open for business?"

She ignores his sardonic tone and bursts into tears. "Rabbi Yehezkel," she wails, "Isser is going to take them away. My boys. He's going to take them to the czar's army. I didn't go to Rebbe Pesach because…because I know what he'll say." She pulls her handkerchief, which is wet from the tears she cried this afternoon, from her sleeve, wipes her eyes, and continues, her voice tight and quivering. "He'll say that there is nothing to do but put my faith in God. He'll say that the entire world unfolds according to His plan, and everything that happens is always for the best, even if we can't understand it. He says that we must fast and pray. For three days now I've eaten nothing all day and read psalms from morning till night. But there must be something else. There has to be a way. I have no money to pay Isser to leave us alone. One day soon he'll come to take my boys, whichever two he finds first, and he'll throw them in the storeroom of the *Beis Midrash.*

He motions for her to come into the house. The room is dark except for a small lamp on the table where a holy book lies open. "Oy, Raizele. The ways of God *are* mysterious, and He has found terrible ways to test us. Every Rosh HaShana we all pray that God will spare us and our children, and still we know more suffering than Job himself."

These words give Raizel no comfort. "What can I do, Rabbi?" she begs. "Tell me what I have to do to save them."

Rabbi Yehezkel sighs and closes his eyes. "Yes. There are ways. But I cannot advise you in those ways."

"What ways? Tell me what to do or I'll go mad. Must I cut off fingers and toes? Or turn my sons into cripples? You know I have no money to pay for an exemption."

"I cannot tell you to do such things. Mutilation is strictly forbidden."

"Then what?"

The rabbi is silent for a moment. And then, in a voice just above a whisper, he tells her, "You have three sons."

"God keep them safe and healthy! Yes. Three all at once. To some He gives none and to me He gave three. But now those sons are like arrows in my heart."

"Exactly. To others He gave none. And to some…He gave only one. And those who have only one are also exempt. The elders of the *kahal* have declared it and Isser has agreed to respect their wishes."

She looks into his face and sees that his eyes are full of the cunning of Moses and Joseph and all the wise prophets of Israel. Suddenly her heart is jumping in her chest and the room seems to sway like a man in prayer. "Rabbi Yehezkel, what are you saying?" she whispers, as though afraid to speak the words.

"I am saying words. Mere words, nothing more."

Raizel stares at the rabbi, burning and perplexed. The words echo in her head, becoming clearer and more definite with each repetition. Rabbi Yehezkel is saying something terrible, something that no mother could fathom, but he is also telling her something wonderful. He is telling her that the disastrous fate that Isser has in store for her sons might be averted. The boys will not have to go to live in the forest. She will not have to have them crippled. Nor watch them roll away from her in Isser's wagon. Nor have to pray each night that the priest has not broken them and forced them to worship the *goyisher got*. They can live. They can remain Jews and grow to become righteous men and scholars. All is not lost. "Yes," she murmurs, and she can hear the words of the *Adon Oilam* resounding in her head, *The Lord is with me, I will not fear.*

The icy air makes everything clear and sharp. The streets of the *shtetl* are empty but the lights in the windows seem to be dancing with a crazed, almost ecstatic fury. And then suddenly, he is right before her. It is Isser in his heavy coat and fur hat, tramping through the snow. The moonlight falls on his face, giving his shadow a dark glow. He looks at her and smiles a thin, cold smile. A violent chill tears through her.

She will have to be strong and very brave. Brave in the way that women are brave. If she can just be brave enough, the boys will be saved. And even if her heart breaks she'll know that she has saved them. All she has to do is to convince Anshel that this way is the only way. It won't be easy, but in a world where everything is either possible or impossible, this belongs to the possible. She needs only the right moment, the right words to convince him.

— • —

The first person Anshel meets as he makes his way home that Friday afternoon is Chaim Kogan, driving a cart loaded with logs to sell in town. "Reb Chaim," he calls out. "*Vos macht a Yid?*"

"Don't ask," Chaim tells him. "A catastrophe has happened. Little Motke Shapiro went into the forest to hide from Isser and he froze to death. Your Raizel was the one who found him."

Chaim's terrible tidings are like a knife in Anshel's heart. When he bursts in the door, Avrum, Itzik, and Yankele are playing a game with buttons while Raizel is in the midst of plucking a chicken. For some reason the scene brings tears to his eyes. "You've heard?" Raizel whispers, glancing up at him.

"I met Chaim Kogan on my way into town."

"God preserve us."

When Anshel recites the *Kiddush* that night the boys say it along with him. They know it by heart and just like on all *Shabbes* nights, there is an air of suspense about who will get the first sip of wine. Raizel tries not to think of Faigle standing by her *Shabbes* table, staring at the empty chair and collapsing in grief.

Now, with Anshel finally home, Raizel wants only to fall onto the bed and sleep forever. The task in front of her is great, too much to bear. It's only later, after Anshel has told the story of David and Goliath (a story the boys have heard a thousand times and could happily hear a thousand more), the boys have finally fallen asleep, and Bubbie Hudis is snoring on the other side of the kitchen, that Anshel draws the thin curtain that separates their bed from the rest of the house. Friday night, when the boys and Bubbie Hudis are sleeping, is the time when, if Raizel is ritually clean, they perform the commandment to be fruitful and multiply. For many years God had denied her. It was only after she went to consult with old Henye, and she told her that she must eat a clove of garlic with every meal, that the miracle had happened and she had become pregnant. Though Raizel continues to eat a piece of garlic with each meal, God has not blessed her again.

Now Anshel climbs into bed and turns to her. The night is pitch black, and as she feels his hands reach out to embrace her, she pulls away. "No," she whispers. "Listen to me, Anshel. Since I found that poor boy in the forest I've thought of nothing but how we can save our own. I haven't known a moment's peace. I swear to you, my heart is drowning, choking in its own tears. I had to do something. And so I went to Rabbi Yehezkel. My Rabbi Yehezkel. God in heaven be praised! In his great wisdom he has given me a way, a way to save them."

"Rav Yehezkel? The *misnaged*? Why did you go to him?"

"He was my father's rabbi." Though this is something Anshel well knows, Raizel hopes that reminding him will quell his displeasure. "And he is wise."

Raizel can feel her husband frowning. "What did he tell you?"

"They will go to live with other families."

For a moment Anshel is silent, rolling it over in his mind, but then he whispers, "No. We will trust in God. Miracles happen all the time."

"But what if there isn't a miracle? What if Isser comes for them and the soldiers take them off to make them Christians?"

"God forbid!"

"But it happens, Anshel! It happens all the time. And it will happen to us."

"We will trust in God."

"God can be cruel."

"Only He knows the reasons for what He does. We must accept His will." To this Raizel says nothing, but her brain is on fire. She wants to say more, but there is nothing to say. Soon Anshel is snoring beside her.

He has decided to behave as if nothing will happen, as if Isser and the soldiers are somebody else's problem. On *Shabbes* afternoon he sits at the table and reads aloud from one of his books. He rocks back and forth, reading the ancient Aramaic words aloud, and then translating them in the sing-song voice of the yeshiva:

> *In the days of Rabbi Tanhuma the rains failed to fall in their time. The people of Israel came to Rabbi Tanhuma and asked him to declare a three-day fast. The people fasted, and still there was no rain. My sons, Rabbi Tanhuma told them, have compassion for one another and the Almighty will have compassion for you. The people set out to collect alms for the poor, and they soon saw a man give charity to the woman whom he had divorced, and was therefore forbidden to support. They came to Rabbi Tanhuma and told him, "While we were collecting alms a sin has been committed."*

"What did you see?" he asked them. And they told him, "We saw so-and-so giving alms to the woman he divorced." The men led Rabbi Tanhuma to the man. "Who is this woman for you?" he asked him. "This is the wife I divorced."
"And why have you given her alms?"
"Because I saw her suffering and I was filled with pity."
And Rabbi Tanhuma looked up to heaven and said, "God Almighty, if this man, who does not owe this woman anything, saw her and was filled with pity, how can you, who are called the compassionate one, not take pity on us, the sons of Abraham, Isaac, and Jacob?" And the rains fell, and the world's thirst was quenched.

Raizel knows that this story is for her. That is how Anshel likes to discuss things with her, in stories and legends. She must fast. She must be righteous and compassionate. But what if one fasts and behaves with compassion and still the devil comes for your sons? Perhaps after such a catastrophe there can be no more stories.

On *Motza'ei Shabbes*, after they bid farewell to the Sabbath and sip the wine and warm their hands by the light of the braided candle and inhale the smell of cinnamon and wish each other a good week, Raizel and Anshel go to the home of Motke Shapiro to console his grieving parents. At the door they separate; Anshel goes to sit with the men, and Raizel slips behind the curtain to the small bedroom where the women gather. Faigle's face is grey and sallow. She looks like a woman who has no reason to wake up in the morning. "Raizel," she calls to her weakly, "come and sit with me, Raizel. You're the one who found my Motke in the snow."

Raizel falls on her neck, grips her thin shoulders and breaks out into loud sobs. "He was a good boy, Faigle."

"An angel," Faigle cries. "He did only good in this world. So serious. So responsible. And such a good brother to the little ones." She sniffs loudly and wipes her tears on the sleeve of her dress, worn and soiled from the long days of mourning. "Just for a few days, I told him. I said, 'Motke, go to your uncle for a few days and lie low, until we send word. Then you'll come home and go back to the *kheyder*, and when spring comes we'll take Basya and Rivale and little

Pinchas and we'll all go to the forest to pick berries.' Oh, Raizel, how could I have sent such a child into the cold?"

"We all have to do terrible things," Raizel tells her, trying with her very last drops of fortitude to offer consolation. "Who wouldn't do terrible things to save a son from the draft?"

"I sent him to my uncle, on the other side of the forest. He knew the way. We've walked it a hundred times. He just got lost. And he was scared. For weeks he couldn't sleep at night. He heard the stories last year when Mendel Sagorsky came home. He was ready to do anything to avoid Isser. He just had his twelfth birthday last month and so he knew that Isser would be coming for him. Who knows?" she says, blowing her nose into a wet rag. "Maybe it's best this way. How long can a boy run from devils who are bent on tearing him from his home? At least he won't be a soldier for the czar. At least he died a Jew and not among goyim who wanted to make him forget who he is."

These are the words that she repeats to Anshel as they walk home together and then she adds, "but our sons are still alive, still with us, and we can still do something." This is the moment, the moment to tell him her plan, but she can't find the right words. "If *we* choose the families, then at least they'll be raised as Jews. They'll have homes…parents. But if we do nothing…if we do nothing…" She glances at him, looking to see if he has understood. She wants to speak clearly but it sounds as if she's talking nonsense.

He shakes his head and stops in his tracks. "Raizel, do you even hear yourself? What you are saying goes against all natural laws. What animal gives her young to another mother? You grew up without parents and so did I. Is that what you wish for our children?" And again, he speaks of God. "No one, not me or you, or even the czar himself can avert what God Almighty has decreed. We must trust in Him, Raizel. His will is mysterious, but His ways are just."

Raizel wants with all her heart to take the words that Anshel is saying and cling to them as a lame man clings to his walking stick, but she cannot trick herself into believing them. She has witnessed too much, knows too much; she's seen this God turn His face too many times. She is weak, as helpless as a leaf in the wind, a Jew who cannot trust in God.

When Anshel leaves early the next morning he kisses the boys, still sleeping in the bed near the stove. "Watch over them," he tells Raizel. "Make sure they study hard and say the *Modeh Ani* every morning."

After the boys have gone off to *kheyder* Raizel takes Bubbie Hudis outside for her morning visit to the outhouse. She's getting to be like a big baby but there's nothing to be done. Life is no picnic. "Did you buy potatoes?" she asks, clinging to Raizel's arm as they cross the yard. "You used the last ones for the cholent yesterday. Hanukka is coming and we'll need to make latkes. And we're out of onions. Go into town and buy some from Basha, I saw her go by this morning with her big basket."

Sure enough, Basha is sitting in the corner of the square by the synagogue where the women come to sell what they've harvested from their gardens. They sit on low stools, wrapped in heavy shawls, rubbing their hands together to keep their fingers from freezing. "Nu Raizel, how goes it?" Basha asks as Raizel examines the onions.

"Praise God."

"And your boys? Everyone is healthy?"

"Praise God."

"And Bubbie Hudis?"

"She's getting old."

"Aren't we all. We're all headed toward the same place." Basha looks up, squinting against the bleak winter sun. "They say Isser's going to start with the recruitment after Hanukka. I heard a rumor. But who knows? Maybe it will happen before that."

Raizel spits on the ground, taking care to avoid the onions. "Don't say that name. It's the name of the devil."

"You had better think of something to pull on Isser. But something smart; you don't want them to end up like poor Motke!"

"God forbid!"

But Basha is right. Everyone with eyes in their head knows what is coming. Raizel looks up and sees two red-haired girls with long braids moving across the snowy square in front of the synagogue, the older holding the hand of the younger. The younger one catches sight of Raizel and she turns excitedly and points, and then calls out to a man coming out of the synagogue. He is chatting with a few others whom Raizel recognizes as peddlers from the market in Gomel. But what are they doing here in Propoisk? They must have come to comfort the mourning parents at the Shapiro house. She watches as the girls break into a joyful run and then stop short before her.

"You're the doll lady," the younger exclaims. "I'm my dolly's mama, and you're her bubbie."

Raizel stares at the braids, neat and shimmering in the sun and remembers, Rich Gittel, the sourpuss mother, the dolls. The man across the square must be the water-carrier father. "I'm too young to be a bubbie," Raizel corrects her. "I could be her aunt."

"No. Shaindle is her aunt," she insists, glancing at her older sister. "Now she just needs an uncle."

Raizel laughs, happy for the moment of lightness under the warm sun in the middle of the square. But then something flickers in her head. A wild, terrifying idea. She freezes and breaks into a sweat, trembling from head to toe. Would you like to have a brother at home?" she asks in a whisper, her tongue stumbling over the words.

"Yes," she says. "So that my dolly will have an uncle."

Raizel feels the ground moving, as if the whole square is about to collapse. "Tell your mother that I need to speak with her," she says to the older girl. "Will you tell her that?"

"But she doesn't know where to find you."

"Then tell her that I will come to her…I will come to Gomel. What is your mother's name?"

"It's Mindel," the girl tells her.

"Mindel what?"

"Mindel Grupstein." She is not oblivious to the tremor in Raizel's voice. "Why? Why do you want to speak to her?"

But Raizel has gone, moving quickly across the square, terrified by the clarity of it all. With every step the pieces fall into their places and it all fits, it all makes sense. She sees it all come together and she wants to scream, to throw herself to the earth and tear her hair out.

Even as she falls into bed that night she knows that sleep is impossible. The walls of the house seem to be closing in as though choking her. She rises from her bed, wraps herself in a shawl, and shoves her feet into Bubbie Hudis's boots that she bought years ago from a travelling peddler. The floorboards creak and groan as she moves toward the door. Yankele shifts and calls for her, but then falls back asleep.

Outside a gentle snow is falling and the chimneys exhale a wispy haze, as though breathing gently in the moonlight. The houses, with their low, crooked roofs and broken shutters line up like unruly children along the winding street. The whole world is right here. The Friedmans. The Golds. And then the Chaikofs, the Weingartens, the Gorodeskys, the rotting house of the Blusteins. Leibel Friedman's parents were ruined trying to keep him out of the army, and then he fell ill with scarlet fever. Misha Gold is his mother's only son. Arke Chaikof sent her son away to her cousin in Poland. Yoshke Weingarten is lame from a mysterious accident. And Yuda-Leib Gorodesky's gone to work in the house of a Polish nobleman. But Monish Blustein, poor Monish, was only ten years old, taken away in the wagon. Raizel still remembers his cries, and the way Moishe, his father, pressed a book of *Tehillim* into his hands, and how Manya fainted and fell ill for weeks after. God knows where Monish is now and what he is suffering.

The little houses of the town are sleeping, their thin walls cradling mothers, fathers, sisters, brothers, grandparents. As Raizel stands on her porch looking out over the snowy street, it all seems as tenuous and ephemeral as the wispy seeds of a dandelion. It would take only a single gust of wind to send them scattering over the earth. She imagines the shabby houses flying up and away. Like birds, or pages from a forgotten book. Or ashes, floating in the wind.

$$\sim \cdot \sim$$

What is left to tell of this story? How the next afternoon Raizel set out for Gomel, asking here and there for the house of Mindel Grupstein with the four daughters. How she knew the house by the long lines of skirts and underclothes drying in the icy breeze and, as she had been told, by the broken window stuffed with an old pillow.

If a stranger were to have stopped on the road by the house that evening and peered in, he would not have been able to hear the words exchanged between Raizel the orphan and Mindel Grupstein. They would only have seen Raizel's face, despairing and determined. And he would have seen Mindel's reaction, doubtful, skeptical, and suspicious. He would have perhaps noted that moment when Mindel nodded her head and held Raizel's hands in her own. And how Raizel sobbed as she threw her arms around Mindel's neck. It was a small, furtive event, born far from the eyes of men who record the important affairs of history. Yet all of these things happened in the crooked little house with the pillow stuffed in the broken window. No papers were signed. The deed was sealed with only the dark sooty walls as witnesses.

When Raizel left Mindel's house the sun was already sinking into the snowy fields, coloring them with a dull orange light. Raizel felt faint and her head was hot with fever. But when she returned to Propoisk she did not go home, but turned instead in the direction of Gittel's cottage on the edge of town, where her father once ran his tavern.

Was there in Raizel's mind a moment of bewilderment, as she tramped through the snow in the last light of dusk on the road from Gomel to Propoisk? A hesitation in her step? A moment when, in the very depths of her soul she asked herself, *how can this be*? Perhaps, but if so, Raizel banished the question and closed her heart like a fortress.

In the last weeks before her father's passing, Gittel had used her money to make the home more comfortable. She had hired a girl to scrub the floors and wash the windows, and had hung delicate lace curtains where there were once cobwebs and dusty glass. Now as Raizel neared the cottage, the warm yellow glow of Gittel's lamp seemed to her the only thing in the world that was true and steadfast and worthy of her faith.

⁓ · ⁓

Raizel has a secret place in her *neshoma* where words fly around like birds and butterflies, and change from one thing into another as if by magic. They come together and break apart of their own accord, arranging themselves this way and that until, satisfied with their sound, she wills them to be still. It has always been like that. When she was a little girl words would dance for her and she would watch them like a princess enjoying a performance. She doesn't know how or when, but there came a day when she discovered that instead of merely delighting in the words, she could master them. She could tell each one exactly where to stand and then play with their sounds until she liked the way they fit beside each other.

Bubbie Hudis, who once, a long long time ago, was known as clever Hudis, taught her how to read and how to use a pen. Even now, when she is a mother with children of her own, it sometimes happens that she is so pleased with what she has done that as soon as she can get her hands on a writing quill and some paper she jots them down. It reminds her of the verse they sing in the synagogue on *Shabbes* morning, *I will compose songs and weave poems, for it is you that my soul desires.* Though she is a mere ignorant woman, she senses that words, even when they are simple and unadorned, are where the true fire of the world resides.

⸻ • ⸻

It's a warm summer day, and the *melamed's* wife has sent word that her husband is sick and there will be no lesson that morning. "We'll all go down to the river," she tells the boys, and they shout and dance around her like playful puppies. Raizel carries a basket of laundry and they all head to a spot where the water is shallow. The boys strip off their shirts and look for dry branches that can float on the water like boats. Sunlight falls on their curly dark heads and white shoulders like rays of gold, and even Raizel succumbs to the warm light and takes off her shoes and stockings. I'm going to make a boat and sail far away, Avrum tells his brothers.

"I'll sail to Volozhin," Yankele cries, "to the great yeshiva."

"You can't sail to Volozhin. You need a horse and wagon," Avrum corrects him.

"But there has to be a river that goes to Volozhin. Isn't there, Mama?"

"How should I know? Do you think I've ever traveled any further than Gomel?"

"Then I'll ask *Tateh*. He'll know. He's been everywhere."

Itzik puffs out his chest like a little man. "I'll be a captain. And I'll go in my boat to *Eretz Yisrael*, where it never snows and it's warm all the time. Mama said that it never snows in *Eretz Yisrael*, didn't you, Mama?"

"And she said that all the rivers there are milk and honey," Yankele adds. "And the sun shines every day. And only good and righteous people are allowed to live there. Only boys who study Torah and Gemara. Didn't you say that, Mama?"

Raizel loves to watch their faces when she tells them about *Eretz Yisrael*. It's good for them to be able to imagine a better place than Propoisk. Raizel herself can scarcely imagine it. But God gave every person a mind with which to envision the things that they will never see.

And then, from out of nowhere, as Raizel is scrubbing a wine stain from Anshel's shirt, she feels words coming together inside her head.

> *I drew a green clover from the black earth*
> *new and fresh, with three green leaves*
> *I plucked each one and wished a wish*
> *and scattered them to the wind*

And then, as if God Himself has shone His divine grace upon her, she finds a second verse:

> *I saw three ducklings*
> *playing on the shore*
> *They waddled into the river and swam off*
> *one swam west, one east, and one to the warm south*

Maybe three ducklings isn't a good choice. Maybe it should be something more graceful. Three swans. Then she might have to change the word *waddled*, which is good for ducks, but not elegant enough for swans. But the clover is good. The black earth. The green clover. The white swans. Now it needs a third scene. Three verses for three boys. But the day is warm and touched with golden light and no more words come to her.

Raizel wondered then if the golden light had chased away the third part. But now, walking home along the cold deserted street, past the little wooden houses with their crooked gates and low roofs, she can hear the missing words in her head:

I saw three stars in the night sky
looking down on me with their light
and though they were so far away
they knew the reasons
for all I had done

In the coming days there are piercing moments of doubt. Never again will she live in a house with three little boys. The walls of her home will no longer hear the sound of their chatter as they dress themselves in the morning for *kheyder*, as they tell each other riddles before falling asleep at night. She will not come home to find the three of them playing by the fire, building snowmen in the yard in winter, picking berries in the summer. And the future, which she had always imagined as a place of imminent joy, stretches before her, barren as a scorched field after a fire.

Raizel closes her heart to sad thoughts. She packs two small sacks, and in each she puts two pairs of pants, two long shirts, two knitted sweaters, three pairs of socks, two undershirts with *tzitzis* fringes, and a prayer book. And then she takes the paper with the three verses and tears it into three. She folds the papers carefully and puts each in a small leather purse. One verse for Avrum, one for Itzik, and one for Yankel.

Raizel tries not to think about what is to come. Tomorrow is the first night of Hanukka. All the Jews of Propoisk, and Gomel, and all of the Jews in the czar's territory, and the kaiser's territory and the king of Austria's lands, and also the Jews who live in the Western countries, and those in the warm Turkish countries to the south and east where they don't even know what snow is, all of them will wait until the stars come out, and then they will light candles to remember the story that took place long before the one who walked on water was even born. And from each house, no matter how decrepit, how stricken and cursed, will come the murmurings of three blessings:

Blessed are you, Lord, King of the universe who sanctified us with his instruction to light Hanukka candles.

Blessed are you, Lord, King of the universe, who performed miracles for our fathers, in those days, at this time.

"Blessed are you Lord, our God, Ruler of the Universe that has given us life and sustained us and allowed us to reach this day."

When she leaves Avrum with Gittel, she tells him to be a good boy and promises to visit him very soon. She's warned him that if he refuses to live with Gittel an evil spirit with red eyes will come to snatch him from his bed in the night. "But what about Itzik and Yankel?" he asks, and it takes the very last of her strength to keep herself from tearing the papers that Gittel's lawyer has drawn up to shreds. Nonetheless, she wills herself to sign her name in firm, unswerving letters.

At the Grupstein house there are no lawyers and no papers, but the way the girls crowd around Itzik, jumping on him, stroking his hair and asking him what he likes to eat, makes Raizel certain that he is saved. "It's just for a few days. I'll be back to get you soon," she tells him, her voice thin and shaky, and she leaves quickly, so as to flee the terrible sight of his bewildered face.

Anshel will be furious. He may never speak another word to her as long as she lives. Perhaps he will even go to Rebbe Pesach and ask to divorce her, but it doesn't matter. As Raizel tramps through the snow, the cold eats through her thin worn boots and the winds blow mercilessly over her face. Her eyes tear up and her freezing limbs throb with fiery pain, but still a peal of triumphant laughter rises in her heart.

A Note on Sources

T his novel is comprised of seven different worlds which could not have been constructed without the help of eyewitnesses who conveyed what they heard, saw, felt, thought, and imagined in the books they wrote.

It was the work of the Yiddish writers, well and lesser known, poets and novelists, that opened a window into the lives of Jews living in the nineteenth-century Pale of Settlement. Not only the work of Shalom Aleichem, Y.L. Perez, and S.J. Abramowitch (otherwise known as Mendele Mokher Seforim), but also the writing collected in anthologies such as *A Treasury of Yiddish Stories*, edited by Irving Howe and Eliezer Greenberg, and *Yiddish Tales*, first published in 1912 by the Jewish Publication Society of America, which aimed to "introduce the non-Yiddish reading public to some of the writers active in Russian Jewry and – and to leave it with a more cheerful impression of Yiddish literature than it receives from Perez alone."[2]

Also invaluable were the collections of women's writing in Yiddish, anthologized in *Found Treasures*, edited by Frieda Forman, Ethel Raicus, Sarah Silberstein Swartz, and Margie Wolfe, and *Arguing with the Storm,* edited by Rhea Tregebov. Both collections revive women's neglected voices and perspectives which would have otherwise been forgotten, and illuminate the complex physical and social conditions in which their lives unfolded. Likewise, Devorah Baron's collection, *The Thorny Path*, translated from the Hebrew, depicts the period through yet another lens.

My depictions of the lives of the Jews of Eastern Europe in the pre-Holocaust years of the twentieth century were greatly aided by the work of I.B. Singer and I.J. Singer. *Deborah*, a novel written by their far less renowned sister, Esther Kreitman, offers a rare first-person perspective on the lives of women in prewar Poland. S.Y. Agnon's *A Guest for the Night* conveys bleak depictions of the day-to-day realities of Eastern European Jews in the post-World War I years.

For real-time descriptions of the first steps taken by Eastern European Jews after immigrating to America, I turned to Abraham Cahan's *Yekl*, Alfred Kazin's *A Walker in the City*, and Anzia Yezierska's *Hungry Hearts*. Meyer Levin's *The Old Bunch* takes readers inside the minds and hearts of first-generation Jews in Chicago, and I could not have written Nat's story without it.

The most challenging period of all for finding real-time (that is, pre-Holocaust) sources was that of secular Jewish Vilna in the 1920s and 30s. Lucy Dawidovicz's *From That Place and Time* provided detailed descriptions and analyses of life in the months leading up to the war. Chaim Grade's memoir, *My Mother's Sabbath Days*, was also of great assistance, as was *Awakening Lives*, the miraculous collection of essays written by Yiddish-speaking youths in the framework of YIVO's autobiographical essay contests of the 1930s, edited by Jeffery Shandler.

For descriptions of the lives of early twentieth-century Zionists in what was then Palestine, I turned to a wealth of photos, recollections, and documents found online in the Kibbutz Givat Brenner story archive, as well as two books I'm fortunate to have in my possession: *Letters from the Desert*, a 1945 collection of translated letters written by Moshe Mosenson to his family and friends while serving in the British army in North Africa, and *The Plough Wom*en, a collection of essays, translated from the Hebrew and written by "Jewish women workers of Palestine"[3] who "felt a need to set down in writing the story of their movement," put out in 1932 by the Women's Pioneer Association. It was once part of my grandmother's personal library, and I am gratified that I was able to put the material found there to use, and in this small way, give it new life.

Acknowledgments

Adebt of gratitude is due first and foremost, to Matthew Miller, for taking on this project, to Caryn Meltz for overseeing it, and to Rachel Miskin, Adina Mendelsohn, and Tani Bayer for their work in bringing this book into the world.

A very special thank you is owed to Sandy Bluestein-Klein, Penny Smith, Lynn Mousmanis, Gary Klein, Vivian Lang, Louisa Hostik, Norman and Simone Stern, Eric and Penny Bowman, Shmuel Bowman, Tzipora Ne'eman Feder, Nechama Feder-Twito, Eydie Zamikoff-Nadborny, Harvey and Shirley-Anne Haber, Arthur Segal, and Linda Segal, who gave their kind permission to include the photo of the 1969 Beth Tikvah Synagogue trip to Israel – a small but pivotal part of my own little history – on the cover of this book.

I want to express my gratitude also to Barbara Krasner who appreciated and believed in this work. To Nina Warncke, Ellen Cassedy, and Yermiyahu Ahron Taub for their help with Yiddish terms. To Jeanette Goldman and Julia Koifman for their help with the cover translation. To Diane Glazman, Laura Walter, and Maya Rock for their input. To the memories of Rabbi James Diamond and Rabbi Herbert Feder, who read early versions and encouraged me to continue. To Eli Jacobs, Miryam Sivan, Joanna Chen, Avner Landes, Michael Schmidt, and Monika Ittah for weighing in. To

Arthur, Linda, Heather, Elana and Tamara Segal, Annette Sherman Segal, and Michael Posner, for their helpful feedback and support. To my uncle, Gerry Posner, for his passion in finding and sharing the stories. To Adi, Danielle, and Aran, and to Pino for making it all possible.

Endnotes

1   Translation by Nathan Halpern. Quoted from: Moyshe Kulbak, 'Vilne', Vilnius: Vaga, 1997, p. 17
2. Yiddish Tales, 2nd ed, edited and translated by Helena Frank (Philadelphia: the Jewish Publication Society of America, 1945), p. 5.
3. The Plough Women, edited by Rachel Katzenlson-Rubashow (New York: Nicolas L. Brown, 1932).

About the Author

Pino Weizman

Janice Weizman was born in Toronto in 1964 and moved to Israel at the age of nineteen. An interest in the history and culture of the Middle East, as well as a desire to explore the untold dramas of women's lives, inspired her to write her first novel, *The Wayward Moon*, which first came out in 2012 with Yotzeret Publishing. The novel was awarded the Independent Publishers Award and the Midwest Book Award, and was reissued with The Toby Press in 2023. *Our Little Histories* is her second novel. More about Weizman's work can be found at www.janiceweizman.com.